SILVER

PRAISE FOR CHRIS WOODING

THE HAUNTING OF ALAIZABEL CRAY
"One of the most intelligent novels published for teens in recent years . . . breathtakingly brilliant" *Guardian*

"enormously inventive and gripping . . . more tension and suspense than a Hitchcock movie . . . not to be missed" *Daily Telegraph*

"shiveringly exciting" *The Times*

STORM THIEF
"[a] powerful blend of thriller, science fiction and fantasy" *TES*

"all the compelling paranoia of a fever-based fantasy" *Books For Keeps*

"dizzying imaginative detail with action-adventure . . . for kids who find fiction second-best to Playstation games, Wooding is ideal" *The Times*

POISON
"breathlessly exciting" *Guardian*

"thrilling" *TES*

"Wooding's explosive visual imagination knows no bounds" *The Times*

SILVER

CHRIS WOODING

SCHOLASTIC

First published in the UK in 2013 by Scholastic Children's Books
An imprint of Scholastic Ltd
Euston House, 24 Eversholt Street
London, NW1 1DB, UK
Registered office: Westfield Road, Southam, Warwickshire, CV47 0RA
SCHOLASTIC and associated logos are trademarks and/
or registered trademarks of Scholastic Inc.

ISBN 978 1 407 12428 5

A CIP catalogue record for this book
is available from the British Library.

Printed and bound by CPI Group (UK) Ltd, Croydon, CR0 4YY
Papers used by Scholastic Children's Books are made
from wood grown in sustainable forests.

1 3 5 7 9 10 8 6 4 2

www.scholastic.co.uk/zone

ONE

1

Darkness.

Crushing pressure on his neck. The sour tang of another boy's sweat. The rough fabric of a blazer rasping against his face.

Pain, as a fist thumped hard into his back.

Paul struggled wildly against the headlock. He swung with his arms, hit his attacker a glancing blow. But the other boy was bigger than him, and all he got in return was another punch, right in the kidneys.

Through the blazer that was tangled round his head, Paul heard his classmates shouting, their cries muffled.

Fight! Fight! Fight!

He lashed out, and this time he made a solid connection, driving his knuckles into soft belly fat. His opponent *whuffed* out his breath, and for a moment the pressure on his head loosened. Paul yanked back violently, punching again, and suddenly he was free.

Daylight. The lake was at his back, sun-bright woods all around, leaves glistening with the memory of rain. Clouds skidded fast across a summer sky.

Paul backed away a step, cheeks flushed and hot. Falling for that headlock had made him embarrassed and angry. Adam glared at him, fists bunched, his thuggish face screwed up in a fighting scowl. He was bigger than Paul, and more thickly built, but there was no retreat now.

Fight! Fight! Fight!

The pupils had abandoned their biology assignments the moment the scuffle broke out. The boys chanted like they were the audience to a gladiatorial combat. The girls made a show of their disgust but watched anyway. Paul looked for Erika in the crowd but found only Caitlyn, her narrow, sharp features a picture of concern, bird-bright eyes fixed on him.

"Go on, Paul!"

"Do him in!"

"Come on, Paul!"

Fight! Fight! Fight!

Maddened, Adam charged. Instead of meeting the charge, Paul sidestepped, leaving a trailing leg for Adam to trip on. The bigger kid went down, crashing to the ground. The crowd broke into laughter. They all wanted to see Adam eat dirt. Paul danced away a step, exhilarated, knowing that he'd scored a point.

A sharp, cold gust of wind whipped through the

woods, rippling the lake and setting the branches lashing overhead. Paul felt a grin coming. The day felt unsettled, like a storm was on its way. There was chaos in the air.

His kind of day.

Adam began to pick himself up, his small eyes hateful. His ears burned red with rage and humilation. Paul expected Adam to get to his feet, but Adam surprised him by lunging from a crouch. Paul wasn't ready, and wasn't quick enough to avoid it. Adam wrapped his arms round Paul's legs and drove into his thighs, knocking him backwards.

Suddenly Paul was on the ground, and Adam was on top of him, punching, frenzied. Paul barely felt the hits. He fought back, thrashing like an animal, and managed to shift Adam's weight before he could be pinned. They rolled, and then Paul was on top, raining blows on his opponent. But Adam was too big to keep down: a moment later, they were rolling again. They scuffled and scrabbled, a mass of jabbing elbows and knees, trying to land hits on each other in a sweaty, furious tussle. And all the time, the hypnotic chant of the crowd:

Fight! Fight! Fi—

"YOU TWO!"

Mr Harrison's voice sliced through the morning air, killing the heat of the fight in an instant. The chanting was instantly silenced. The spell was broken: the crowd looked guilty and abashed.

Paul and Adam got to their feet, dusting leaves off their blazers, neither taking their eyes from the other. Mr Harrison stood at the top of the slope, beyond which lay the school and the sprawling grounds of Mortingham Boarding Academy. The headmaster didn't trouble himself to come through the wood to the lake. He just stood there like some disapproving god gazing down on his wayward flock.

"I'll see you both in my study at the end of this period!" he said, in that hammered-steel drill-sergeant voice that every Mortingham pupil had learned to dread. "Is that understood?"

Neither Paul nor Adam said a thing. They just glared at each other, panting.

"*Is that understood?*" Mr Harrison barked.

"Yes, sir," they both mumbled reluctantly.

Just then, Mr Sutton came hurrying through the trees, led by Erika, who'd run to fetch him from the other side of the lake when the fight started. He took in the scene with a glance and sighed.

"Everything under control here, Mr Sutton?" Mr Harrison asked. Nobody missed the pointed sarcasm in his voice.

"Everything's under control," Mr Sutton said. "Isn't it, boys?" He looked from Adam to Paul, and Paul thought he saw disappointment in that calm gaze. He was surprised by a pang of guilt.

"Yes, sir."

Mr Harrison stared down at them for a long

moment, then stalked off and out of sight. Mr Sutton raised his gaze to sweep the assembled crowd.

"Well, what are you all doing here? That biomass won't weigh itself, you know! I want every worm, every beetle in your sample zone collected up and recorded. Get to it."

He clapped his hands and the crowd dispersed, heading back to their sample zones. Each zone was staked out with four poles, red thread strung between them, marking out a square metre of undergrowth. One pupil was in charge of collecting the insects; one was in charge of recording what they found.

"Come on," said Mr Sutton to Paul and Adam. "You've had your fun. Get back to work. We'll talk about this later."

As he was led away from the others, Paul saw Erika watching him. He flashed her a savage grin. She narrowed her eyes and looked away.

2

Mr Harrison's study was located in the heart of Mortingham Boarding Academy. The massive central building had once been a workhouse for the poor, then a sanatorium for tuberculosis sufferers, before ending up as a school, which Paul hardly counted as an improvement. It seemed to him that all that concentrated unhappiness had soaked into the walls over time, and turned its stony halls oppressive and gloomy. There was a sense of confinement here that wasn't present in the more modern buildings which surrounded it. One way or another, this place had always imprisoned its occupants.

Paul stood in front of Mr Harrison's mahogany desk and looked out of the thin, arched windows while he waited for the headmaster to finish paging through the folder of reports in his hand.

The grounds were huge, big enough to encompass a small lake, playing fields, tennis courts, half a dozen dorm buildings and accommodation for staff and visitors. There was a state-of-the-art sports hall with an Olympic-sized swimming pool. There was a theatre, an ancient library, even an old ruined chapel that the Year Sevens told ghost stories about.

But all of it was inside the wall. Three metres high, solid stone, it had a single gate which was the only exit from the campus.

And outside? Nothing. Green valley walls swept up to grey, rocky peaks. Sheep wandered in meadows bordered by trees and dry stone walls. The only sign of human life in that beautiful, desolate world was the weather monitoring station that sat on a ridge several miles down the valley. It was stark white against the landscape, all domes and angles.

There was a single road that snaked away down the valley, following the slender river. At its end was Mortingham town, and the gateway to civilization and the rest of the world. Or so Paul had heard, at least. He'd been here six months, and he'd never left for so much as a day trip.

"Now, then," said Mr Harrison.

Paul returned his attention to the headmaster. Mr Harrison was sitting back in his chair, gazing at Paul with those grey, dead-fish eyes of his. He was a big man with wide shoulders, a little overweight, and he had the kind of face Paul associated with authority. He looked like the bad cop in all those 80s TV shows Dad used to watch: bald on top, brown moustache, an expression like a bulldog chewing a wasp. Even his clothes seemed thirty years out of date.

"Now, then," he said again, with the oily manner of a bank clerk eager to please a customer. "How can we help you settle in to our fine establishment, Mr Camber?"

Paul wasn't fooled by his tone. He didn't want to give Mr Harrison the satisfaction of playing along with his game, but he had to say something. So he just said "Dunno, sir."

"He doesn't know," Mr Harrison said to Mr Sutton, who was standing quietly to one side. Mr Sutton was Paul's housemaster as well as his biology teacher, and as such he'd felt it necessary to come along. Paul felt sorry that he'd been dragged into this. Mr Sutton was a decent bloke.

"The reason I ask," Mr Harrison continued, his tone hardening, "is because I have on my desk a series of reports from your previous school. Let me quote

7

a few for you." He began to leaf through the pages. "'Well-behaved' this one says. 'Exceptional pupil', 'Gets on well with others', 'Natural Leader'." He closed the folder and gave Paul another dose of that unblinking stare. "Do you have a twin brother I don't know about?"

Paul supposed that was what passed for wit among headmasters. "No, sir."

Mr Harrison whipped out another sheet of paper. "Your preliminary report from Mortingham Academy. We do these on all new pupils. Let me see... 'Does just enough work to get by', 'Has potential but refuses to apply himself' Oh, here's a good one. 'Doesn't listen to instructions'." He put the report down. "Anyone would think you didn't want to be here."

Paul didn't answer that. He *didn't* want to be here. But then, he didn't exactly have anywhere else he could go, either. He was suddenly taken by that awful feeling that sometimes crept up in the night, as if he was falling into endless emptiness and he couldn't stop himself. Panic fluttered in his chest. He swallowed it back and stared straight ahead.

"Well, you *are* here, Mr Camber," said Mr Harrison. He got to his feet and leaned over the desk, his voice rising towards a shout. "And while you're here, you will *obey the rules*!"

It was hard not to be intimidated by a man of Mr Harrison's size bellowing in your face. He was a man permanently on the edge of boiling point. It wasn't uncommon to see Year Sevens reduced to tears after a roasting from the headmaster. Paul just looked down at the floor.

"Yes, sir," he said, because that was what was expected. That was what would get this whole thing over with.

"I've been a teacher here for twenty-five years," Mr Harrison said. "I've seen a hundred boys like you. You all think you know better. You all think you're something special. But year after year, you're all the same."

Paul didn't rise to it. There wasn't any point arguing; he'd learned that. Nobody was interested in his opinion. His job was to stand still and be talked at until the talking was done.

"I won't bother asking who started it, I already know," said Mr Harrison. "We had Adam's brother here for a few years. Nasty piece of work, he was, and they're cut from the same cloth. I expected better from you."

Paul kept his silence. Eventually, seeing that he'd get no reaction, Mr Harrison humphed dismissively. He walked across the office and looked out of the window. "Strange kind of day, isn't it? Weatherman can't make up his mind if it'll be hot all weekend, or if the sky's going to fall." He turned away. "Won't matter to you, anyway. You'll spend the rest of July indoors. You're confined to dorms till the end of term. Go back to your hall straight after lessons. I don't want to see you outside. Not at breaktime, not at lunchtime, not after school. You can catch up on work while your friends are out having fun." He looked away, back out of the window. "Off you go."

Paul accepted his punishment without much emotion. Mr Sutton led him out of the office. Sitting on a bench by the door was Adam, who stared at him with sullen suspicion and threat in his eyes. *What've you been saying in there? You better not have grassed me up.*

"You can go in now, Adam," said Mr Sutton, in his soft and sympathetic voice.

Adam levered his bulk out of the chair and sloped inside. "Ah, Mr Wojcik! What a surprise to see you here!" Mr Harrison cried, before the door closed and left Mr Sutton and Paul alone in the corridor.

Paul rolled his shoulder. He was still a little sore from the fight, but it would fade in a few hours.

"What have you got next?" Mr Sutton asked.

"DT," Paul replied. Design and Technology.

Mr Sutton checked his watch. "Not long left till end of break. I'll walk you to the science block."

Paul would have rather been alone, but he couldn't think of an argument. Besides, he felt he owed his housemaster something. He knew his behaviour had made Mr Sutton look bad in front of the headmaster.

They walked together in silence. With all the pupils outside, it seemed eerily deserted in the school.

Footsteps echoed. The laughter and shouts from the grounds could be heard only faintly in here, stifled by the stone walls.

They came to a corner at the end of the corridor. There, sitting on a window seat in an alcove, was a boy Paul vaguely recognized from his classes. He was skinny and ginger, with a high forehead, and he was anxiously tapping his heels against the wall. As Paul appeared, the boy stopped tapping and looked up at him expectantly, fixing him with an eager gaze. In that moment, Paul was convinced that he was about to spring off the window seat and say something.

But he didn't. The boy's eager expression faded, and Mr Sutton gave him a look which Paul couldn't read. Then the moment passed, and they walked on, leaving Paul with the distinct sensation that he'd missed something.

3

They came out of the main entrance of the school, on to the gravelled forecourt where older pupils loitered in groups and Year Sevens ran about playing tag. Paths wound off across the grounds, leading to other buildings nearby. A long drive stretched away south to the gate, splitting halfway down to encircle a round lawn dominated by a massive ornamental fountain.

Paul glanced at Mr Sutton, who was loping

alongside him on the path. He was tall and rangy, with a long face and floppy brown hair. He had sad, watery eyes, but he always seemed to have half a smile on his face, as if he was secretly pleased at something. His clothes were always dull and a bit shabby. He was probably in his late thirties, but he had that droopy English professor look that made him seem older. A pipe-and-slippers kind of man.

"You want to tell me what happened?" Mr Sutton asked, eventually.

Paul didn't, really. "It's stupid," he said. "Shouldn't have done it." He met the teacher's gaze, then looked away, over towards the mountains in the distance. "Sorry, sir."

"Still, I'd like to know. I put you two together for a reason."

That surprised Paul. "What reason's that?"

"To see if you could get along with him."

Paul snorted. "That didn't work out too well, did it, sir?"

"Apparently not," said Mr Sutton. They walked on a few more steps. "So what happened?"

Paul realized that Mr Sutton wasn't going to let this go. "He kept getting it wrong," he said. "I was meant to collect up the insects, he was supposed to identify them. You gave us those checksheets with pictures and everything." He felt himself reddening. It sounded so petty now he said it aloud. "He kept putting ticks in the wrong boxes. I don't know if he was doing it on purpose or if he's just too stupid to count the spots on the back of a ladybird, but—"

"Paul. . ." Mr Sutton warned.

"Well, he *is* stupid!" Paul snapped. "I know you're supposed to tell us that we're all precious unique little snowflakes and that, but the truth is, some people are just dumb."

Mr Sutton didn't say anything, but somehow his silence made Paul feel ashamed of his outburst.

"Anyway," he said. "So I took the sheet and started marking them in myself."

"That was Adam's job."

"He couldn't *do* his job."

"So why didn't you help him do it, instead of taking it away from him?"

"Didn't seem worth it," Paul said. "Easier to do it myself."

They walked on a little way. Paul watched some kids kicking around a football, and remembered how he used to play all the time until recently. It felt sort of pointless now.

"I was talking with Bobby Farrell today," Mr Sutton said. "You know him, don't you?"

"Faz? Yeah. I mean, we hang out a bit."

"Would you say he was your best friend at Mortingham?"

That seemed a weird thing to ask. "Erm," said Paul uncertainly. "He's alright. Wouldn't say he was my *best mate* or anything."

"So who is?"

Paul began to feel awkward. He wasn't sure what Mr Sutton was driving at, but he didn't really want to be discussing his personal life with a teacher. "Dunno, sir. I hang out with a lot of different people, I s'pose. Why? What did Bobby say?"

"Oh, nothing very specific. He asked if I knew what your parents did."

Paul froze up inside. The kids playing football seemed suddenly far away, as if they were separated from him by something more than distance. He felt like if he called out to them, they wouldn't hear him. He kept walking towards the science block, one foot in front of the other, but a sense of terrible loneliness had descended on him.

"You haven't told anyone about your parents, have you?" Mr Sutton said quietly.

Paul suddenly wished he was anywhere but here. He wished Mr Sutton would shut up and get lost and quit hassling him. He nurtured that thought, thawing himself with anger. It felt good to think thoughts like that. He looked down at the ground and kept a furious silence.

"I'm worried about you, Paul," Mr Sutton said. "You've been trying to handle everything by yourself ever since you got here. You need to trust somebody."

Paul couldn't help a short, nasty laugh at that.

"Is that funny?" Mr Sutton asked.

"No, sir," said Paul, in the same dry, mechanical way he'd spoken to Mr Harrison. "Sorry, sir."

Mr Sutton heard the tone in his voice, and was defeated. He was smart enough to know there would be no getting through to Paul now. "No, *I'm* sorry," he said. "I'm sure you think it's none of my business."

That's right, thought Paul. *That's exactly right. None of your damn business.*

They approached the science block, an unremarkable rectangular two-storey building with a flat roof. Apart from the science labs, it also housed the technology department and workshops for metalwork and woodwork. The elegantly designed sports hall off to the left made it look drab by comparison.

They went through the doors to the science block, and into the foyer, where swing doors led into different corridors and a set of stairs led up to the floor above. There they stopped. Mr Sutton looked awkward.

"Yes, well, then," he said, wearing a troubled expression. "I suppose you ought to get to class."

"Right," said Paul, and headed off. He was just pushing open the swing doors when Mr Sutton said, "You should thank Mark, by the way."

Paul stopped in the doorway. "Who?"

"Mark Platt."

Paul looked blank.

"You saw him in the corridor just a minute ago. Outside Mr Harrison's office."

It all fell into place suddenly. The skinny ginger kid with too much forehead. "What about him?" Paul asked.

"He stuck up for you. Told me what happened."

Paul was genuinely puzzled. They had a couple of classes together, but he'd never even spoken to Mark Platt. "What did he say?"

"He said that Adam started it. That he threw the first punch."

"Well, he lied, then," said Paul. "'Cause that was me."

Then he walked through the door, and let it swing shut behind him with a thump.

TWO

1

Adam Wojcik had learned early on that life wasn't fair, but somehow he'd never been able to accept it. A childhood full of small injustices had made him constantly suspicious, always on the lookout for the next insult, the next blow, whether real or imaginary. He sought out reasons to get mad. He nursed his grievances and held his grudges close to his chest. The world to him was a mean and unforgiving place, and you had to fight at every opportunity to defend the respect you'd gained. Otherwise people would just walk all over you.

Today was a perfect example. People talked about "innocent until proven guilty" but somehow that didn't apply to him. It didn't matter that most of the time he *was* guilty. The times when he wasn't, nobody believed him. So what was the point of behaving yourself if you were just going to get blamed for everything anyway?

He felt bitter enough when they accused him of

something he did do. It was twice as bad when it was something he didn't.

Adam stamped away from the school building with his fists stuffed in the pockets of his blazer. Smaller kids moved surreptitiously out of his way, recognizing the look on his face. He barely even saw them.

All he'd been doing was defending himself! That bloody Camber kid punched him! Was he supposed to sit there and take that? So what if he'd said something about Paul's mother first? Whenever Adam hit someone for insulting *him*, it was all "You can't use your fists to solve your problems" and that kind of crap.

But Harrison hadn't even bothered asking for his side of the story. Naturally.

Confined to dorms, then. As if they were gonna keep *him* inside for the rest of term. Maybe he'd have to keep his head down for a few days, but there was no way he was staying in for three weeks just 'cause some teacher said so. He wasn't getting done for something that wasn't his fault.

When things weren't fair, you had to make your own justice.

Lost in frustration, he hadn't been paying attention to where he was going. He just wanted to put distance between himself and the school. Now he found himself heading back towards the lake, which lay in a hollow at the south-western edge of the grounds, invisible behind the small wood that encircled it. On the edge of the wood was the old chapel, gnawed by time into a fraction of its former glory. There, hidden in the ruins, he spotted a group of three kids clustering excitedly around something that one of them was holding.

Adam sensed a secret. And if there was one thing he didn't like, it was being left out.

He changed direction and headed towards them. His mood lifted in anticipation. A few seconds ago he'd been seething with rage at what had been done to him, but now he saw an opportunity to take it out on someone else. He couldn't pay Harrison back, so he'd pay it forward. That was the way it worked: the academy's very own food chain, with the strong preying on the weak. Mr Sutton would have been proud of his observation.

He wondered if the teachers ever thought that by punishing him they were only making it worse for kids like these? Probably not. And even if they did, they'd somehow make out that it was Adam's fault.

He recognized two of the kids from the biology class that morning. One had flaming acne, braces and spiky hair; the other had a long face and enormous gums that suggested at least one of his parents had been a horse. Adam didn't know their real names, only the nicknames he'd bestowed on them: Pusbag and Buckaroo.

The third kid was a massive, flabby, milky-looking

thing whose tiny eyes had disappeared in the folds of his cheeks. Adam was amazed that this new kid had passed beneath his notice for so long. It seemed that Pusbag and Buckaroo had made a new friend.

Well, a kid like that needed a nickname. Jabba was already taken, as were Slug and Hungry. Adam wasn't feeling especially creative, so he just christened him Planet. A kid that size must surely generate his own gravity, presumably enough to attract any nearby snacks.

They didn't spot him till it was far too late to run. They tried to hide what they'd been looking at, but it was too late for that, too.

"What you got there, then?" Adam demanded.

They stared at him, pale and fearful. Like rabbits caught in the headlights of a car.

"Give it here," he said.

They glanced at one another uncertainly. He slapped Buckaroo round the side of the head. Planet took a quivering step back. He looked ready to wet himself.

"Give it *here*," Adam said again, with more threat in his voice this time.

Buckaroo held out what he'd been hiding. A Tupperware box, like the kind you kept your lunch in. Adam snatched it off him.

"Don't open it!" Pusbag squeaked, as Adam was about to do just that.

Ordinarily that would have earned another slap,

but something in his tone stopped Adam. He shook the box, and felt something small and heavy sliding about inside. "What's in there?"

None of them were brave enough to speak first. Nobody wanted to invite his attention. He had half a mind to hit them all.

"A beetle," said Pusbag at last.

"A *rare* beetle," Planet chipped in breathlessly.

Adam scoffed. "A *beetle*?"

"We found it in class," said Buckaroo. "Down by the lake. It wasn't on the checklist, so I scooped it up with my sandwich box."

Something scuttled inside the box. If that was a beetle, it was a bloody heavy one. He held the box up to the clouded sun. Through the plastic, Adam could see the shadow of something the size of a mouse. Bigger than any beetle he'd ever seen, that was for sure.

He put his hand on the lid to open it. "Careful!" Pusbag said. Adam gave him a warning look and he shut up.

"Let's see what you got," he said. He lifted up the lid a little and put his eye to the crack.

A sudden movement; a flash of silver. The beetle jumped at his face. Instinctively, Adam jerked his head back, letting out a yell of surprise. The beetle thumped into the lid of the box and it tumbled from his hands, breaking open as it hit the dirt. The other kids cried out in alarm, but none of them moved.

Adam looked down. The box and its lid had parted

company. Between them was the beetle, lying on its back with its six legs waving helplessly in the air. It was huge, ten centimetres long or more, and its carapace had a grey metallic sheen.

He didn't look at it any closer. He stamped on it hard, and felt it crack beneath his shoe. When he raised his foot again, Planet let out a moan of dismay. He'd crushed it flat.

Adam's face was hot with anger. The damn thing had scared him. He'd been shown up in front of these wimps. Shown up by a *beetle*.

In the distance, the bell rang to signal the end of break. He glared at the other kids, who blanched and cringed from him. None of them dared to laugh. If anyone did, he'd break their jaw.

Without another word, he stalked away. There was nothing left to be done.

2

"Pass it! Pass it!" Miss Watson shouted at the players on the court. "Hayley! Defence!"

The squeak of trainers on the polished floor echoed round the sports hall. Caitlyn passed, ran, then took the return ball. A moment later Hayley, the opposition centre, was in her face, trying to block her. Hayley was quick, but she couldn't defend to save her life. Caitlyn feinted one way and then fired a bounce pass to her left, where Beth had dropped back along the court to receive. As soon as the ball left her hands she was off again, looking for space.

"That's good movement, Caitlyn!" called Miss Watson. "Come on, everyone! You're standing around like dummies! This is netball, not cricket!"

Beth had dithered so long that her three seconds were almost up. Caitlyn ran to the edge of their opponent's goal circle, but by the time Beth saw her she'd been cut off by the goal defence. Instead, Beth sent a cross-court chest pass to Soraya on the other wing, who almost dropped it before she got it under control. By that time, her opposing number was all over her, so Caitlyn repositioned, making herself available to her wing attack in case she needed somewhere to send the ball.

Stop, start, stop, start. The jerky rhythm of the game. The cool, spacious hall versus the heat and sweat on her skin. So what if this was just a practice runaround? There were few things that Caitlyn enjoyed more than a hard game of netball, and she took it seriously. Netball was something she was good at. Really good.

But not the best. Never the best. Not while Erika Robinson was around.

Erika was in the goal circle, where she spent most of the game. Erika played goal shooter, of course. It was the role of greatest glory, the team's primary goal scorer. She was also irritatingly good at it, but then, she was irritatingly good at *everything*.

Erika Robinson. Where Caitlyn was bony and sharp-faced, Erika was lithe, long-legged and immaculately proportioned. Her blonde hair was pinned back from the icily gorgeous Scandinavian features she'd inherited from her icily gorgeous Scandinavian mother. She was the star of the netball team, a straight-A student with the looks of a model, except without the anorexia. Erika Robinson, Little Miss Bloody Perfect.

Soraya didn't have an angle on Erika in the circle, so she passed back to Caitlyn, who was just inside the opponent's goal third. As soon as the ball hit her hands she was turning to throw it back to Beth, the only other player on the team who was allowed to shoot apart from Erika. But Beth had got herself blocked off again. Caitlyn hesitated for the briefest of seconds.

"Give it to Erika!" Miss Watson yelled.

Give it to Erika, Caitlyn thought, with a surge of anger. *Yeah, I'll give it to Erika. Sixty miles an hour in the face.*

And for one wild moment, she actually thought she'd do it. Sling the ball hard, smack her in the nose, black her eyes. God, that'd feel good. That'd be worth any punishment that followed.

But a moment was all it was. Erika shifted to the right to lose her marker. Caitlyn anticipated the move and put a pass straight to her. Erika pivoted and took the shot.

She scored, of course. Miss Watson blew her whistle, and that was the end of the game.

The celebrations were all for Erika, naturally. Caitlyn didn't join in. She walked back along the court to get some water while the other girls were busy high-fiving their star shooter.

She couldn't stop thinking about the look that Paul had given Erika after his fight with Adam that morning. That look of triumph, as if he'd done it all for her. Wasn't it enough that Erika was going out with Tom Barker, captain of the rugby team, two years older and handsome enough to resurrect the dead? Did she have to have everyone *else's* boys as well?

The thought of Paul conjured a picture in Caitlyn's head, a mental snapshot that she kept like a portrait in a locket. The first time she'd seen him, he'd been sitting on the back steps of the theatre, reading a book. The sun had been behind him that day, a low January sun shining over the wall that encircled the Mortingham campus, and he'd been wrapped up in a coat.

Caitlyn had been heading to drama class, walking quickly and purposefully. The sight of him had brought her to a stop. To this day, she didn't know why. He just struck something in her. He was so absorbed, so *complete*, sitting there alone with his book. His black hair had been stirring against his forehead in the chill wind, and the sun cast long shadows across the tarmac that lay between them.

Then he'd looked up, and his gaze had met hers, and there was something so bleak and haunted in those grey eyes that he'd seemed like something otherworldly. Caitlyn knew then that he was wounded somehow, and felt an urge to help him, to understand him. But she didn't know how, and all she could offer was a shy smile.

After a moment, he'd smiled back. It did nothing to ease the sadness she felt surrounding him, but it made her heart pound anyway. Then she'd put her head down and hurried away, her chest tight and her cheeks hot.

Later, she spotted him in a corridor and discovered the title of the book he was carrying. *The Chrysalids,* by John Wyndham. She'd bought it and read it herself, mining the text for clues and connections, seeking a route into his mind.

Eventually, she talked to him, and they became passing acquaintances, if not exactly friends. But what she didn't know then was that she was already too late. Paul's attention had been caught by Erika, and while she was around he'd never be interested in another.

The youngest of four girls, Caitlyn had spent her whole life competing and losing. Alex was the pretty one, Sadie was brilliant at everything she turned her hand to, Joanne had all the brains, and Caitlyn ... Caitlyn was just *average*. Moderately talented, moderately good at school, moderately attractive. Everything she tried to do had been done before, and better, by her older sisters.

When Joanne won entry to an exclusive London sixth-form college, it was the happiest day of Caitlyn's life. Since the start of term, Caitlyn had had Mortingham Academy to herself. At last, she had the chance to step out of the shadow of her siblings. At last she might make a mark, distinguish herself, rise above second best.

But then there was Erika. Everywhere Caitlyn looked, Erika was in her way.

She *should* have thrown that ball at her face.

Miss Watson gave a short team talk and then sent them to the changing rooms. On the way, Soraya caught up with Caitlyn.

"Good game, huh? You were aces, as always."

"Yeah, it was fun," said Caitlyn, brightening. It was hard to stay in a bad mood with Soraya around. She always told you exactly what you wanted to hear.

"You should totally try for the county team."

"Oh, shut up," said Caitlyn with a smile.

"Just saying," Soraya declared innocently.

Erika jogged up between them and swung her arms over their shoulders, pulling them all together. "I'm hanging out with Tom and his friends this lunchtime," she said, her voice low as if she was delivering a dreadful secret. "Don't leave me alone with them."

"Wouldn't dream of it, would we, Caitlyn?" Soraya

said, her dark eyes lighting up at the thought of all those Year Thirteen boys.

"Oh, no," said Caitlyn with a grin. "Wouldn't dream of it."

"Great. See you after," said Erika, and slipped off ahead of them to get to the showers first.

Caitlyn watched her go with a mental sigh. Hanging out with the sixth-formers again. Most of the girls in her year would have killed to be in her position, but for Caitlyn it meant another lunch break full of forced laughter and fake smiles.

Sometimes it was hard work being best friends with your worst enemy.

3

"Got. Got. Need. Got. Need. *Need*!"

Andrew practically squealed at the sight of a six-headed hydra slapping down on top of the deck of trading cards. A satisfied smirk passed across Graham's face and he gave an evil cackle. Presumably he was trying to approximate the dreadful laugh of some kind of Dark Lord, but the effect was ruined by the fact that he was actually a massive nerd.

"And what will you give me for this fine beast?" he asked. "Oh, wait, I seem to remember you have a particularly rare Cradlejack card in your possession. . ."

Mark paid his friends no attention. Monster

trading cards. Honestly. Mark loved a good acid-belching swamp troll as much as the next guy, but there were some things you just didn't *do* in public when you were fifteen years old. Not if you ever hoped to land a girlfriend, anyway.

Girlfriend? Don't get ahead of yourself. One step at a time. Stick to the plan.

Yes, the plan. Mark remembered the flow chart he'd drawn up. His personal map out of geekdom. It'd be a hard path, he knew that. But now he had a plan, he felt like anything was possible.

If you're failing to plan, you're planning to fail, he thought, and then winced. Fridge-magnet wisdom? Not cool. He'd have to be careful about that. They'd spot him a mile off.

Oh, who am I kidding? They'll spot me a mile off anyway. If you looked up "Loser" in the dictionary, there'd be a picture of me, with my eyes halfway shut from blinking and someone making donkey ears behind my head.

He looked dejectedly around the lab. Mr Levitt had been called away and had left his DT class to get on with their assignment in his absence. Of course, the minute he was gone, everybody had left their drawing boards and started messing around and chatting. Mark watched the other boys as they lounged on the backs of chairs, laughed with their mates and flirted with girls. It all seemed so easy for them. Like it was the most natural thing in the world.

When did I get left behind?

They didn't even notice him. That was what hurt. If he was spectacularly ugly, if he wore his trousers at half-mast, then at least he might come in for a bit of bullying now and then. If he was some speccy swot or one of those kids that looked permanently filthy because they ate fried food all day and never washed, then the girls might snigger at him as he passed. But Mark was none of those things. Instead, he seemed to occupy a blind spot in the school heirarchy. He was just *there*, like an extra wandering about in the background of a TV show while the stars talked amongst themselves.

Up until a few months ago, he hadn't really minded. He had his mates Andrew and Graham, he had his hobbies, his parents were nice and there were no particular problems in his life. All in all, he was content.

Then something changed. He didn't know what. He didn't even notice it at first, but every day this new awareness bothered him more and more. It was as if he was waking slowly from a long and pleasant dream to find himself in a cold, damp bedroom with peeling wallpaper and the rain pouring down outside.

Gradually, he became self-conscious. He began to imagine how he must seem to other people, the way he looked, the way he acted. It made him cringe. He began to wonder what he was missing out on.

Andrew and Graham didn't understand. When Mark tried to broach the subject they just gave him blank smiles of incomprehension. They wondered why he wasn't so keen to join in their games any more, but they didn't wonder for long. They just carried on playing without him.

I've grown out of them, thought Mark one day. It was a shock, and it made him sad, but there it was. *I'm embarrassed by my best friends.*

The problem was, he had no idea how to make new ones.

Since then, he'd undertaken a thorough re-evaluation of his life. How was it that he'd never noticed before how geeky his hobbies were? He was into electronics, computers, online games. He built models, took photos of them and put them on his Facebook page. He flew his radio-controlled plane about for hours at a time. He got excited when the guys from NASA announced that they'd detected a new quasar in the Crab Nebula.

If you made a list of all the hobbies least likely to get you a girl, just about everything Mark did would be solidly in the top ten. The only comfort was that he'd never been interested in trainspotting or stamp collecting (although monster trading cards were arguably just as bad; the jury was still out on that one). Only his passion for photography could possibly be classified as cool-ish, since it was kind of arty, and he reckoned that girls liked arty.

But it wasn't too late to do something about his situation. Mark wanted to be part of the in-crowd.

Or at least make his way in from the edges a bit. He wasn't asking for much, just for someone to notice him. Someone other than a teacher or another forgotten kid like himself.

And so, being the meticulous sort, he'd identified a target. Paul Camber.

Paul was the perfect candidate, really. He'd joined the academy at the start of the spring term, and he hadn't really settled in yet. He seemed a friendly type, since he was always hanging out with different people, but he didn't have a close group of mates as far as Mark could tell. That meant he was still a bit of an outsider. Just like Mark.

Mark had waited for him in the corridor outside Mr Harrison's office after biology. He'd felt sure that Paul would recognize a gesture of friendship when he saw it. Mark had lied on his behalf, after all. He'd taken a big risk, grassing up Adam like that. He'd done his best to get Paul out of trouble.

But Paul had walked past like he didn't even recognize him.

Mark had been disappointed at first, but he soon bounced back when he realized what had gone wrong. Nobody had told Paul what Mark had done for him. And it seemed that Paul was still in the dark, since he hadn't so much as looked at Mark all lesson. Surely, if he'd known, Paul would have come over and thanked him by now.

Well, then, time for Plan B. Mr Levitt's departure

had given him the opportunity he needed. He couldn't let himself pass up the chance.

He took a deep breath. His mouth had gone suddenly dry. He felt too hot in his clothes.

Just do it, he thought. *Go over and say hi. Say you saw him in the corridor. Ask how it went with old Harrison.*

How hard could it be?

His feet were taking him across the classroom before he could change his mind. He could sense Andrew and Graham's puzzled gazes following him as he walked. The world crowded in and everything seemed close and tight. He wanted to turn back, but he couldn't now. Not without looking like a fool.

Paul was talking with Ben Hooper and Sandra Appleby as Mark approached. He was telling some funny story about a teacher from his previous school. Mark realized too late that he should have waited until Paul was alone, or at least until he wasn't talking. It would be rude to interrupt. Instead he found himself hovering on the edge of the group, just behind Paul's shoulder, waiting to be noticed.

Seconds ticked by. Agonizing, endless seconds. And nobody so much as looked at him.

His nerve broke. He looked desperate, standing there. He was sure that everybody was watching him and sniggering, but he couldn't just walk away. That would be crushing. Instead, he turned his attention to the drawing board that Paul, Ben and Sandra had been working on.

They were supposed to be designing a simple control system for a Meccano car engine, something to move the car forward and back and turn the wheels. It was child's play for Mark, who'd been doing that kind of thing at age eight, but these three hadn't got very far with it at all. He pretended to be furiously concentrating on it, so he looked like he was doing something.

Maybe he'd been standing in the wrong place. That was why they didn't notice him. On reflection, he should have stood a bit more to the right, instead of just by Paul's shoulder. Standing behind someone that way, that was just creepy. Why wasn't there a manual for this kind of stuff?

Well, he'd screwed up Plan B, that was for sure. Just a few more seconds, and he could walk away and pretend that he'd just come over to take a look at their schematic. A few more seconds and—

"Er. . ." said Paul. "Hi."

They'd noticed him. Just when he didn't want them to any more.

"Can we help?" asked Sandra, in a rather sarcastic tone that he didn't like.

"Oh, I was just looking at what you were doing here," Mark said in a false-casual voice. "I like this part, but you've connected the capacitors all wrong, and you haven't earthed it anywhere."

His words plunged into silence like stones into a black well. Sandra gaped in horrified amusement, half a smile on her face, as if she just couldn't believe she was lucky enough to hear anyone say anything that geeky. Ben gave him a flat look that said: *Seriously? You're actually talking to us?*

Paul just looked a little bit puzzled.

"Ha!" Sandra gave a short, sharp laugh. And that was all.

Mark turned and hurried away from them before they could say anything else. He burned so furiously red, he must have been giving everyone a suntan.

Stupid, stupid, idiot, stupid, STUPID!

He returned to his drawing board, picked up his pencil and started drawing straight lines with the slide rule. He didn't look at anything but the paper.

"What happened?" asked Andrew.

"Did you talk to them?" Graham asked, amazed.

They hadn't even realized that he'd humiliated himself. How could they? They didn't know what embarrassing *was*. Instead of making him feel better, that just made him feel worse. It was like they lived in two different worlds now.

"I told them how to fix their remote," Mark mumbled eventually.

"Really?" Graham was astonished at his friend's bravery. "Well, what did they say?"

"Oh, you know," Mark replied, "they just said thanks."

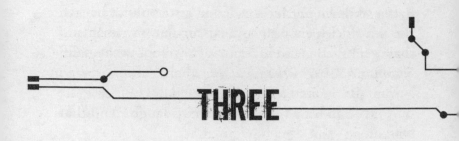

THREE

1

By lunchtime, all the talk was about the silver beetle. Well, it was among Mark's friends, anyway. He doubted if kids like Paul got excited about stuff like that.

The boys who'd found the beetle had taken its squashed body to Mr Sutton for identification. They spent the next double period telling everyone who'd listen about their amazing find, and their encounter with Adam Wojcik. It wasn't long before it occurred to somebody that there might be more of those beetles down by the lake.

Mark knew that looking for beetles wasn't the kind of thing the cool kids did, but when Andrew and Graham asked if he was coming, he said yes anyway. He'd had enough of trying to be someone he wasn't for one day.

When the lunch bell rang, Mark headed back to his dorm and picked up his camera. Like everything else he did, he took photography seriously, and read his

Amateur Photographer magazine cover to cover each week. Last Christmas, he'd persuaded his parents to stump up for a Canon EOS 350D camera with an EF 75-300mm lens. He hid it in a satchel as he scampered across the grounds towards the lake, in case he bumped into someone like Adam who'd demand to "have a go" and somehow break it.

There were about twenty pupils of various ages rummaging through the undergrowth when Mark got to the wood that surrounded the lake. Andrew and Graham were waiting for him down by the shore, beckoning to him frantically. He picked up his step at the sight of the urgent expressions on their faces.

"Get a photo!" Andrew squeaked, pointing at a clump of rushes near the water. "Quick!"

Despite himself, Mark's pulse sped up a little as he hunkered down next to the rushes to take a look. He was sure that the stories had been exaggerated – you'd have to go to the rainforests of the Amazon to find a beetle *that* big – but it definitely didn't sound like something you'd see every day in the English countryside. He had visions of his photograph appearing in a double-page spread in *Amateur Photographer*, with his name printed at the bottom.

It took Mark a moment to find the beetle amid the thick tangle of greenery. When he did, he let out a low whistle.

"That's some beetle," he said.

The stories hadn't been exaggerated at all. On the

contrary, it was *bigger* than the rumours painted it. The one that had been given to Mr Sutton was the size of a mouse, by all accounts. This one was the size of a small rat. It was labouring clumsily through the foliage, which bent under its weight as it clambered along.

"You know what the biggest beetle in the world is?" Graham said. He was full of facts like this. "The Titan beetle. The biggest reported ones have been about seventeen centimetres long. That thing can't be far off that."

"Photo!" Andrew urged.

Amazed, Mark dug out the camera and put it to his eye. He studied the beetle through the magnified viewfinder. Its ridged carapace had the metallic sheen of mercury, and there was something stiff and awkward about the way the creature moved, as if it was somehow dazed or disoriented. Blank silver eyes were set above outsized mandibles that chewed the air in slow and constant motion.

Maybe it was because it was so big, but it really was one evil-looking insect.

He focused in and took a snap. The flash went off unexpectedly. Andrew sucked his breath through his teeth. "Oi! Don't let the others know we've found one!" he complained.

Mark glanced up at the sky. Dark clouds had gathered, making it dim enough to trigger the automatic flash on his camera. He checked the digital picture on the display – too bright – then turned off the flash and lined up again.

But the beetle wasn't moving any more.

"You killed it," Graham muttered. Mark gave him a look.

"Hey! Did you find something?" said a Year Nine, who was coming over to investigate, attracted by the flash. But before Mark could say anything, a shout went up in the trees – "There's one over here!" – and the Year Nine changed direction and joined the stampede to check it out.

Mark returned his attention to the beetle. It was unnaturally still. A few seconds passed, and then suddenly it jerked into motion again. It rotated itself towards him, turning like a miniature tank.

"Here's another!" someone called from the undergrowth nearby. It seemed like they were all over the place. More kids hurried off to examine this new find, leaving Mark and his friends alone.

Mark aimed his camera again. The beetle was larger in the viewfinder now. Slow as it was, it was lumbering towards him with unsettling purpose. He took a snap. The beetle kept on coming.

"Flash it!" said Graham.

"What?"

"You used the flash before."

Mark turned the flash back on, and took another shot. The rushes flickered with light. The beetle froze.

"That," said Andrew, "is weird."

It really *was* weird. In fact, there was something weird about all of this.

Then the beetle was moving again, as if nothing had happened. Most beetles ignored you or tried to move away, and they tended to potter about investigating this and that. But Mark could swear this one was heading right for him, curiously intent on its destination. It made him feel uneasy. Beetles didn't usually do that.

He put his eye to the viewfinder to ready another shot. He was just focusing in on the beetle when there was a quick movement, and something thumped into his camera, knocking his aim off. Mark jerked backwards, away from the rushes, and tripped into Andrew, who caught him and held him up until he could get his feet back under him.

His first thought was that someone had thrown something at him, and he checked his camera automatically. His stomach sank as he saw that the lens was cracked. That lens cost his dad a hundred quid. How was he ever going to explain this?

Neither Andrew nor Graham had even noticed the damage. They were staring at the beetle, which lay on its back, trying to right itself.

"Did you see that?"

"Guys, my *camera*!" Mark complained.

"The beetle broke it."

"The *beetle*?"

"It jumped right into the lens!"

Impossible, thought Mark. It was too big to even get into the air, let alone jump a metre off the ground with sufficient force to break a lens. And yet this whole situation was beginning to feel very, very wrong all of a sudden. He was getting the distinct impression that these strange beetles were not half as harmless as they'd first appeared.

No sooner had Mark thought this than he heard a shriek from nearby. A group of kids came scrambling out of the wood, one of them flailing wildly at himself. At just the same moment, an older pupil stood up suddenly, shaking his hand in the air.

"Bloody thing *bit* me!" he cried.

Another shriek. Mark's head snapped around to find the source of the sound, and couldn't. Instead he saw one of the beetles launch itself from a blackberry bush, a little silver missile flying towards a blond-haired Year Eight. The kid saw it coming and swatted it out of the air with the plastic binder he was carrying.

Suddenly everyone was pushing their way back through the wood, up the slope towards the school. Absurd as it seemed, they were under attack, so they did they only thing they could. They legged it.

2

"Mr Sutton! Mr Sutton!"

Mr Sutton looked up from his book – *Species of Coleoptera* – as the three boys burst into the lab. Mark

Platt, Andrew Taylor and Graham Nicks. They came running in with the childlike urgency of boys much younger than they actually were, and practically fell over each other in their rush to tell him what had happened.

He suppressed a smile. Sometimes it was nice to see kids acting like kids, instead of trying so hard to be grown-ups. Once you got to adulthood, there was no going back. Mr Sutton was of the opinion that you might as well take your time about it. You had the rest of your life to wish you were a kid again.

"Calm down, fellers," he said. "One at a time."

They composed themselves for a moment, then went on exactly as before. In amid all the blurting and interruption Mr Sutton gathered a picture of what had happened down at the lake a few minutes ago.

"Alright, now," he said in his slow, considered manner. "Let's be scientists about this. First thing's first: how many beetles can you think of in the British Isles that have a bite that's dangerous to humans?"

"None!" said Graham quickly. He was the naturalist among them, forever poring over books of birds and insects.

"How many in Europe?"

"None," said Graham again.

"Is there a beetle in the world capable of causing serious harm to a human being?"

They thought about that for a while, and decided that there probably wasn't. "Not unless you ate one,"

42

Graham volunteered. "Some of them would poison you if you ate one."

"Did anyone eat one?"

"Don't think so," said Graham, sounding disappointed.

"Right," said Mr Sutton. "Let's not panic too much, then. I'm sure the nurse can handle a beetle bite or two." He got to his feet and brushed the crumbs of his lunch from his shabby jacket. "I was just about to take a look at my specimen, actually. It's a bit squashed, but worth a poke. Care to sit in?"

The boys eagerly agreed, and followed him over to a workbench, where the beetle that had been crushed by Adam Wojcik's heel lay waiting for dissection.

"I've given up trying to identify it," Mr Sutton said, settling himself on a stool. Then, just for effect, he added, "It's possible we've discovered a whole new species here."

That set the boys to gasping. Mr Sutton didn't for one moment believe it was true, but he never missed an opportunity to get his kids enthusiastic about science.

They gathered round him as he got started. There was a magnifying glass on a flexible arm attached to the table, which he pulled into position to give him a closer look. With the tip of a scalpel and some forceps, he began to prod and pull at the strange insect.

"Notice the unusual silver colour of the chitin," he said. "It's abnormally reflective."

"Chitin?" Andrew asked.

"That's the stuff insect shells are made of," said Graham.

"Full marks, Graham," said Mr Sutton. "Although I'm not one hundred per cent sure it *is* chitin." He peeled away a cracked section of wing casing, then picked it up with his fingers. "Feel that," he said, handing it to Graham.

They passed it among themselves while Mr Sutton carried on probing.

"Feels a bit like metal, sir," Mark ventured.

"Good. That's what I think, too. Wafer-thin metal. Put it aside and we can run some chemical tests on it."

"But how can it be metal?" Andrew complained.

It couldn't, but that wasn't going to stop Mr Sutton implying that it was. "That's something we shall have to find out."

He could sense the excitement in his audience and, he had to admit, he was feeling some of it himself. He'd given up his dreams of becoming a great scientist when he realized that his talents lay in teaching, but he'd never lost the thrill of discovery. And this beetle was something truly unusual.

Delicately, Mr Sutton prised away another section of the wing casing to get a look at the abdomen underneath. What he saw made him frown in surprise.

"Hmm," he said.

"What, sir?"

"Mark, why don't you take a look at this?"

He moved aside and let Mark take his place at the magnifying glass. Graham looked crestfallen that he hadn't been asked to look first – after all, he was the insect expert among his friends, and he was proud of it. Ordinarily, Mr Sutton would have recognized this and honoured him accordingly, but this was something more suited to Mark's expertise than Graham's.

"Beneath the wing case, on the surface of the abdomen. What do you see?"

"Silver lines, sir. There's dozens of fine silver lines running all over. And little blobs."

"Notice anything strange about them?"

Mark thought a minute. "They don't look right," he said. "I mean, when they bend, they bend at sharp angles, not curved, like in nature. . ." Mark fought to explain himself. "It's all too *regular*."

"And what does it remind you of?"

Mr Sutton waited for the answer, perched on the edge of his stool in anticipation. Underneath his calm facade, he'd become ever so slightly anxious. Could he have been mistaken? Surely it was too incredible to be true? He needed someone to tell him that he wasn't completely deluded.

Mark was blushing. He knew what he thought; he was just afraid of being laughed at.

"Go on," Mr Sutton said gently. "There's no wrong answer."

"They look like circuits, sir. Like you get on the motherboard of a computer. Except really, really small."

"Yes," said Mr Sutton. "Circuits. That's exactly what they look like."

And if that's true, he thought, *then what on earth* are *these things?*

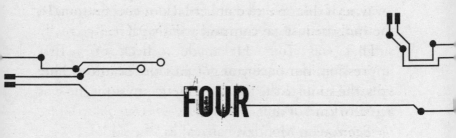

FOUR

1

Tom always kissed the same way.

At first it was gentle, just a press of his lips on hers. Then a little harder, then harder still. More often than not he'd give a little sigh through his nose about then, the signal that he was heating up. Erika would feel his lips parting, and she'd part hers too, and their tongues would meet. They'd go at it for a while, proper French kissing (but who called it French any more? Every country did it) and at some point he'd give her a little bite on the lip, and she'd bite him back. Then he'd pull away, brushing his lips softly against hers a couple of times, and he'd stare into her eyes earnestly, and it would be over.

At first, when he'd done it that way, it had been electrifying. *Wow, he can kiss*, she'd thought. Nowadays, it was just nice. It had taken her a while to notice, but he always did the same things in the same order at the same time. Whenever she tried to change the rhythm, he just looked puzzled and broke away, as if disappointed at her lack of cooperation. In the end, she just gave up and went with it.

That was Tom. He made a heck of a first impression, but once you got past the beautiful blue eyes, the smile to die for, the athletic physique, he was actually kind of dull.

"See you on Monday, babycakes," he said.

Oh yes. And he liked to call her babycakes.

She let him go first, so they wouldn't be seen coming out from behind the dorm hall together, and risk wolf whistles from his friends at the gate. Tom liked to kiss her in front of everyone, but it made her feel awkward and on display, so she insisted on doing it somewhere nobody could see them. In this case, it was round the back of the visitor's accommodation block, which was empty on a Friday afternoon.

He turned at the corner and gave her a little wave. She waved back. He really was handsome, she thought. Just the kind of boy you'd expect a girl like her to be going out with.

So why didn't she feel lucky?

She made her way round the back of the dorm hall and came out on to the main drive of the academy. At one end of the drive was the looming school building, with its stern, narrow windows, exuding an air of disapproval. At the other end was the gate. Halfway between, the drive split in half and looped round a circular lawn, at the centre of which was a grand old stone fountain surrounded by wide stone steps. Several pupils were sitting there, watching the activity at the gate. She headed over and joined them.

Friday afternoon was always busy at the gate as parents and drivers arrived to take the children home. Some kids at Mortingham were day pupils from the nearby towns, but most were here all week and only went home at weekends. Then there were those who never went home on Fridays. They stayed at school the whole term, usually because their parents were too busy and important to look after them.

On weekends, Mortingham Boarding Academy lost about four-fifths of its pupils. Its raucous corridors went quiet. Its halls echoed emptily.

Erika sat on the steps and watched as Tom said his goodbyes to his rugby mates by the gate. The drive was lined with cars, and everyone was out of uniform and looking relaxed in their own clothes. The dark clouds overhead didn't dampen the light-hearted mood that prevailed at the end of a school week. A chilly breeze whipped strands of blonde hair across Erika's eyes, and she brushed them away and thought of the weekend to come.

She wasn't going home today; her parents were on holiday. It was a relief to stay at school for the weekend. Home was where there were hours of violin practice, the tennis coach, the maths tutor. Home was where her life wasn't her own.

But then, was it ever?

All those girls who were jealous of her for being

good at school, good at sport, good at music. If only they knew the hours she was forced to put in, the hours she never spoke of, just so she could be the best. Even when she'd brought Tom home for the weekend, she was forced to practice most of the time while he made nice with Mummy. Elegant old Mummy and handsome, polite Tom, sharing tea and scones while she played Debussy in the conservatory. How bloody delightful. The way they went on, you'd think they liked each other more than her.

She wouldn't complain, though. She couldn't. Who would listen? Who'd ever have sympathy for her?

She knew what they thought about her. Little Miss Perfect. Everyone was waiting for her to slip up. Everyone wanted to see her hit a bum note in a recital, to fluff a penalty shot, to get a B. Even her best friends watched like vultures, ready to exult in the slightest failing, eager for a sign that she was human like them. Sometimes the pressure was enough to make her want to scream and tear her hair out.

But she had a face made for smiling, so she smiled instead.

She spotted Soraya, and gave her a wave. Soraya was heading home too – Erika had already said goodbye, knowing that Tom would want some snogging time – but Caitlyn was around. Erika wasn't sure how she felt about that. Ordinarily she'd have been glad, but sometimes she got the sense that Caitlyn was holding something back, and never more so than this lunchtime. Something was off between them; Caitlyn had barely been able to disguise it.

Erika suspected it was to do with Paul Camber, of course. Probably because he'd given her that look after his stupid fight with Adam. The smallest little thing like that could set Caitlyn off when Paul was concerned. It didn't matter that Erika didn't fancy Paul, didn't even *like* him much. Somehow, in Caitlyn's eyes, she was encouraging him. Somehow it was Erika's fault that the boy Caitlyn fancied didn't fancy her back.

There were times when Erika wished she lived in a world where being pretty didn't matter, where your grades didn't matter, where nobody gave a damn who you were supposed to be but only cared about what you *were*. But she didn't suppose a day like that would be coming anytime soon.

She looked up at the sky as she felt the first of the raindrops land on her nose.

Better get inside, she thought. *Looks like a storm*.

2

Paul sat in the window seat in his dorm room, his feet up, watching the rain run down the glass. It was darker than the hour suggested, only seven o'clock, yet it might as well have been night. Lightning flickered in the distance. Paul counted nine seconds before thunder growled overhead.

He shared his dorm room with three other boys, all of whom went home every weekend. He liked having the room to himself for a couple of days each week. There wasn't much privacy in a boarding school. Paul had a knack of getting on with everyone, but sometimes he needed to be alone.

The lights were on across the campus, illuminating the paths and the buildings. He watched a pupil in a raincoat hurrying from the library, hood up and a satchel clutched in her arms. A Year Eight, late for dinner. It would be another forty-five minutes before Paul's year were allowed in to eat.

Well, if I have to be confined to dorms, at least it's better in here than out there.

When she was gone, Paul let his eyes roam. Ever since January, the walls of Mortingham Boarding Academy had been the limits of his world, and he knew it well. It was a prison that he had no interest in leaving. Here he was, and here he'd stay.

He looked over at the school, black beneath the storm. A dozen narrow yellow windows slit its glistening walls. Mortingham Boarding Academy had grown and changed over the two hundred years since it was built, but its chill heart remained. The school building stood at the centre of everything, a terrifying Gothic pile that dominated all around it. Its vast grounds had once been used as vegetable plots tended by the occupants of the workhouse, and later as gardens for suffering patients to wander in. Now, among the old dorm halls and the ruins of the chapel, there were buildings of a later age. The most modern was the sports hall, built in gleaming steel and glass, with swooping curves that defied the strict, rigid lines of the school's facade.

Paul had never been much of a fan of old stuff. History lessons frustrated him. It wasn't that he didn't think it was worth learning, it was just that history was history. A great big heap of traditions and grudges. For every good thing it had to teach there were three bad ones. All over the world, people were killing each other because of history. Families threw out their children because of history. Lovers couldn't be together because of history.

But what he distrusted about it most of all was this: history didn't change. And if there was one thing the past six months had taught him, it was that everything changed, whether you wanted it to or not. Change was the only thing you could ever rely on.

If it was up to him, he'd wipe the slate clean and start again. No more history. Start from zero, without any of the baggage, without any of the old hatreds.

But that was the problem with history. Once something had happened, it had happened. And no amount of wishing could make it unhappen.

He thought about his confrontation with Mr Harrison earlier that day. *"I've seen a hundred boys like you,"* the headmaster had said. *"You all think you know better. You all think you're something special."*

But Mr Harrison was wrong. Paul didn't think he knew better than anyone else. He just couldn't help the way he was. The way he'd become. It felt like it was all out of his control.

Mum and Dad were gone. One day, they'd been alive and well and happy and breathing and living and loving. The next, they disappeared from the face of the earth. How the hell could anything ever make sense after that?

The thought brought hot tears to his eyes. They took him by surprise, and he blinked them back angrily before they could fall. He wasn't allowed to cry. That was what you were *supposed* to do. You were meant to cry and get angry and do all that stuff for a while, and then eventually you'd feel okay and the world would be right again and you'd go on as normal. But he didn't *want* to feel normal. He didn't *want* things to be right. And he certainly didn't want to stop feeling angry.

Because that would mean they were gone. Just gone, winked out of existence. And that would mean that he accepted it was *just one of those things*. And he didn't. He never would.

Paul was still staring out of the window when something went loping past the dorm hall and across the lawn, heading in the direction of the old chapel. Between the dark, the blurring effect of the rain on the window and the tears still in his eyes, Paul could barely make it out, but he could tell by the way it moved that it was a dog. A *big* dog. He wiped his eyes and pressed his face closer to the glass, trying to see through the restlessly switching channels of rainwater.

The sight of a dog on campus grounds was strange enough. But there was something else. . .

Lightning stuttered in the distance, and the scene was suddenly lit in sharp white. The dog froze still. Paul blinked the dazzle from his eyes and looked again. Yes, there it was, just standing there like a statue. He fought to see through the water running down the pane. And he was certain he saw. . . It *couldn't* be, but. . .

He could have sworn that dog was silver.

Thunder boomed overhead, violent enough to make him jump. When he looked again, the dog was out of sight, swallowed by the dark.

Paul jumped to his feet and snatched his coat up from where he'd thrown it across a chair. It briefly crossed his mind that he wasn't allowed to leave his dorm hall, but that didn't come close to stopping him.

After all, what could Mr Harrison, what could *anyone* do to him that was worse than what had already happened?

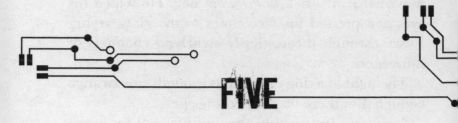

FIVE

1

Mr Harrison sat back in his chair, the leather creaking as he settled his weight, and took a sip of whisky. There were few things in life as fine as a good whisky. He kept a bottle of Laphroaig Quarter Cask in the drawer of the mahogany desk in his study, and it was his secret pleasure to pour himself a finger of the good stuff before dinner, when he was attending to the last of the day's paperwork.

It was a whisky kind of day, too: the kind of day when you were glad to be inside. The storm boomed and rolled and threw rain against the narrow arched windows of his study. It was chilly in here – the school building never got warm – but the drink put a bit of fire in him. He had a hot dinner to look forward to in the dining hall, and after that he'd head over to his house in the northwest corner of the campus. He'd put his feet up, stick on some Bach or Brahms. When it came to music, his motto was "Nothing less than a hundred years old." All that new bleep-bleep rubbish gave him an ulcer.

He put down the whisky and flicked through the papers in his hand. Staff performance reports, which he had to complete for the board of governors. Boring, boring. . .

Aha.

Mr Alistair Sutton. Now *that* might be an interesting one to write. Mr Sutton's report would be less than glowing. Mr Harrison wasn't a man to mince his words: Mr Sutton was too soft, and he was going to say so. The brawl by the lake that morning was just another example of the lack of discipline in his classes. He indulged his pupils far too much. He spent too much time trying to be their friend and too little time trying to be their teacher.

If there was one thing Mr Harrison's years of experience had taught him, it was this: give the little sods an inch, and they'd take a mile.

He'd been idealistic once. Wasn't everyone, when they were young? Time took care of that. When he first became a teacher, he dreamed of inspiring young people to learn. History was his subject, and back then he'd had quite a passion for it.

The problem was, nobody else seemed to.

Oh, he found a few bright young things over the years, kids who were eager to be taught, but they were tiny shards of diamond in a mountain of coal. Most pupils simply didn't care. He was shocked that they didn't get the same joy from history that he did. They memorized dates and names because they had to, and remembered them just long enough to pass their exams. But they didn't understand anything.

And then there were the louts, the troublemakers, the ones who tried to disrupt the class. The anti-learners, who wanted everyone to be as ignorant as they were. Those were the worst of all.

Don't you see? he wanted to cry. *Don't you see how wonderful it all is? How people discover their true worth in times of crisis? How civilizations rise and fall, each one forming the ashes for the next to rise from? It's the story of us, don't you see that?*

But they didn't see. The Ancient Greeks had come and gone, Rome had risen and been sacked by barbarians, there had been plague and war and empires that had crumbled to dust. Each of his pupils was the product of a line that had lasted thousands of years, slipping through the deadly minefield of history for generation after generation, a game of impossible chance that resulted in *this* exact person, *that* particular child. All that, so they could sit idly at their desk in his class and flick rubber bands and yawn and wait for it to be over.

Slowly but surely, he'd stopped caring too. He stopped believing he was doing any good. He stopped thinking of them as pupils and began to think of them as opponents. His job was to make them shut up, learn, and pass their exams. Their job was to stop him.

After a while, they were no longer people. Their names meant nothing. Instead he labelled them: Quiet, Slow, Bad Attitude, Cocky, Hard Worker. That was all he needed to know. If they did what they were told, he ignored them. If they got out of line, he crushed them.

School was a battlefield. Each new generation thought they knew it all, but they were just rookies in comparison to him. He was the general. They didn't have a trick he hadn't seen before.

Mr Harrison got up and walked across his study to the window, bringing his whisky with him. He sipped it as he looked out at the rain. Maybe he didn't like Mr Sutton because Mr Sutton reminded him of himself. How he used to be, before he'd given up.

As he considered this, his gaze fell on a boy scampering across the grounds in a raincoat, a hood pulled over his head. There was something furtive in the way he ran that pricked Mr Harrison's instincts. Whoever that was, they were up to no good.

Then the boy turned his head, and lightning flickered. Inside that hood, Mr Harrison saw the face of Paul Camber.

Thunder cracked the sky, almost overhead now. Mr Harrison's knuckles went white as he gripped harder on his glass. He drained the whisky from it, slammed it down, swept up his coat and stormed wrathfully out of the door.

2

Rain splattered against Paul's coat as he hurried across the grass, hunched over against the assault from the sky. Bullying gusts of wind shoved past him and then went whistling away down the valley. His feet sank into the drenched earth; his shoes and trousers were already ruined with mud.

Paul barely noticed. *I saw it*, he thought. *I know I saw it*.

He wiped a hand across his face and scanned the campus, eyes sharp and hard beneath his hood. By now he'd strayed off the paths, and was surrounded by the furious gloom of the storm. The dorm halls were clusters of lights that hung disembodied in the distance. Behind him, the looming mass of the school building was still visible through the obscuring rain, windows aglow, stone blacker than the dark.

Ahead of him were the woods that surrounded the lake. On the edge of them stood the ruin of the old chapel. The dog had been heading in this direction, and there wasn't a lot else in this corner of the campus. It had to be nearby, and he was determined to spot it again.

Paul couldn't have said what it was that drove him out into the rain that night. Curiosity? No. There wasn't much that excited his curiosity these days. It was just that he needed to prove to himself that he hadn't imagined that silver dog. He needed to know.

Once, he'd believed the world was a sane and ordered place. But that was before his parents vanished, quietly chalked off the planet. After that, nothing made sense any more.

Mr Sutton thought there was something wrong with him, for not putting his faith in anything or anyone. But it was everyone else who was crazy, for blindly believing that things would be alright as long as they followed the rules, as long as they just kept on doing whatever they were doing.

That silver dog was proof of the world's madness. It was an impossible creature, made of metal. He'd *seen* it. Now he just had to make sure.

Paul headed for the old chapel first. He told himself that it was because the chapel was closest, but the truth was, he was scared of the woods. They hissed and thrashed in the storm. Anything could be hiding in there.

It had been a *big* dog, he reminded himself. For the first time, he wondered if it was entirely wise to be out here alone with a creature like that on the loose.

He neared the old chapel, its ghostly broken walls becoming more solid with every step. He stopped and listened in case there was something within, but he could hear nothing over the din of the storm.

A sense of foreboding was gnawing at him. This

might be his last chance to turn back and walk away. Better that way, perhaps. Better if he was never sure what he'd seen from the window of his dorm room tonight.

But the hesitation lasted only a moment. He went to a gap in the wall and looked inside.

The ruin was deserted. Just an empty shell of stone.

Paul wasn't sure if it was relief or disappointment he felt just then. He walked through the gap and into the ancient chapel. The floor had been broken up and consumed by the earth long ago, and now it was covered with a lumpy carpet of mud and grass. Only the half-fallen walls remained, an outline of the building that had once stood here.

Lightning flickered and thunder crashed overhead. Paul pushed back his hood, closed his eyes and lifted his face to the storm. Chaos. This was the way of the world. Not the calm ease of a sunny day. The driving, switching wind, the ripping violence of thunder, the rain that washed everything away and left the land sparkling and changed.

Bring it on, he thought. *Wash it all away*.

A heavy hand slapped down on his shoulder, making him jump. He whirled. Hulking in the gloom, like an ogre out of myth, was Mr Harrison, his face dark as the clouds.

"Paul Camber!" he roared. "What on earth do you think you're doing out here?"

Then Paul saw a flash of silver from the corner of

his eye, and the dog lunged out of the dark, knocking Mr Harrison to the ground and pinning him there. Paul stared, too shocked to move, as Mr Harrison bellowed and struggled beneath its weight. Its snarls sounded unnatural, low growls accompanied by a high-pitched whine like a buzzsaw. Mr Harrison had his arm up in front of him to ward the beast off, and as Paul watched, it dragged its claw along the headmaster's forearm.

Mr Harrison's cry of pain was enough to spur Paul to action. He searched around frantically and saw a rock lying on the ground. He ran over to it and snatched it up. Holding it in his fist, he turned, ready to bring it down on the dog's rain-slicked back. But by then, Mr Harrison had already flung his attacker off, and was scrambling away along the ground. Paul found himself looking right into the dog's eyes as it crouched at bay in the centre of the ruin.

His blood slowed to a crawl. For the first time, he got a really good look at the creature he'd seen from his window.

In shape, it resembled a Border collie, one of the sheep-herding dogs that farmers used for their flocks in the pastures up the valley. But Paul had never seen a Border collie that big, and never one so horrifyingly *strange*. Most of its body was covered in a silver mesh, hundreds of wiry tendrils that spread unevenly across its skin like some alien form of circuitry. Its hind legs had cables instead of tendons. In some places, there were irregular plates of silvery metal that seemed fused into the flesh beneath.

And yet there was muscle and bone there too, patches where the silver mesh hadn't spread, where scrappy tufts of black and white fur were still visible.

Paul might have thought this was some kind of robot, impossible though that was. But now he saw it, he knew it wasn't. This was both flesh and metal, animal and machine.

The creature bared its fangs. Silver fangs. Suddenly the rock in Paul's hand seemed a pathetic excuse for a weapon.

And then it turned and bolted, racing away through one of the gaps in the chapel walls. In an instant, it was gone.

Paul stood where he was, the rock still half-raised to strike, his chest rising and falling as he panted in frightened breaths. Then Mr Harrison gave a strained groan of pain through gritted teeth, and Paul remembered the headmaster. He dropped the rock and ran over to him, crouching down by his side.

"You alright, sir?"

Mr Harrison was clutching his forearm, wiggling the fingers on his wounded hand. "Bloody *dogs*!" he snapped angrily. "I'll find out who owns that mutt and I'll *have* 'em!" He took Paul's outstretched hand and pulled himself up.

"Is it bad?"

Mr Harrison slid back his sleeve. Rain washed away the blood from his hairy forearm. He flexed his hand again and hissed in his breath through his teeth. "It'll be alright," he grunted.

Paul looked at him, waiting for something more than that. Mr Harrison looked back.

"Didn't you see it, sir?" he asked. "The dog?"

"Course I bloody *saw* it, you fool. It *attacked* me!"

"No, sir. The dog . . . it wasn't right. It was . . . it was like it was *mechanical*."

He saw a moment of doubt on Mr Harrison's face. Just a moment. Then the headmaster's expression hardened. "Don't be ridiculous, Camber. It was a dog. That's all. Now get back to your dorm, and don't think I've forgotten why I came out here in the first place. I'm going to see the nurse, and then we're going to have a long talk about what happens when you disobey me."

He turned and began to stalk away towards the medical block, where the school nurse lived. But he'd only gone a few steps before he swayed, staggered, and had to put out his hand against the chapel wall to stop himself falling over.

Paul rushed to his side. It didn't matter what had happened between them before; Mr Harrison was obviously in trouble, and Paul could hardly leave him that way.

"Here," he said, offering his arm. "I'd better go with you, eh?"

Harrison pushed away the arm, straightened himself up and walked off, slowly and unsteadily. Paul trailed along behind him, ready to catch him if he stumbled again, and in that manner they made it to the medical block.

3

The nurse on duty was Nurse Wan, a small lady of Chinese descent who flitted about restlessly like a moth. She was already in something of a fluster when Mr Harrison came in from the rain, dripping all over the carpet and holding his bloodied forearm. She let out a little squeak when she saw him and then came rushing over.

"Mr Harrison! What's happened?" Her accent was crisply English.

Paul slipped in behind him while Mr Harrison explained how he'd been scratched by a dog. Paul waited to see if he'd mention that the dog was unusual in any way, but he didn't. He'd already convinced himself that the thing he'd seen was only in his imagination. Easier to deny it than to face the fact that it might be true.

Paul hovered around while the nurse guided Mr Harrison to a chair. She rolled back his sleeve, took a look at the wound, and frowned.

"Are your tetanus shots up to date?" she asked.

"Had a booster last year."

"How do you feel?"

"He was stumbling a bit on the way over here," Paul volunteered.

Mr Harrison gave him a poisonous glare. "I don't feel a hundred per cent, put it that way."

"Probably the shock of it all. Come on, I need to clean that up. There's some dirt or something in the wound."

Mr Harrison got to his feet with some difficulty – he did seem unusually weak – and he was led away down a corridor by the tiny nurse. Paul was left alone in the waiting room of the medical block. He didn't quite know what to do next, so he sat down in a plastic chair, ruffled his wet hair, and waited. He didn't want to go back to his dorm yet. He was too disturbed by what he'd just seen.

For a minute or two, he just sat around, processing everything. The clock ticked on the wall, showing twenty past seven. Rain blew against the windows. He studied his reflection in the darkened glass. He examined small imperfections in the short green carpet.

The dog. He should tell her about the dog when she came back. It might be important. Whatever Mr Harrison said—

He heard Nurse Wan's rapid step from the corridor, and she whisked back into the waiting room.

"Is he alright?" Paul asked.

She glanced at him as if she'd just noticed he was there. "Did you get scratched, too?" she asked sharply.

"No," said Paul, a little surprised by the tone of her voice.

"Bitten? Did it touch you?"

"The dog? No."

She seemed relieved. Paul opened his mouth to tell her about the strange metal on the dog, but she'd already gone to a phone behind the reception desk and picked it up. She dialled a number, listened, hung up the phone and picked it up again. She rattled the cut-off switch and listened again. Then she looked up at Paul.

"Does your mobile have a signal?" she asked.

"No one gets a signal here," he said. "We're in a valley. Half of us don't even bother carrying them around."

Nurse Wan sighed impatiently, as if she'd already known the answer before she asked the question. She thought for a moment.

"Is he alright?" Paul asked again, more concerned this time.

"It's not just him," she said. "It's Jason White. He was brought in with Eddie Grant a few hours ago. The two of them got bitten by some beetles near the lake at lunchtime, and by the afternoon they were both feeling very ill. Eddie Grant got picked up by his parents, but Jason. . ." She rubbed the back of her neck, worried and agitated. Suddenly she snapped her fingers. "Run over to the school for me, will you?" She scribbled down a number on a slip of paper and gave it to him.

"What for?" Paul asked.

"All the phones in the campus go through a switchboard in the school building. This phone's dead, but you should be able to call from there. That number's the duty doctor at the hospital. If that doesn't work, find the caretaker and get him to check the switchboard."

"Hospital?" Paul felt a chill seep into him.

"Just in case," said Nurse Wan. "Jason White's getting sicker, and I'm a little worried. He might need to spend the night there. Go on. I need to stay here."

Paul got to his feet and hurried off to do as he was told. *Hospital? Is it really that serious?*

It was only when he was halfway to the school that he realized he'd forgotten to tell Nurse Wan that the dog had been silver.

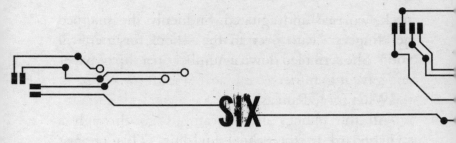

SIX

1

The heavy double doors at the entrance of the school building were locked, of course. Pupils were forbidden inside after seven o'clock, when the first dinner bell rang and all the after-school activities were done. Paul knew there was another door which the teachers used when they were working late, but he'd never troubled to find out where it was.

He tugged on the old iron bell-pull, and kept on pulling until he heard a key rattle, and the door was pushed open a crack. It was the caretaker. Paul recognized him but didn't know his name. He was a tall, thin man with a patchy ginger beard, wearing dirty blue overalls. Like all school caretakers, he was regarded by the pupils as slightly creepy and possibly unhinged.

Paul hastily explained the situation. The caretaker listened with a wary scowl on his face, as if he suspected a trick.

"Nothing wrong with the phones last time I checked," he said.

"Well, there's something wrong with the phone in the medical block," said Paul. "Can you let me in? It's important."

The caretaker considered that. "You're not supposed to be in here after seven."

Paul was getting frustrated. He was already wet through, and the caretaker wasn't helping his mood. He held up the slip of paper that Nurse Wan had given him and spoke very slowly and firmly, as if to an idiot. "We need . . . to call . . . a *doctor*!"

The caretaker's scowl deepened, but he stepped back and let Paul through, then locked the door behind him. He glared at the puddle Paul was making on the the floor. "Come on, then," he said sullenly, and stalked off down the corridor.

Paul followed. The silence in the school sounded louder in contrast to the storm outside. The classrooms they passed were dark. This was the twilight world of school after hours, the eerie, empty land where caretakers lurked. Paul had walked these corridors a hundred times in the six months he'd been here, but never like this. It felt like he was being given a glimpse behind the veil of the ordinary.

They came to a public phone in the corridor, one of several that pupils could use to call home. There were many similar ones scattered throughout the dorms. Paul wondered if it would have been easier to find one of them instead of having to deal with the caretaker.

"You'll have to put in the money yourself," said the caretaker, as he pulled the handset from the cradle and held it out to Paul. Paul took it, listened, and gave it back with an expression that said: *I told you so*. The caretaker put it to his own ear. He tapped the cut-off switch a few times, just like Nurse Wan had.

Why do people do that? Paul thought. *Did they learn it from the movies? It never works.*

"Dead," said the caretaker. "There's another one round the corner."

Paul opened his mouth to say *that* one wouldn't be working either, but he decided to let the caretaker find out for himself.

"Huh," said the caretaker, when it turned out Paul was right.

"Nurse Wan said you should check the switchboard, or something," Paul offered helpfully.

"Right," said the caretaker. "The switchboard." He walked off down the corridor. After a few steps, he stopped and looked back. "Well? Can't leave you here on your own, you know. Not allowed to."

Paul caught up with him. "Where are we going?"

"Basement," he replied.

"There's a basement?"

"Oh, yeah," said the caretaker, with a grin that

exposed his crooked teeth. "You'll like it."

2

The route to the basement took them deep into the heart of the school. They passed along a corridor with windows that looked out on to the quad, an enclosed square open to the sky where special assemblies and graduation ceremonies were held. They walked down dour and forbidding old corridors hung with portraits of former headmasters with grim and haughty faces. Presently, they came to the Osbourne Gallery, or, as it was better known, the Hall of Show-Offs.

The Hall of Show-Offs was a long, wide corridor with a high ceiling and decorative stone pillars set into the walls. Placed along its length, in the centre of the gallery, were seven glass cases on pedestals. In each was displayed a famous invention from one of the academy's former students.

One contained a model made of coloured plastic balls linked by a series of metal rods, representing a molecule of some important chemical. In another was a novel called *The White Bird Singing*, which had won a big prize or something. Paul had never stopped to look.

At the end of the hall was the most impressive display. A full-sized combustion engine, polished and gleaming inside its glass case. It was put there to commemorate some Mortingham genius who'd designed a new and more efficient fuel conversion system for small aircraft and seaplanes.

"Knew him," the caretaker grunted, thumbing at the engine as they passed it.

"Did you?" Paul said, half-interested.

"Yeah." The caretaker wiped his nose on the sleeve of his overalls. "He was a little git."

The basement was reached by an unmarked door of sturdy wood, set into an alcove. The caretaker unlocked it, turned on the lights, and led him down a stairwell. There was none of the grandeur of the old academy here. The walls were bare brick, lit by stark fluorescent lights.

They descended to a corridor which ran both ways into darkness. The caretaker thumped a press-switch and one end of the corridor lit up. Paul heard the switch ticking as its timer counted down. It would turn the lights off again after thirty seconds or so, to save energy.

"You don't want to get caught in the dark down here," said the caretaker, grinning again.

He set off, and Paul followed nervously. The caretaker was right: he really *didn't* want to find himself down here in the dark. Maybe he was just unsettled by the sight of that strange dog, but this place made his skin creep. It felt *hungry*, as if the cold, sucking, empty blackness at the end of the corridor was just waiting for its chance to swallow him.

They passed through a maze of corridors, with

closed doors to either side, bearing signs like DUCT ACCESS 2/A and CABLE STORAGE. He saw one with a childish silhouette of a man being hit by a bolt of lightning, and the legend: KEEP OUT! DANGER OF DEATH! Each time they turned into a new corridor, the caretaker hit another press-switch to light it up. A few seconds afterwards, the lights in the corridor they'd just passed through would go out. Paul had a disturbing feeling that they were racing against the dark, and only just winning.

They passed several large grates set into the wall at floor level. Paul didn't notice them until he saw one with the grate removed, leaning against the wall. Inside was a shaft of reflective metal, big enough to crawl through.

"Billy," the caretaker said, and tutted. "I keep fixing it, he keeps taking it off."

"Who's Billy?" Paul asked automatically.

"You don't know about Billy McCarthy?" The caretaker sounded surprised.

"I haven't been here long," Paul said.

The caretaker just chuckled to himself and walked round the corner. He stopped in front of a door with a sign on it that read: DANGER. It wasn't new and plastic like the other signs down here, but old and made of discoloured copper.

"In here?" Paul asked doubtfully.

"Oh, no. Can't go in there. That's the boiler room. Behind that door is the whole heating system for the entire building. Great big Victorian gas-fired monster, takes up half the basement, pretty much. All those huge old air ducts, they were built at the same time, though I don't think they ever got used." He gave Paul a sidelong look. "Not by us, anyway."

Paul waited to hear what he meant by that.

"Billy McCarthy. . ." said the caretaker. "Billy McCarthy was a boy about your age. He was at the academy back in nineteen-fifty-something, before my time. Little tearaway, so they said. Anyway, one day he found his way down here, don't ask me how. The caretaker left the door unlocked, I suppose. They didn't have any lights in the basement back in those days, so Billy gets himself a torch and decides to have a bit of a look around. And that's when he sees this sign."

He tapped the sign on the door, as if Paul didn't know what he meant.

"Well, Billy was one of them boys couldn't resist something like that. So in he goes, and while he's in there, he takes it into his head to start messing around with the boiler. Maybe he thought he could shut it off and they'd have to cancel lessons the next morning. It was winter, see?"

Paul was beginning to get the sense that the caretaker had told this story many times before. There was a slick and rehearsed quality to it, as if he were a tour guide.

"Anyway," the caretaker continued, "next day the heating doesn't come on, right enough. So when the caretaker comes in that morning he goes down to the basement to investigate. Straight away, he notices the smell. It reeks of gas. Thick enough to choke you. But this caretaker, he weren't the sharpest tool in the box, and it wasn't all health and safety in those days. So he decides to shut off the leak himself. Coughing and spluttering, he is, by the time he gets to this spot. He pushes the door open, and it bumps against something, so he shoves it a bit harder, and then he sees what's blocking the door."

The caretaker leaned closer, until Paul could smell his sour-milk breath. "It was Billy McCarthy's body."

The lights went out.

Paul stood stock-still, shocked by the sudden and complete loss of sight. He'd never known a darkness as complete and total as this.

From nearby, he heard a slow cackle. "Some say he's still down here," the caretaker said, his voice disembodied. "You hear him sometimes, creeping round in the air ducts. Sometimes you catch him, looking up at you, them eyes glittering in the dark. Might be he's watching us right now."

Fright was suddenly overtaken by anger. The caretaker had played him. Brought him down here, spun him a ghost story, and timed it so the lights went out at just the right moment. Evidently he was getting his revenge for Paul's rudeness earlier.

Well, Paul wasn't going to give him the satisfaction of showing he was scared. He just stood where he was, silently, and folded his arms to show he was unimpressed.

"He'd messed with a gas valve, hadn't he?" said the caretaker. His voice was further away now: he was moving off down the corridor. As Paul's eyes adjusted, he saw a tiny orange light in the darkness, a little way away. "He got himself trapped inside, suffocated on the fumes. But it could've been worse, you know. If that caretaker had made so much as a spark, this whole school would've been blown to bits. Even the spark from a light switch would've done it. If we'd had these handy-dandy press-switches installed back then, he'd have hit the button and *BANG*!"

The lights flared again, dazzling Paul. The caretaker was standing at the end of the corridor, near where Paul had seen the orange light. He realized it was a guide light, so you could find the button in the dark. Which was exactly what the caretaker had done.

"And *that's* why you don't go into the boiler room," the caretaker said, and he went off up the corridor, cackling to himself. Paul gave the boiler room door one final glance, then swore under his breath and followed.

3

A little way further on, they came to a metal door

marked COMMUNICATIONS. The caretaker reached in and flicked a switch – a normal light switch this time. The room lit up for a second and then went dark with a glassy *tink* as the bulb blew out. The caretaker cursed and dug out a small Maglite torch from his overalls. It was the size of a tube of lipstick, but when he turned it on it was startlingly bright.

"These lights are always going out," he grumbled. "Can't understand it sometimes."

"Must be Billy McCarthy's ghost," said Paul sarcastically.

The caretaker grinned at him and they went inside. After a few seconds, the light in the corridor went out, leaving them with only the Maglite to see by. Eerie shadows lunged and swayed across their faces as the caretaker shone it around. Paul felt a lot less brave all of a sudden.

The room was large and dank. There were piled-up cardboard boxes that had sunk with the moisture, and thick heating pipes running along the back wall. Near the door was a large junction box, with a key hanging off it on a chain. The caretaker opened it up. Inside was a bewildering mass of wires.

"There's only one phone cable out of this place, see, on account of how isolated we are," said the caretaker, shining the light around inside. "Everything gets routed through this automatic switchboard, then it's sent on its way down the line. Storm's probably done something to it."

"No," said Paul. He reached over and tilted the Maglite up. "I'd say it was more likely because of that."

A thick cable ran from the junction box up to the ceiling. It had been entirely chewed through.

The caretaker snorted. "Mice," he said.

"We need to get a doctor," said Paul. "There's a sick kid in the medical block."

"Well, someone's just going to have to drive to town, then, cause there's nobody calling out of here until that gets fixed."

Paul opened his mouth to reply, but at that moment they heard a sound, loud in the underground silence. A scrabbling, clicking sound, as of tiny claws.

"I can *hear* them, the little buggers!" the caretaker snarled. He whirled and shone his Maglite in the direction of the sound. The beam played among the boxes and pipes. "Where are they?"

"Let's just go," said Paul. "We need to tell the nurse."

The caretaker ignored him, shining his torch this way and that. Paul stepped back towards the wall. He felt safer if nothing could get behind him. The knowledge that there were other things down here in this darkness, even little things like mice, had made him suddenly afraid.

Something scuttled. The caretaker swung his torch. Paul caught only a glimpse of it before it disappeared behind a pile of boxes on the other side of the room. Something many-legged, something writhing and moving fast. Something silver.

"We have to get out of here," he said quietly. He wanted to run, but the caretaker had the only light. He looked towards where he thought the door was, and saw nothing. Then, a metre to the right, he glimpsed a small orange light. The press-switch in the corridor outside. He could see it through the open doorway.

"Did you see that?" the caretaker said. "What *was* that?"

"We have to get *out* of here!" Paul told him again, pulling him in the direction of the orange light.

There was a squabbling babble of squeaks from the darkness. The sound had a metallic edge, as if it was being played through an old 80s synthesizer. But the caretaker, instead of retreating, was still trying to find the source of the noise with his torch.

"That's not mice," the caretaker muttered. There was a scrabble of claws again, and something scrambled out from behind the boxes. The caretaker shone his torch on it, and it froze.

Paul's blood went cold. They weren't mice. They were rats. Five huge silver rats, their tails wrapped together in a tangle, crouched in a grotesque pile. Their matted fur was covered in mesh, plates of metal sewed in and out of their skin. They were a horrible patchwork of flesh and machine, like experimental animals that had escaped from the cruellest laboratory imaginable.

Then, suddenly, they broke apart, tails whipping as they unwrapped themselves; and now they were racing towards the intruders, squealing, long teeth bared as they came.

Paul ran. He couldn't help himself. He flung himself into the darkness, towards the tiny orange glow that offered light and salvation. For an instant, he was blind. His shoulder struck the edge of the doorway, and he bounced off it, careering through, tripping into the corridor beyond. He crashed into the wall on the far side, and suddenly light blasted the corridor. He'd fallen against the press-switch.

Dazzled, he shaded his eyes and looked back through the doorway. The caretaker hadn't moved. He was still dithering in terror, shining his torch on one rat and then another as they raced across the room towards him. He turned and stared at Paul. Finally he began to run.

Too late. The rats swarmed on to him, racing up the legs of his overalls. Paul scrambled away, his heart pounding, panic bubbling up inside him. The only thought in his mind was that he couldn't let them get him. He couldn't. *He couldn't.*

The caretaker's screams rang in his ears. He fled headlong down the corridor, slapping light switches on the way, racing ahead of the dark.

This time, he didn't think he'd be able to outrun it.

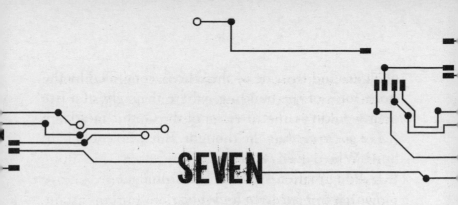

SEVEN

1

Paul ran through the corridors of the school, breath burning in his chest, his footfalls echoing around him. The screams of the caretaker still sounded in his ears, the awful cries of the rats, like angle-grinders on a girder. He'd put a heavy door and a lot of distance between himself and that room by now, but he still felt they were on his tail. If he looked back, he'd see them, their silver eyes glittering, teeth bared.

The rats . . . the dog. . .

What was *happening* here?

There, ahead of him: a fire door, hidden away in an arched stone alcove. Suddenly he knew how the teachers got out at night after the caretaker locked them in. He ran at it, shoved down the bar and pushed it open. Lightning and thunder met him. He slipped through and slammed the door behind him. No handle on this side. No way back.

Gasping, he leaned against the cold, wet metal. A stitch was jabbing him under his ribs. He was in a nook around the side of the school, concealed by the stone folds of the building, where the sight of a fire door wouldn't ruin the effect of the Gothic facade.

I've got to get help, he thought. But who could help him? Who'd even *believe* him?

It didn't matter. He had to tell someone.

The nurse. I have to tell the nurse.

Paul set off for the medical block, guilt gnawing at him. Should he have stayed? Should he have tried to help the caretaker? Wouldn't that have been the right thing to do?

He couldn't deal with those questions now. He was too shocked to make sense of everything. All he could do was what had to be done.

The medical block was not far away. Light from its windows glowed in the dark. Paul ran towards it, and burst through the doors into the waiting room.

It took him only a moment to realize that something was wrong.

There were a dozen or so kids in the waiting room, standing there in dripping raincoats. The younger ones were scared; he saw it in their faces. Nurse Wan was nowhere to be seen.

He stared at them all. "What's happened?" was all he could think of to say.

His answer came a moment later. A roar from somewhere out of sight, a man bellowing at the top of his lungs, with the kind of savagery that only the deranged could manage.

Into the silence that followed, Paul said quietly: "What the hell was that?"

"Mr Harrison's gone crazy," said someone. "He's locked up in one of the treatment rooms."

Nurse Wan came hurrying out from the corridor where Paul had seen her lead the headmaster earlier. "What are you all still doing here?" she cried, then fixed her eyes on Paul. A flicker of disappointment crossed her face. She seemed to have been expecting somebody, but it wasn't him. "Did you get through?" she snapped at him.

It took him a moment to work out what she meant. "The doctor? No . . . the phones are all out. . ." And then he remembered *why* they were out, and he remembered the caretaker, and his legs went weak.

The door behind him was flung open and Mr Sutton came hurrying in, along with that ginger kid with the big forehead. The one who'd grassed up Adam on Paul's behalf, who'd tried to help him with his DT assignment, and who'd been acting generally weird all day. Mark somebody, that was his name. He had a satchel over his shoulder and was carrying an umbrella, which he shook out and folded up.

Paul put the picture together. Mr Harrison's yells had attracted some of the younger kids on their way to the dinner hall, who had in turn attracted more, the way a crowd gathers around a fight or a car crash. They were all scared, but nobody was leaving: they all had to find out what was going on. Nurse Wan had sent one of them to fetch help. Mark had tracked down Mr Sutton.

The crowd made way for him. Mark followed behind and Paul, motivated by some instinct he didn't understand, went after them. The other kids were frightened. He and Mark were the only older pupils there. It gave them an authority that obliged them to involve themselves.

Nurse Wan stopped a little way down the corridor, in front of a plain beechwood door with a white plastic sign on it: TREATMENT ROOM 2. As she turned back to Mr Sutton, she noticed Mark and Paul there, but she was too flustered to worry about them.

"He started raving and screaming. I had to lock him inside, for safety's sake. I've got another patient here, too, you know! That little boy who was bitten, down by the lake!"

"You did the right thing. It's alright," said Mr Sutton, in an attempt to calm her down.

"It's *not* alright! Listen to him!"

It was hard not to. Mr Harrison sounded like he was throwing furniture about in there. Something crashed into the wall and made the door shake. He roared again, and there was a strange quality to his voice. Inhuman. *Metallic*.

Paul felt himself begin to tremble.

"Mr Harrison!" Mr Sutton shouted through the door. "It's Mr Sutton! Please tell me what's wrong! We want to help you!"

The roaring stopped. Inside the treatment room, everything went silent.

"Mr Harrison! Malcolm!" Mr Sutton called. "You're scaring the children. Talk to me! It's Alistair!"

Nothing.

"Did you call someone?" Mr Sutton asked Nurse Wan.

"The phones are all out," said Paul again, automatically. *The caretaker. The rats.*

Mr Sutton thought for a moment. "I should go in there," he said.

"No!" Paul blurted. "Don't!"

"He could be in trouble, Paul. I have to help him."

Paul opened his mouth and shut it again. *There's something bad in there*, he wanted to say. *Something very, very bad.* But his throat locked up, and somehow the words wouldn't come out. How could he explain it? How could he make them believe? Whatever he told them, they'd go in anyway. They believed the world was a sane and orderly place. In their world, Mr Harrison was maybe having an epileptic fit, or just freaking out, or something else that was not too dangerous, something nice and easy to explain. They didn't know how the world could turn on you in an instant, how everything could change in the blink of an eye.

Nurse Wan fumbled uncertainly with the keys. Paul watched as if in a dream, feeling powerless to intervene.

She unlocked the door and stepped back to let Mr Sutton take the lead. He ushered Mark and Paul back against the wall and put his hand on the handle.

"Malcolm? We're coming in, alright?" he called.

He waited for a response. There was none.

"You shouldn't. . ." Paul said quietly. Mr Sutton opened the door anyway.

The room beyond was dark. The fluorescent light had been smashed. The only illumination was the orange glow from the campus lights, seeping through the slats of the venetian blind.

"Malcolm?" Mr Sutton called. He stepped into the room, hands raised warily. Nurse Wan stayed close to him, ready to help. They peered into the darkness. Inside, there was silence, only the hiss and splatter of rain on glass.

Behind them, the door slammed shut.

Chaos erupted inside. The furious roar of Mr Harrison, a raw-throated scream from Nurse Wan, Mr Sutton shouting, the crash of toppling furniture. Paul and Mark exchanged a terrified glance. Neither of them knew what to do. Neither of them did anything.

And then, seconds later, the door was wrenched open, with Mr Sutton on the other side. He staggered backwards, still looking into the room. Nurse Wan was screaming, screaming, *screaming*. The light from the corridor fell on a writhing, shadowy shape on the floor. Paul stared at it, horrified. It didn't look like a person.

It wasn't. It was *two* people. Mr Harrison was on top of Nurse Wan, who was thrashing wildly beneath him. He had his head bent down close to her throat. Then there was a wet tearing sound, and Mr Harrison's head came up, and Nurse Wan went suddenly rigid. Her legs juddered, heels tapping spasmodically against the floor.

The light from the doorway fell across Mr Harrison's face then. At least, Paul *thought* it was Mr Harrison.

Half his face was silver. Thin metal tendrils slid in and out of his skin, spreading up one side of his neck from beneath his shirt collar. They'd encircled his eye socket and crept across the bridge of his nose. The surface of his right eye was mottled with patches of the same colour. His mouth and chin were red with blood; a flap of muscle and skin hung from his teeth; his face was twisted in a snarl of animal savagery.

Mr Sutton tripped over his heels as he backed into the corridor. He grabbed for the door handle to support himself, but only succeeded in pulling the door shut as he fell into Paul.

"What was...? What...?" Mr Sutton looked stunned. Suddenly his expression cleared and he picked himself up, clambering to his feet. "Nurse Wan!"

"*You can't help her!*" Paul cried, grabbing him as he reached for the door. "If she's not dead, she's like *him* now. It's infectious! Don't you get it? He was bitten, and now he's like them. Like the dog!"

Mr Sutton stared at him blankly. "What dog?"

There was a high-pitched squeal from down the corridor, quickly joined by several more. Girls, shrieking. Mr Sutton raced back towards the waiting room. Paul hesitated a moment, caught between the need to keep Mr Harrison inside the treatment room and the need to get away from him. But Nurse Wan had the key, and she was inside. Mark ran off after Mr Sutton, and that made up Paul's mind for him. He wasn't going to be left standing here when Mr Harrison came out.

When they got to the waiting room, they saw what had happened. Jason White, the kid who'd been bitten by a beetle down by the lake, was up and about.

He was standing there in his school uniform, swaying and looking dazed. He seemed puzzled by the sight of all the other children gathered together in wet raincoats, squealing in fright.

Thin tendrils had spread across his face, too, like a webwork of shining silver veins. His irises were a hard blue, glowing faintly, like the sharp light of a computer monitor in a dark room.

Then, as if he'd solved the puzzle that had been troubling him, his expression changed. His eyes narrowed. His lips drew back to reveal teeth clad in silver. And he ran at the cluster of children, a thin screech coming from his throat, a whine like feedback from a microphone.

The children screamed and scattered, but he was like a fox among chickens. He pounced on a boy his own age and sank his teeth into the base of his target's neck, biting through the coat to the flesh beneath.

"Out! Out! Everybody out!" Mr Sutton shouted, but the others needed no telling. Hysteria had taken hold. They flooded out of the door, shoving each other aside in their haste to escape. Mr Sutton grabbed Jason White by the shoulders and pulled him roughly away from his victim. He came up snarling, teeth bloodied. Mr Sutton flung him away, sending him stumbling across the room. He tripped over and fell in a heap. Mr Sutton scooped up the wailing child on the ground.

"Go! Go!" he urged Mark and Paul. Down the corridor, they heard the sound of a door being thrown open, and another bellow of rage from Mr Harrison. They needed no further prompting to run for their lives.

2

The world had turned upside down.

It had to be a joke, Mark thought. Some kind of elaborate hoax, special effects, something like that. Any moment now, the storm would shut off like magic, and a presenter with a face like a ventriloquist's dummy would emerge to tell everyone they'd been suckered for the cruel amusement of millions of dead-eyed viewers. His brain was racing, flitting from theory to theory, trying to figure out the trick. How it was all being done? There had to be a logical answer. There was *always* a logical answer.

They poured out of the medical block like blood gushing from a wound (*the nurse! the blood!*). Rain swept against them, driven by a fierce wind, and thunder boomed all around. Mr Sutton was shouting "Back to your dorms! Everyone, go back to your dorm halls and stay there!" but hardly anyone was listening. They fled in all directions, spreading their fear to other pupils who'd come to investigate the commotion.

Why do people run towards trouble instead of away from it? Mark asked himself, then remembered that he'd done the same thing. It was Mr Harrison's roaring that had drawn him to the medical block. He'd been passing by on his way to get first in the queue at the dinner hall. With Andrew and Graham gone for the weekend, he knew he'd be eating alone, so he wanted to get it over with as quick as possible. He'd brought his camera along, so he could scan through the pictures he'd taken of the beetle that morning. The lens might have been cracked, but he could still use the screen.

Now he knew. The beetles had only been the start of it.

Mr Sutton ran up to him, the wounded boy in his

arms. He put the boy down on the drive. Mark saw a white, frightened face inside the hood. He glanced up at the door of the medical block. They'd only gone a dozen metres down the drive. Shouldn't they be running, like everyone else?

Mr Sutton tore open the boy's raincoat. He clamped his hands down on the wound. "Mark, come here. Bring that umbrella."

Mark forgot he'd been carrying it. He opened it up and held it over Mr Sutton and the kid.

"Put pressure on this," Mr Sutton instructed him.

Mark stared at the blood welling through Mr Sutton's fingers. He backed off, his stomach clenching, and thought he was going to be sick.

"Paul! You do it! I need you to staunch the wound while I carry him!" Mr Sutton said, and Mark realized that Paul was standing by his shoulder, a sodden ghost in the storm.

"It's infectious. . ." Paul said weakly. Mark was shocked to see Paul's jaw quiver, as if he was about to burst into tears. Then Paul turned away, and his face was hidden by his hood.

"Give him here," said a voice behind them, and Adam Wojcik appeared, pushing them impatiently out the way. He threw his coat aside as he crouched down next to Mr Sutton, then tugged his sweatshirt over his head. He wadded it up and handed it to Mr Sutton, who pressed it against the wound. Adam took over and held it there.

"Keep the pressure on," said Mr Sutton. "We're going to take this boy to my car. Mark, Paul, run to the groundskeeper and get him to open the gate. We need to get this boy to hospital."

"Hey, what's up with this kid?" said Adam, staring down at the wound. Mark looked. Around the edges of the wadded sweatshirt Adam was holding, little silver lines were creeping out, branching and dividing across the skin.

How are they doing that? It has to be a trick!

"It's too late," Paul said quietly.

Mr Sutton ignored him. "Adam, keep your sweatshirt where it is!" He scooped up the boy and stood, with Adam still keeping the wound covered. "Mark! Paul! I meant *now*!"

They'd never heard Mr Sutton raise his voice before, and it made both of them jump. Together, they ran down the drive towards the gate.

Mark's umbrella caught the wind and turned inside out. He let it go, and it blew off across the lawn. A moment later, he remembered the satchel bumping against his hip. The camera was wrapped up inside, secure in a plastic bag. He'd wanted to keep it protected from the elements, but now the satchel was getting soaked. He wished he'd never brought it now.

What are you worried about a camera for? he thought. *What about what happened to Mr Harrison?* But that was his way. He wasn't the kind of person who got caught up in the big picture. Even in a crisis, he put things in little compartments in his mind, and looked at them one by one. He organized tasks like a flow chart. He did things piece by piece.

Paul was freaking out, he could see that. Paul couldn't take it all in. But Mark wasn't thinking about everything at once, like Paul was. Mark was just thinking about the next task he had to do.

He wondered if freaking out was the more *normal* thing to do right now, but he just didn't feel it. Even after seeing Mr Harrison ripping Nurse Wan's throat out with his teeth. Yes, he'd been scared out of his wits. Yes, he suspected that later he'd turn to jelly and cry his eyes out. But right now, he felt surprisingly under control.

Despite the lashing rain, pupils were coming out of their dorm halls. Teachers too. They tried to herd everyone back inside, but it was already getting out of control. The pupils had seen kids running from the medical block, heard their shrieks. They couldn't just sit still and wait to be told what danger they might be in. They had to go and find out for themselves.

Off to their right was Beswick Hall, the dorm that stood nearest the lake and the old chapel. Paul slowed suddenly and moaned in horror. Mark looked, and saw a dog, a big silver dog, racing across the slick, muddy grass towards a group of kids who'd just come hurrying out of the dorm.

"Hey! Watch out!" Mark hollered at the top of his voice, but if anyone heard him, it was too late. The dog crashed into the group, knocking several to the ground. It pounced on one, bit and scratched, and then leaped off and began savaging another kid.

Paul just stood there, paralysed. Mark grabbed his arm. Paul jerked away, and stared at Mark as if it were the first time he'd ever seen him.

"Mr Sutton needs our help," said Mark.

The main gate was locked when they got there. It always was, after six. You couldn't have pupils wandering about in the valley unsupervised. If you wanted to be let out, you had to knock on the door of the groundskeeper's cottage by the gate, or press a buzzer if you wanted to be let in. The groundskeeper or his wife would always be there to open the gate for you.

Paul didn't go to the house. He ran up to the gate and clamped his hands around the bars, looking out to the valley beyond. Mark regarded him uncertainly. He couldn't imagine what Paul hoped to see out there. Even if he could penetrate the darkness and the rain, all he'd find were green slopes and a winding road, and the white, angular buildings of the weather monitoring station, perched up there on the ridge.

Paul was acting strange; he wouldn't be much help at the moment. Mark turned his attention to the groundskeeper's cottage.

It was a tiny dwelling, with walls of glistening stone, deep-set windows of latticed glass and a small picket-fenced garden patch surrounding it.

It was also dark.

Mark slowed as he approached. The grounds-keeper's house was *always* occupied by someone, from six at night till seven in the morning. It was part of the job. Otherwise people wouldn't be able to get in or out of the campus. But no lights were on, despite the gloom of the storm.

He went up and rapped on the door with the knocker. When there was no answer, he pressed the doorbell. There was a loud buzz from inside the house. Mark held it down for as long as he dared.

Nobody came.

Mark looked over his shoulder nervously, as if Paul might provide him with a suggestion for what to do next. But Paul was still staring out past the gate, at the world outside Mortingham Boarding Academy. Lightning flared, freezing the campus in shocking white. Further up the drive, towards the centre of the campus, Mark saw a snapshot of children running. Their cries were carried down on the wind to him. Somewhere, a fire alarm was shrilling.

Mr Sutton would be here in his car at any minute. He'd pick them up and take them all away from this madness. But first Mark had to get the gate open.

Even if nobody was in, Mark reasoned that they might have at least left the key to the gate inside. He hurried along the path that led round the side of the cottage. He didn't think he'd have the nerve to break in, but maybe if he could *see* the key, he could get

Paul to smash a window or something. Paul seemed like the kind of boy who didn't care too much about being disciplined. Mark felt uneasy just trespassing in the garden. He knew it was ridiculous – kids could be *dying* back there near the school! – but he had a deeply ingrained fear of getting into trouble, and even now it was hard to shake.

He pressed his face against the glass of the nearest window. The lights were out in the small sitting room, but he could see through to the kitchen on the other side of the cottage, where he could make out the dreary grey rectangle of another window. He wiped away rain and squinted, waiting for his eyes to adjust.

Something moved inside. A figure shuffled slowly across the kitchen, passing in front of the window, blocking its dull light. The squat, burly figure of the groundskeeper.

So he *was* in! How had he not heard the doorbell?

Mark raised his hand to rap on the window, but something stopped him. Something about the way the groundskeeper was moving. Aimless, lost, as if he were searching for something but he wasn't sure what it was.

Then the groundskeeper tilted his head towards Mark, and the meagre light fell on his face. Even distorted by the rain on the glass, Mark could see how the shining veins of silver caught the light.

He backed away quickly, afraid of being spotted. The back of his legs hit the picket fence and he tumbled over it backwards, landing in a heap on the muddy bank that led down to the drive. He scrambled to his feet, clutching his satchel to his body with his precious camera inside.

Paul had turned away from the gate, and was staring at him.

"The groundskeeper. . ." Mark said. "I don't think he's the groundskeeper any more. And he's got the key in there with him."

"Doesn't matter," said Paul. "They're out there too."

Mark gazed at him dumbly. "In the valley?"

Paul nodded. "Dogs. I saw them out there in the pastures. They're after the sheep. If we try to run for it on foot, they'll take us down."

Mark felt helpless. "We can't get out!" he cried.

Paul was no longer blank-faced and vague, but grim as flint. "We can't get out," he agreed.

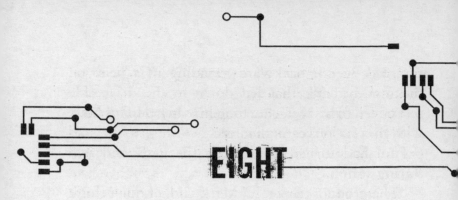

EIGHT

1

"Hey! There's something kicking off outside!"

His yell silenced the dinner queue. The boy – his name was Robert Yates – was a troublemaker by reputation. After he delivered his breathless message, he ran off again, heading for whatever disturbance he'd warned them of.

Murmurs ran up and down the line of pupils waiting to be let in to the dining hall. Tricks like that had been played before. If they left the queue to find out what was going on, they'd lose their place in line. But the draw of conflict was strong, especially for the boys. If there was something that would liven up the routine of their boarding school lives, they had to be in on it. They gathered like iron filings to a magnet, just like they had when Paul and Adam had been scrapping down by the lake that morning.

Fight! Fight! Fight!

Some of the boys hurried off after Robert. Caitlyn

exchanged a sceptical glance with Erika, who stood next to her in the queue.

They'd gone to dinner together, naturally. After Caitlyn's frosty behaviour at lunchtime, Erika had begun to suspect that something was up. But Caitlyn didn't want to talk about it, so she thought she'd better ask Erika to sit with her at dinner, to disguise the fact that she was secretly mad. It was all pretty complicated. But she'd had a lot of practice at it.

Growing up as the youngest of four girls was no picnic. At times there was love and happiness and friendship, but at others there was teasing and bitchiness and vicious emotional bullying. She was always the weakest, never smart or witty enough to hold her own against her more experienced siblings. To avoid getting picked on, she learned to make allies of her enemies. She was nice to those who could best defend her. In a squabble, she decided who she thought would win and came in on their side. It was survival, and she was good at it.

And yet somehow she was still in the shadows. She was free of her sisters but not of being second best. She should have known it would happen when she chose to be Erika's friend. But the lure of the in-crowd was too strong. School was easier when you looked down from the top, everyone knew that. But who ever really looked at Caitlyn? Who ever really *saw* her?

Unless she broke away, she'd always be second best

to Erika. But she just didn't know if she could make it on her own.

More and more people were leaving the queue now. Whispers had turned to excited speculation. Had someone been hit by lightning? Had the storm blown down the old chapel?

Even Erika caught the fever, and soon her initial scepticism was forgotten. "Shall we go see?" she asked, her blue eyes shining.

"Out in the storm? It's just some stupid fight," said Caitlyn.

"Oh, come on, it could be fun!" said Erika, in that oh-so-bloody-perky way she had.

Then the shrilling of the fire bell sounded through the building. Caitlyn swore. Now they *had* to leave, like it or not. Dinner would be late, and they'd have to stand out in the rain, and all because some idiot pulled the alarm. Probably Robert Yates. It was the sort of thing he'd do.

Their minds made up by the bell, most kids in the queue rushed towards the exit. Caitlyn and Erika followed, pulling on their coats as they went.

The moment they got outside, they knew something was badly wrong.

A small crowd of pupils had gathered at the entrance to the dinner hall. They'd sensed it too. Terror was in the air, as real as the rain that lashed at them. There were screams on the wind. In the distance, kids went running this way and that, frantic.

Mr Johnson, who taught PE, came sprinting by. He yelled at them to get back inside and stay there, then he ran off without waiting to see if they obeyed.

Most of them did, fleeing back into the dinner hall, their curiosity overtaken by fright. The girls started squealing as they crammed themselves through the door.

Erika tugged at Caitlyn's arm. Her pretty face was a pale picture of distress. "We should do what he said."

Caitlyn ignored her. Her mind was already on somebody else. Someone who might be out there in the storm, out there in unknown danger. She had to be sure they were safe.

Paul.

"Caitlyn!" Erika called after her, as she headed off into the dark. A moment later, she heard Erika come splashing after her along the gravel path. Her fear of being left alone was clearly stronger than the fear of what was happening out here.

You can follow me, for once, Caitlyn thought.

The dining hall was round the back of the school building. They hurried through the storm, passing the sports hall on their left. Caitlyn saw a girl lumbering along a short way away. She walked as if shell-shocked or wounded, her movements clumsy, swaying as she went, long hair sodden and hanging. Caitlyn wondered if she needed help, but something about the way the girl moved made her instincts jangle.

Lightning flashed and thunder hit at the same

moment. The girl froze still, as if she were playing a game of musical statues. Caitlyn stared. The girl stayed that way for a few seconds, and then started to move again, as if she'd never been interrupted.

Caitlyn didn't go over to help.

They rounded the front of the school. Figures pelted through the rain. Thin screams and shrieks, as if from a flock of birds, blew about with the changing wind. Caitlyn wiped water from her eyes and looked about for signs of Paul, but she couldn't see him.

"Caitlyn." Erika patted her arm and pointed.

Ahead of them was the staff garage, an old converted stable block which sprawled along the east side of the main drive. Lying on the grass nearby, curled up in a foetal position, was a young pupil. He was wearing a muddied raincoat with his hood pulled up. He twitched and shivered violently.

Erika went straight towards him, heading off the path and on to the lawn. Caitlyn fretted for a moment – she wanted to concentrate on locating Paul – but in the end, she couldn't ignore that little boy. In fact, she felt a stab of anger at Erika, for the immediate and unquestioning way she went to offer aid. It made her feel like a bad person for having to think about it first.

Other kids were nearby. Teachers were shouting. Nobody paid attention to the fallen pupil.

Why is everybody ignoring him?

Erika had crouched down by the boy's side by the

time Caitlyn caught her up. The boy was lying with his back to her, the hood obscuring his face. "Hey," Erika was saying. "Are you alright?" She reached out and touched the boy's shoulder. The boy jerked at her touch, and then began slowly getting up, dragging his feet underneath him, as if it was a great effort to even rise to a crouch.

There was something about the way he moved. Something that reminded Caitlyn of the girl she'd just seen wandering in the storm, the girl who froze when the lightning flashed.

"Are you alright?" Erika said again, holding out her hand to him.

The boy turned his head towards them, and Erika gasped. The face beneath the hood was a webwork of silver threads crawling across the boy's skin. His mouth was open, and his lips and tongue and teeth were veined in the same colour. His irises were a bright electric blue, and the whites of his eyes were mottled with tiny, irregular silver plates.

Caitlyn sensed the lunge an instant before it came. She grabbed Erika's other arm and pulled her roughly aside just as the boy leaped towards her outstretched hand. His teeth clicked shut on the spot where Erika's fingers had been half a second earlier, and he toppled forward and fell on to the muddy lawn. He began struggling to get up again with the shaking limbs and clumsy movements of something newly born.

Erika screamed and ran. Caitlyn shouted her name

and ran after her. She caught her a dozen metres later and pulled her to a stop. Erika was out of her mind. She was mouthing words as if she wanted to say something, but no sound was coming out.

"Erika! Erika, you need to calm down," Caitlyn was saying. Her voice seemed to be coming from someone else. It sounded strong and reassuring, which was not at all how she felt. *Calm down? Calm down? What on earth happened to that boy?*

"Oi!" someone shouted. It took Caitlyn an instant to place the thuggish bellow. Adam Wojcik. He came running over, wet through, his shirt plastered to his bulky body by the rain.

"Wh-wh-wh—?" Erika began, juddering out the beginnings of a question. Adam didn't wait for her to finish.

"Get to the science block!" he told them. "Sutton says. Everyone's going there. Science block, got it?" He pointed through the rain. "Tell anyone else you see."

"Is Paul there?" Caitlyn asked, but Adam had already run off, shouting the same message to some other kids. "Is *Paul* there?" she called after him.

Erika swallowed and pulled herself together. "Science block. . ." she said. "Come on."

"You go. I need to look for someone."

"Paul will be in the science block," said Erika. "Everyone's going there. You heard him."

Caitlyn felt a flash of anger at the sound of his

name on Erika's lips, and then felt guilty for it. She had a point. Caitlyn didn't have much of a chance of finding Paul in the storm. Likely he'd headed for the science block himself.

"Science block," she agreed reluctantly, then gave Erika a measured look. "You'd better be right."

2

"Oi! You!"

The kid turned to Adam, frightened. Adam collared him roughly. "Science block! Everyone's going to the science block! Get going!"

He shoved the kid off in that direction. The kid stumbled a few steps and looked back at him, his face slack with that same blank rabbit-in-the-headlights expression that Adam was used to seeing on his victims.

"Go!" he snapped, and the kid bolted.

What was *wrong* with everybody? They were all acting so dumb. Standing there terrified or running about like headless chickens. Even some of the teachers were staggering around stupidly, dazed by the chaos and the storm, shocked by what they were seeing. So many people came apart at the seams as soon as something messed-up happened.

For Adam, fear and anger were the same thing. He responded to intimidation with fury. When faced with something he couldn't comprehend, he got mad.

The other kids weren't used to conflict and threat, that was their problem. Adam had barely lived a day without it. At school, at home, violence lay round every corner. Fear was your friend when your whole life was a fight.

He looked around, trying to spot any other kids he could steer towards the science block. The only figures he saw were the ones who moved funny, the changing and the changed. There were more of them every minute.

No wonder, really. He'd seen what happened to that kid Mr Sutton had tried to save. He'd seen how fast he changed.

After Mr Harrison went mental in the medical block, Adam had found himself holding his sweatshirt to some kid's bleeding throat while Mr Sutton carried him to his car. By the time they'd reached the staff garage, that silver stuff had branched out all over the boy's skin. They entered through a small door in the side, which Adam opened with the key Mr Sutton had given him. Adam didn't bother putting his sweatshirt back on the wound. It wasn't even bleeding any more. Instead, it was clotted with fine silver filaments, like thread.

The boy's breath was wheezing in and out of his body as Mr Sutton bundled him in the back of his car. It hadn't been long since he was bitten, but his eyes had already started to change. Adam didn't know what was happening, but he knew that kid wouldn't make it to any hospital, that was for sure. Mr Sutton knew it too, but he didn't give up trying. Not till the kid lunged at him and tried to take a bite out of his arm.

Sutton was lucky: the kid only got the sleeve of his tweed jacket. He pulled himself back out of the car and Adam slammed the door in the kid's face. The kid started pawing at the window and snarling. All he had to do was reach down and pull the door handle to open the door, but it was like he'd forgotten how. Mr Sutton fumbled out his zapper and locked the car.

"We have to save the others," Mr Sutton said, his eyes fixed on the boy, who was dragging his fingertips down the glass. His voice was slow and all the feeling had gone out of it. "We need to get everyone to the science block."

Well, Adam had done what he could on that score now. It was getting too dangerous out here. Time to head back.

It was easy enough to avoid the kids who were turning. He'd seen a dog running about, which moved pretty quick, but most of them were clumsy, slow and uncoordinated. Most of the kids who got caught had been taken by surprise, or had been too stupid to recognize the danger in time. You could run round them easily enough, if you were careful.

Other people were losing it in the confusion, but not Adam. He wasn't one for deep thought. He fought when he had to, and sometimes when he didn't. He faced tonight's events with the same blank acceptance that he faced everything else. It just was. He didn't need to understand it, he just had to deal with it.

When he got to the doors of the science block, Mr Sutton let him inside. There were a half-dozen kids there with him, piling up planks and nails from the workshops where they did woodwork and metalwork. Everyone was soaked, and the floor was slippery wet.

Adam looked at the stack of planks. This was why Mr Sutton had picked the science block to gather everyone. It was small enough to defend, there was only one entrance, and there were all kinds of materials on hand. Adam had to admit, it was a smart move. For a teacher.

"Couldn't find any more," Adam grunted, a little out of breath. "There's a lot more of them others out there now."

Mr Sutton looked anxiously out through the science block doors. A pair of kids and a teacher – or at least, what was left of them – were staggering along the path in Adam's wake.

He dithered for a moment. Adam knew what he was thinking. It was the same instinct that had almost got him bitten in the garage. He was too soft: he didn't want to leave a single kid behind. He wanted to leave the door unlocked till the very last moment in case anyone else turned up. But by doing so he was endangering everyone inside.

"Sir. . ." Adam said, a warning in his voice.

Mr Sutton shook his head angrily at himself. "Yes, you're right," he said. Then, to the others: "Let's board this up."

They got to work immediately. Someone jammed a bar through the handles and they started nailing planks across the swing doors.

"Adam, can you—" Mr Sutton began, but Adam already knew what to do.

"I'll go check on the others, make sure they're boarding up all the windows."

"Good man, Adam. Good man," said Mr Sutton, and then turned back to the task of securing the door.

Good man? Adam thought, as he headed off down the corridor. He couldn't remember anyone ever saying that to him. He wasn't sure he deserved it. All he was doing right now was pushing people around. He'd done that all his life.

Still, though – it was kind of nice to be given a pat on the back like that. Not something he was used to at all.

Yeah. Kind of nice.

3

The science block echoed with the sound of hammers. It came from everywhere, vibrating through the walls, causing ripples in the puddles on the corridor floors. Mark wasn't sure how many pupils had made it inside, but almost every one of them was occupied with boarding up windows, working with feverish and frightened enthusiasm.

Mark was kneeling on a workbench that ran beneath a row of three large windows. Two were boarded up tight; they were working on the third. He was holding up one side of a heavy plank, pressing it flat against the wall. Holding the other side was Caitlyn Stross, a sharp-featured girl with black hair whom he'd never spoken to before. Paul was hammering the nails in with reckless force. Also in the room, hugging herself and looking at the floor, was Erika Robinson.

Paul had barely said a word since they'd returned from the gate. He moved with purpose now, but his face was hard, his expression dark. Mark had no idea what he was thinking. For his part, Mark was just concentrating on getting the next thing done, and then the next, following his mental flow chart of tasks. Anything else was just too complicated to handle.

It was like a computer. Computers could do things that seemed to be nothing short of miraculous, but when you broke them down, they were just a lot of individual components, each doing a job. Ones and zeroes. On and off. Mark was a component, that was all.

There were things moving out there in the storm, beyond the windows. He tried not to think about them.

Mark glanced over at Caitlyn, and caught her

looking at Paul, who was occupied with banging in more nails. Mark reckoned she probably fancied him; that was why she kept looking. Hard to tell, though. Girls were in a different orbit these days. It was like they reached a certain age and started speaking another language. The words were the same, but the meaning was all different, full of hints and suggestions he couldn't understand.

Paul finished hammering in the plank. There was one more to do, right across the centre.

"Pass us up that last plank, Erika," said Caitlyn, reaching back for it.

"Let me help nail it up," said Erika. Mark thought he heard anger in her voice, and wondered at its cause. "I feel useless."

"We've got it under control," said Caitlyn.

"I need to *do* something!" Erika said. "I can't take just standing around like this!" She climbed up on to the worktop with them, the plank under her arm, pushing in between Caitlyn and Paul. Caitlyn had to move to make way, which caused her to knock a Bunsen burner into a sink, and to hit her ankle on a gas tap.

"For God's sake, Erika!" Caitlyn cried. "How many people does it take to hold a plank?"

Erika stared at her friend, shocked and hurt by the tone in her voice. Caitlyn drew in a breath to say something, perhaps to apologize, perhaps not. They never found out. Through the gap in the planks,

Mark saw something loom close to the window outside. Two small, bright circles of blue shone through the rain-blotched glass.

Eyes.

The glass smashed as a thick arm was driven through it, and through the gap in the planks. Through the shredded sleeve, Mark saw plates of silver, veins replaced by cables, circuitry everywhere. It grabbed for Erika. She tried to pull away, but she wasn't fast enough. The hand caught the sleeve of her coat and yanked her against the boarded-up window.

Suddenly everyone was yelling and screaming at once. "Paul!" Erika shrieked. "Paul, get it off me!"

The thing beyond the window screeched as Paul tried to drag Erika away from it. Caitlyn whacked at its arm with a metal tripod, which was the only thing she had to hand. Mark was knocked back in the struggle and slipped off the workbench to the floor. He landed on his feet in a crouch, looked up – and saw his satchel poking over the edge of a nearby table.

In an instant, he knew what he had to do. He pulled it open and tugged out his broken camera. The lens was cracked, but that didn't matter. He clambered up on to the workbench again. Erika was screaming fit to burst. She was trying to work her arms out of her coat, desperately fighting to keep away from the creature outside, but she was stuck inside the sleeves. Paul was losing the tug of war, and

Caitlyn's attacks were ineffective.

"Paul!" Erika shrieked again.

Mark wedged himself in between Caitlyn and Erika, thrust the camera up to the window, and pressed the shutter release. The flash flickered, lighting up the thing outside, stunning it with brightness. A horrible mechanical mockery of a human face, more metal than flesh. He recognized it anyway.

Mr Harrison.

Erika's arm came free, and she went tumbling backwards into Paul, and the two of them went off the side of the workbench and landed on the floor in a heap. Mark put the camera aside and snatched up the last plank, shoving it into place in the gap, shutting out Mr Harrison's face. Caitlyn caught on quickly, and held up the other end.

"Paul! Nails!" she cried.

Paul was up on his feet in a second, clambering back on to the workbench. He picked up a hammer and started driving in nails.

There was a shuddering impact on the other side of the plank. Mark and Caitlyn held firm. Paul hammered in another nail, working with desperate speed.

Another impact, weaker this time. Paul hammered in another nail.

There were no more impacts after that. Mark and Caitlyn held on as Paul beat the last nails into the wood, making the window secure. Now there were only narrow gaps between the planks, less than a finger's width. The wind got through, but nothing else. Paul peered through, but Mr Harrison – the thing that had *been* Mr Harrison – was gone now.

Adam appeared in the doorway. He swept the room with his small, suspicious eyes, studying the four of them. Erika was quietly choking back sobs and clutching herself.

"All done?" he grunted.

"All done," said Paul.

Adam nodded. "Then that's the last of the windows. Looks like we're sealed in tight." And he disappeared off down the corridor.

Mark felt a shiver pass through him as he listened to the whistling wind. *Looks like we're sealed in tight*.

Other people might call it trapped.

Outside, they heard the buzzsaw shriek of one of the creatures, rising over the storm. It was answered by several more.

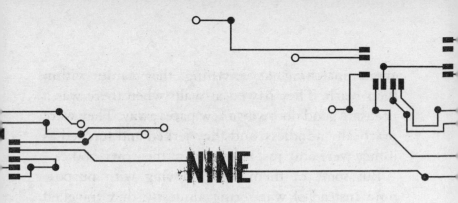

NINE

1

They were out there. Paul could see them.

The storm had died, leaving the campus glistening in the yellow glow of the electric lights that stood on poles or in recesses along the pathways. Though it was dusk now, the passing of the storm made it seem a little less dark than before, and he could see all the way out past the wall that surrounded Mortingham Boarding Academy. Beneath a steel-grey ceiling of cloud, the ridges of the valley stood stark and sharp in the last light.

He sat at an upstairs window, crammed on to a wide sill. A Design and Technology lab. The room was chilly and empty. Benches and drawing boards stood silent in the light of the fluorescent bulbs.

All over the campus, *things* were moving. They were getting faster. Faster and smarter.

He'd watched it happen, as he sat up here alone on his perch. At first, they'd been shambling things, some of them barely able to stand. They staggered about snatching at anything that came within their reach. They pawed at walls when there was a perfectly good doorway a few paces away. They were practically mindless, and they jerked and lurched as if they were only just in control of their own bodies.

But some of them were moving with purpose now. Instead of wandering aimlessly, they travelled in packs of three or four. He'd seen a group of them running across the campus, hunting down something or some*one* he couldn't see. The creatures in packs didn't crawl around or scratch at doors they couldn't get through. He could see them prowling about, looking for ways into the buildings.

He heard the smashing of glass from somewhere over the other side of the campus. A thin scream rose into the darkening sky.

There were other kids out there. Other kids who'd holed up just like the pupils in the science block. Except some of them hadn't barricaded themselves in quite so well.

He thought of Erika. With everything going on, she'd been pushed to the back of his mind, but now he had a moment to think, she came back to dominate his thoughts.

He'd helped to save her, hadn't he? And what thanks had he got? When he asked if she was okay afterwards, when he put out a hand to touch her arm and comfort her, she just gave him an icy look and walked away. Hadn't she screamed out his name when the creature was trying to pull her through the window? Hadn't she begged him for help?

But he couldn't get mad at her. Not Erika. The whole time he'd been at this school, she'd been the one good thing he'd found. It didn't matter that she wasn't interested in him. His world might have fallen apart, but at least there was her, reminding him that he might one day feel again, that he might one day let himself care deeply for someone. Not yet, perhaps. Not now. But one day.

Paul looked down on the creatures roaming the campus, and he smiled.

He'd been right all along. The world had turned over again. One moment, everything was cosy and normal, and the next ... *nothing* was normal. He saw the shock and bewilderment on the faces of the other kids. They couldn't understand how it had happened.

Last time the world had changed, Paul wasn't ready for it. This time, he was.

So this is how it's going to be from now on, eh? Nothing sure, nothing certain? Well, alright then. I can deal with that.

He felt good. He actually felt *good*. At first he'd been horrified by what had happened to the caretaker, knocked off-balance by the shock of it. But that had worn off now. In its place was a strange sort of excitement.

Ever since his parents had died, he'd been

sleepwalking. But suddenly the world seemed alive with possibilities. It had shown a new side, and this one was hard and sharp, not dull and soulless like before. He liked it better that way. He'd rather have danger he could do something about than safety he was helpless against. The whims of fate couldn't be battled, but these creatures could.

So bring it on, Paul thought fiercely. *Bring it all on. 'Cause I don't really have a lot to lose, these days.*

He heard footsteps at the door to the classroom and looked up. There, in the doorway, was the shabby, lanky figure of Mr Sutton.

"Paul. There you are," he said.

"Here I am."

"Are you alright?"

"I'm just fine," he said, and he meant it.

Mr Sutton gave him an odd look. "We're having a meeting downstairs. To decide what to do." He paused, then added, "We all need to work together now, Paul. As a team."

Paul didn't say anything to that. He just got down off the window sill, and followed him out.

2

They gathered in a classroom downstairs, arranging themselves on chairs and tables in a semicircle around Mr Sutton. He was the only teacher. There were about fifty kids here, none of them older than fifteen.

Mark was among the oldest, along with Paul, Adam, Erika and Caitlyn.

Mark was surprised at how few they numbered. He wondered briefly how the rest were doing, and where they were. Then he made himself stop thinking about it.

"Alright, everybody," said Mr Sutton, clapping his hands together. "Now I think it's fair to say that we've all had a bit of a scare—"

Some kid began to blubber. "Quiet!" Adam barked. The kid froze and shut up. "Teacher's talking," Adam said, with a threat in his voice. The kid nodded dumbly and looked back at Mr Sutton.

"Yes, thank you, Adam," said Mr Sutton uncertainly. "Anyway, the point is, everyone's a bit shaken up, but let's not get silly, eh? You've all done a very good job in sealing up this place, and from what we've seen so far, those things outside aren't especially bright. They can't get in. We're safe here."

There was a general sense of relief at that. Some of the kids smiled bravely at one another.

"Sooner or later, someone's going to come and rescue us. I know this academy is very, er, remote, but the worst-case scenario is that we're stuck here till Monday morning, when the rest of the staff come ba—"

The blubbering kid burst into tears at the thought of that, which set a couple of girls off too. Adam drew a breath to yell at them but Mr Sutton held up his hand and shook his head. Adam deflated, looking disappointed.

Mark decided that Mr Sutton wasn't all that great at this speech-giving lark.

"Now, now! It won't come to that, I'm sure. More than likely the police will hear about it very soon, and everything will be alright. In the meantime, we have water, and there's enough junk food in the snack dispensers to keep you hyperactive for days. I can't stress this enough: we're *safe* in here. Nothing's going to get you."

The kids gradually stopped crying, though some of them still glanced uncertainly at the boarded-up windows. The shrieks of the creatures outside could occasionally be heard over the sniffling in the classroom.

"Meantime, let's work on how we can help *ourselves*," said Mr Sutton. "First thing's first, what do we know about what's out there? Come on, everybody, chip in."

"They're zombies!" piped up a thirteen-year-old with freckles.

"They're *not* zombies," said his pudgy companion.

"They're slow and stupid, and when they bite you, you turn into one of them," argued Freckles. "Sounds like zombies to me!"

"Zombies aren't made of metal," replied Pudge snottily. He folded his arms as if the case was closed.

"They're cyborgs, then!" said Freckles, who was getting frustrated.

"They're not cyborgs, buttface. You don't get infected with cyborgitis."

"They're *both*," said Mr Sutton, before a full-scale fight could break out. "And they're neither. I spent a bit of time studying one of those beetles that was found this morning. In fact, it was so amazing, I was planning to take it to a professor friend of mine in London tomorrow. I suppose we're a bit past that now."

"So what are they?" asked Erika, brushing her hair back behind her ear.

"Well, I only have limited equipment, but the best I could make out is that it's some kind of virus causing this. It turns organic matter – flesh, bone, chitin, fur – into something resembling metal. But it doesn't behave like any virus I know. It builds *structures*, like circuits. It's like it's operating under some sort of control, or like it somehow *knows* what it's doing."

"But how's that possible?"

"I don't know," said Mr Sutton. "But I do know this. Those people out there, they're infected. And maybe infected people can be cured."

Mark didn't hold out much hope of that, but it was a nice touch, and it made everyone feel a bit better. Some of them had friends out there who hadn't gone home for the weekend. At least his own friends, Andrew and Graham, would be safe at their parents' houses. He felt a bit guilty for not having thought about them till now.

"Infected," said Freckles, nodding to himself. "The Infected. I like that."

"Yeah," said Pudge, nodding along. "Cool."

Mark stared at them. While most of the kids were upset or shocked, these two appeared to be taking it rather well. In fact, he wondered if they thought it was all just a video game or something. Maybe it was better if they kept believing that.

A Year Ten boy raised his hand. He had an impractical emo haircut that was slicked forward so that it almost covered his face. Mark wondered if he ought to trim that a bit, get some peripheral vision back. Monsters could sneak in from the side and he'd never see them coming.

"Johnny," said Mr Sutton, acknowledging him.

"Eddie Grant and Jason White got bitten by beetles at lunchtime, right? Jason White didn't turn until hours later. But when those things were running about outside, people they bit changed in, like, *minutes*."

"Eddie Grant got sent home!" one of the younger kids wailed. "What if . . . what if he spread it too?"

"Let's worry about ourselves for now, eh?" Mr Sutton said hastily, before the implications of that could sink in. "Concentrate on getting out of this little muddle."

"Mr Harrison was scratched by a dog," Paul said, dragging the conversation back to its previous track. "Took him about half an hour to change."

"It must depend on the severity of the wound," said Mr Sutton, who seemed grateful to be on safer ground again. "The worse it is, the more the infection gets in, and the faster you change."

"But why are they attacking people at all?" asked Caitlyn, who was sitting up on a table, swinging her legs and looking anxious.

"I suppose the virus makes them do it," said Mr Sutton. "Since it needs organic hosts to multiply, it needs to spread itself by bite or scratch. So it makes its victims aggressive. Like rabies."

"Like zombies!" Freckles said, triumphantly.

"They're not zombies!" Pudge cried. "*He* said!" He thrust a finger a Mr Sutton, and then began to sulk.

Something heavy scratched along the outside wall of the classroom.

Everyone fell silent immediately. The atmosphere went taut. Some of the younger kids clutched at one another.

They listened as the dragging noise moved along the wall. Slowly, slowly. Like something metal was sliding against the bricks, moving in jerks and scrapes.

It reached a window. Shrieked along glass.

The window gave way with a smash and a tinkle, and something thumped against the boards on the other side. Several of the younger kids screamed and scrambled away, pressing themselves against the far wall, where Mr Sutton stood.

"Sssh!" he was saying. "Sssh! It's alright."

Mark was astonished at how calm Mr Sutton seemed to be. Inside, he must have been as terrified as the rest of them, but you'd never have known it from his manner.

Silver fingers pawed at the planks, slipped through the gaps. The kids screamed and cried anew, but the planks held firm. The thing outside thumped and pulled at them a few moments longer, and then stopped.

The wind whistled through the gaps in the planks. They heard the sound of something trudging away, feet squelching on the wet grass.

And it was gone.

"They're not zombies, they're Infected," Mr Sutton reminded them quietly. "But that doesn't matter, because they *can't get in*."

Some of the kids made reluctant murmurs of agreement. Slowly they settled back to their seats. They'd seen the barriers in action now, and despite the scare, they felt a little safer.

"So what are we going to do, then?" asked Erika impatiently, once the frightened whispers had subsided. "Just sit here?"

Adam gave her a sharp glare, warning her not to use that snappy tone. He seemed to have set himself up as Mr Sutton's enforcer. Incredible that he didn't see the irony. The boy most likely to get expelled had suddenly started acting like a prefect. Although Mark reckoned that a prefect was just another kind of bully, so he actually suited the role pretty well.

"Well, let's look at what we have," said Mr Sutton. "We have one of the best-equipped science and technology labs of any school in England, for a start. Surely we can make use of that somehow."

"I can build a foxhole radio," Mark said. It came out louder than he'd intended, more like an eager squeak. Suddenly everyone was looking at him. He felt his face grow hot.

"You'll have to explain to us what that is, Mark," said Mr Sutton gently.

"Um. . ." said Mark. "Well, in World War Two the American GIs used to build these little sets made out of junk so they could listen to radio stations. All you need is a few bits and bobs like cardboard tubes and thumbtacks and wire. You don't even need to plug it in: it's powered by radio waves."

"No way!" gasped Pudge, who was now staring at Mark as if he were the fifth member of the A-Team.

"Er . . . yeah. It's pretty easy if you know how."

"We're in a valley," Paul pointed out. "Our mobile phones don't get a signal here. Is a radio going to work?"

"Should do," said Mark, who was growing in confidence by the second. "Radio waves are different to phone signals. They bounce off the atmosphere, which means they'll get over the valley walls."

"Can't we listen to the radio on our mobiles?" someone chimed in.

"Tried that already," muttered somebody else.

"Mobile radio runs off the same signal you use to make calls," said Mark. "It won't work here. We need to do it the old way."

Caitlyn hunkered forward. "When that thing reached through the window in the lab, you flashed it with your camera. . ."

"Er, yeah," said Mark. "Yeah, I did. I noticed it when I took some photos of the beetles earlier. They freeze if they get flashed with bright light."

"He's right," said Paul. "I saw it happen to one of them when lightning struck."

"Me, too," said Caitlyn. There were general murmurs of agreement from others who'd seen the same.

"How many of you have mobiles with flash cameras?" Mr Sutton asked. Only half a dozen hands went up, including Caitlyn's. Most kids in Mortingham only carried mobiles in order to play app games in their free periods, or to take the odd photo. In such a remote valley, they were useless for anything else.

"Well, then," said Mr Sutton. "It seems we have a weapon. Not much of a weapon, but—"

"Still a weapon, though," said Paul, with a grin.

His unexpected optimism infected the others. Mark saw the first beginnings of hope spreading among the group. Some them even smiled.

Mark opened his mouth to say something, then closed it again. He didn't want to seem boastful, or a teacher's pet. But Mr Sutton had spotted him.

"You were going to say something else, Mark?" he prompted.

Why not? thought Mark. "I can make some flash bombs, if you like. They blind you for a few seconds when they go off. Might work the same as a camera flash."

"*Cool!*" said Pudge, who was now fully convinced he was living a video game.

Mr Sutton actually laughed. He clapped his hands together with delight and pointed at Mark. "Boys and girls, *this* is why you should be paying attention in science class. Of course, while I officially disapprove of schoolchildren messing about with dangerous chemicals, unofficially I think that's a brilliant idea. Well done. I'd better come help you out, though, just to be safe."

Mark glowed. Some of the younger pupils watched him with naked admiration in their eyes. He was a little embarrassed to be the centre of attention, but at the same time, he loved it. They *noticed* him. Even Paul seemed to be looking at him with new respect.

The mood in the room had turned around. Instead of being victims, they were taking the initiative back. Even these small things made them feel less helpless.

"What about the rest of us, sir?" Erika asked.

"We should search the science block," said Paul, before Mr Sutton could speak. "Top to bottom. Collect anything that might be useful: torches, batteries, whatever. Reinforce the doors and windows. Make sure there's no way in that we haven't blocked up. It's not just people that got infected, remember. I've seen rats that had the virus, and we've all seen the beetles. They can get in through places that others can't."

"That's a good idea, Paul," said Mr Sutton. "That's exactly what we should do. Everybody find a partner, and I'll assign you to a task."

They started to mill about, pairing up, motivated now. Mr Sutton walked over to Mark and dropped a comradely hand on his shoulder.

"Looks like it's you and me in the lab, Mark. Let's get to work."

3

Of all of them, it was Erika who found herself alone.

There were an odd number of pupils, and Caitlyn had attached herself to Paul almost before Mr Sutton had finished speaking. Paul looked across the room at Erika, puzzled. He'd expected Caitlyn and Erika to pair up. After all, weren't they meant to be best friends?

But Caitlyn wouldn't even look at Erika. And Erika didn't want to be around Paul right now. So she told Mr Sutton she'd go search on her own. He protested, but she went anyway.

She walked along the corridors with a quick step, hugging herself, eager to put distance between her and Paul and Caitlyn. She could hear her own voice in her ears: *Paul! Paul, get it off me! Paul!*

She was ashamed. She knew Caitlyn was crazy about Paul. She knew that Paul fancied her instead. She knew that she *didn't* fancy Paul. And yet, during that moment of utter terror when that creature had hold of her, it was Paul's name she called, Paul she begged for help.

Little Miss Perfect. The damsel in distress, looking for a hero to save her. She'd tried to help out, and only ended up getting herself in trouble. Better if she just sat in the corner and let everyone else get on with things. *Ugh*.

She was disgusted. She'd betrayed her friend, and she'd betrayed herself. She knew Paul fancied her, so it was him that she reached out to. Not Caitlyn, or that little ginger kid . . . Mark, that was his name. No, she'd gone for Paul.

That was why she couldn't be around him right now. All her life she'd wanted people to see past her face. She wanted people to like her for who she was, instead of feeling jealous or using her as a route to the in-crowd. But when the chips were down, she'd acted just like they expected she would. She'd traded on her looks to try and save herself.

No wonder Caitlyn hated her. She hated *herself* right now.

Well, no more. Whatever happened, she wouldn't do that again. She'd stand up for herself. She didn't need anyone to look after her. Not her daddy, not Tom, and certainly not Paul.

She was stronger than they thought she was. And somehow, she was determined to prove it to them all.

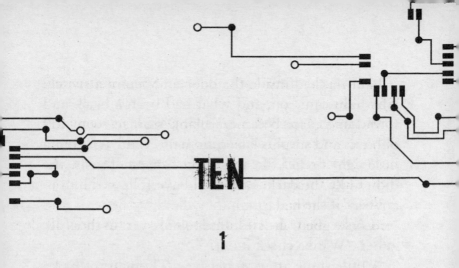

TEN

1

Caitlyn peered over Paul's shoulder into the dark doorway, her heart fluttering for more reasons than one. Down the corridor, she could hear other pupils scavenging, kids let loose to raid the classrooms and labs. From outside came the muffled cries of the Infected beyond the walls as they roamed the campus. But here, there was only the two of them.

Finding herself alone with Paul was precious and rare. There were always other people around, getting in the way, and she never had the nerve to approach him directly when nobody else was nearby. She didn't know what to say.

But for once, there was no Erika to distract him. For once she had him to herself.

Erika. Caitlyn couldn't stop thinking about how she'd called out Paul's name when that thing was trying to pull her through the window. *Paul! Oh, Paul, save me! Save your darling!*

Bitch.

Paul reached inside the door and found a switch. The light came on, and what had been a black and forbidding place became a blank storage room full of boxes and surplus lab equipment. Caitlyn let out a little sigh of relief. She wasn't the bravest of souls. She didn't like the dark. But she'd have followed him in anyway, if she had to.

"Looks good," he said. He looked over his shoulder at her. "Wanna check it out?"

A little smile grew on her face. Thoughts of Erika were banished when he turned his eyes on to her. "Why not?" she said.

They went down the stairs into the storage room and set to, rummaging through the shelves. She rummaged alongside him. Most of the boxes contained bits and bobs like test tubes and pipettes, but Paul found a box full of orange rubber tubing, used to connect Bunsen burners with gas taps, and put it aside.

"What's that for?" she asked.

He shrugged. "You can tie up door handles with it. Make tourniquets. That kind of thing."

She brushed her hair back behind her ear and smiled nervously. She hadn't thought of that. God, he was so *practical*.

She carried on searching, barely paying attention to the things on the shelves in front of her. She was more concerned with trying to think of something witty to say. Paul seemed quite happy to get on with the work of gathering supplies. She sensed that if she didn't make an impression on him now, she'd miss her chance. She just couldn't think how.

"All this. . ." she said. "It's all really messed up, huh?"

"Yeah," he agreed, neutrally.

"Why's this happening to us?"

"Why?" he asked. He stopped searching and gave her a strange look – sort of sad, sort of intense; she couldn't decide which. "Sometimes there doesn't need to be a *why*. Stuff doesn't happen because we deserve it or we don't. It just happens."

She sensed the tension in his voice, and felt like she'd brushed up against something personal. She was intrigued, but now wasn't the time to ask. "Something must have caused this, though," she said. "Something must have started it."

"Yeah," he said. "We might never know what it was, though. We might never find out. People drive themselves crazy looking for *why* and *what happened* and all of that, but in the end it doesn't make any difference. You still have to deal with it, one way or another. Knowing where those things came from isn't going to make us any less dead if they get in."

She thought that a curious reaction to her question, and wondered if she'd annoyed him somehow, or if it was linked to the secret he was keeping. "You think those people out there are dead?" she asked. "The Infected?"

He gazed at her a long moment; she had no idea

what was going on behind those eyes. Then he looked away. "No," he said. "But I think I'd rather they were."

His tone chilled her. With all the fright and despair, she hadn't really thought too hard about the nature of their enemies. But now she found herself wondering. Were there still people inside those things? Did they know what they were doing? Did they feel the slow creep of machinery as it took over their bodies?

Don't, she told herself. *It's too horrible*.

"Hey, look at this," said Paul. He pushed aside some boxes in a corner of the room.

Caitlyn came over to see what he'd found. There was a large hatch in the floor. He crouched down next to it, then suddenly grinned up at her.

"A way out," he said.

"Or a way in," she replied.

"Or a way *out*," he insisted. "Let's be positive, huh?"

Positive? How can you be positive? There are metal ghouls walking around out there!

He pulled the hatch, and it came open. It wasn't even locked.

"There are stairs here," he said.

Caitlyn looked over his shoulder. He was right. Below the hatch was a crawlspace, and set in the floor of that was the opening to a stairway. They could only see the first few steps in the light from the room, but it was obvious the stairway was much older than the building above.

"It must go to the tunnels," she said. Having the hatch open was making her uneasy. She expected something to come rushing up the stairs, out of that thick darkness.

"Since when did we have tunnels?" Paul asked, amazed.

"Oh, everyone hears about the tunnels at some point. School legends, you know? I didn't think they were really here. It's like that story about Billy McCarthy. You heard that one?"

"Yeah, I heard it," said Paul. "Can you see a torch anywhere around?"

She looked about, and to her surprise, she spotted one almost immediately. A big yellow-and-black thing encased in toughened plastic, sitting on a nearby shelf. Pleased at her success, she handed it to him. He shone it down into the dark.

"So what do they say about these tunnels?" he asked, his voice echoing back.

"Oh, right. Well, er, when they first built Mortingham House, it was supposed to be a country manor or something. The owners were a bit weird, so they had tunnels made to the outbuildings where the servants lived, so they didn't have to see them tramping across the gardens or carrying stuff or whatever. But building this place bankrupted them, so it got turned into a workhouse instead. I guess the tunnels were already here by then, though." She knelt down next to him and peered around inside the crawlspace. "Look, you can see how it doesn't connect up with the building properly. There must have been a building on this spot that they knocked down, and then they built the science block over it."

"So this could go to the school building?"

"Might go anywhere," she said.

Paul shone his torch around a little more and then seemed to come to a decision. "Let's go find out."

"Wait, shouldn't we . . . I don't know, go back and tell the others or something?" She heard the words coming out of her mouth and mentally winced at how lame she sounded. "I mean, we should stick together, right?"

Paul was already climbing down into the crawlspace. "You go run it past Mr Sutton if you like. I'm gonna see where this leads."

His tone was dismissive, and hurt her. He wasn't being nasty: he just wasn't bothered whether she came with him or not. She couldn't understand why he wanted to be so reckless. Why was somebody who got on so easily with everyone always so eager to do things on his own?

She hesitated, thinking of the dark down there. It terrified her. She should go back. She should do anything but follow him.

But this was a test. A chance to prove herself to him. A chance to make him notice her, *respect* her.

A chance to show she was braver than Erika.

"Wait," she said again, and this time he stopped and looked up at her. She swallowed against the dread that tried to prevent her speaking.

"I'll come with you."

2

The tunnels were chilly and dank and crushingly dark. They smelled of earth and rot, and there was a musty animal odour in the air, which could only be mice or rats. Droppings were scattered in the corners.

Paul shone the torch on the droppings and stared at them for a long time. His face was grim and closed, as if he was considering something. For a moment, she thought – *hoped* – that he'd turn back, and she could go with him. But then he started walking.

"If you hear anything, tell me," he said. "If you hear rats, I mean."

Caitlyn was surprised by the tone in his voice. Tight, full of suppressed emotion. Was he scared of rats? Somehow, that vulnerability made her feel closer to him. As if she'd been given a glimpse into his secret self, and now they shared that knowledge.

Then she remembered what he'd said about seeing rats infected with the virus, and she just felt stupid instead, and even more afraid.

Paul had the only torch. Beyond that, the blackness was total. The beam played over bare walls of old grey brick, mortar flaking to dust. Every so often, they passed little alcoves that were set into the wall at shoulder height. In one they found a rusted iron candle holder, but there was no candle inside.

Her imagination began to run wild. She pictured Infected things creeping up behind them, but since Paul had the torch, she couldn't even shine it back there to look. It took an effort to slow her breathing, which was getting sharp and short.

She should never have come down here. She should make him take her back upstairs.

Don't embarrass yourself. You've got to show him. You've got to show him you're better than her.

Drawn by an urge for reassurance, she clutched herself to his upper arm. Surprised by her touch, he stopped and frowned at her.

"You alright?" he asked quietly.

The concern in his voice flooded her with warmth. Though she must have looked terrified, she steeled herself and nodded.

"Hold on to me," he said, even though she was already doing just that. And they kept moving down the corridor, with Caitlyn attached to his arm, her heart thumping with the thrill of the contact.

The scratch and skitter of rodents sounded from up ahead. Caitlyn felt Paul go tense. She didn't need to tell him. He'd heard it.

Paul suddenly jerked backwards and pulled her aside as the creature burst into sight. He caught it in the light of his torch: a fat black rat, racing towards them. Caitlyn let out a little scream as it bolted past them and ran up the tunnel.

It was just a regular rat. Paul let out a long, shaky breath.

"Let's go back," said Caitlyn, hopefully, and was immediately disgusted with herself for wheedling.

He was tempted, she could tell. But in the end, he said, "We have to find out where this goes. We might need a way out if those things get into the science block."

They moved on through the dark. Every step forward was another step they'd have to take to get back. Caitlyn prayed to whoever was listening that there was nothing worse than the occasional rat down here.

Up ahead the tunnel angled right, which Caitlyn guessed would take them towards the school building. They heard the sound of rodents moving about again, but this time there were more of them. They weren't running, just scratching about.

Paul shone the torch round the corner, saw nothing, and went on. After a few steps they found a doorway to their right, and looked inside. There was a small room there, empty, with scraps of sackcloth decaying in the corner. Storage for servants' supplies? Caitlyn didn't know, and didn't care to speculate. She just wanted to be gone from here.

The room was the first of a row of three doorways, after which the tunnel kinked left and went out of sight. The sound of movement was close by, quick little scrabbles now and then, the shuffle of shifting bodies. It was hard to tell how many there were, whether they were big rats or tiny mice. The corridor echoed, and seemed full of wet whispers. She looked over her shoulder again. Anything could be lurking in the dark back there.

Paul shone his light into the second doorway. The room beyond was as empty as the first, except for a few shelves that had split and collapsed. She could feel the muscles bunched in his arm, the tension there. He swung the beam up the tunnel, and on to the third doorway.

The scratching stopped.

For a moment, neither of them moved. They listened to the silence. The door was too far up the tunnel to see in, but the rodents had been alarmed by the light. She pictured them frozen there, sniffing the air, wondering what manner of thing had come down into the depths to disturb them.

"They're just rats," Paul said. At first she thought he meant it to comfort her, but then she realized he was talking to himself.

The rats stayed silent as they came closer. He kept the light trained on the doorway.

Step after careful step, each one more tentative than the next. They reached the doorway. Paul shone the torch inside.

And Caitlyn saw it.

At first it was almost impossible to tell what it was. The torch showed only a writhing, lumpen mass of flesh and fur and metal. Then she found its head, and suddenly *oh dear God* she could make out its shape.

The creature was huge, the size of a bear. It was vaguely ratlike in shape, but half-formed, a mutated heap of animal and machine matter. Raw muscle stretched between metal components; dirty clumps of fur sprouted between plates of armour; servos whined as it raised its awful face to the light. Smaller rats were attached to its flanks, some of them partly absorbed into the body. Where their flesh had joined it seemed as if they'd melted into the larger mass. Tiny legs waved uselessly in the air; pink tails curled and flopped.

Blind, deformed eyes were set without symmetry to either side of a silver-toothed mouth. The jaws gaped wide and the thing *squealed*, shrieking at a deafening pitch, a savage and half-mechanical howl.

Paul staggered backwards in the face of that hurricane of noise. As he did, he tripped against Caitlyn and fell. She was pulled down with him, her arm still wrapped around his. Paul's hand swung out to balance himself, his torch hit the edge of the doorway, and with a tiny *plink* the light went out.

The light.

Went.

Out.

Caitlyn was so stunned by the terror of the moment

that it was all she could do not to scream. The impact of hitting the ground was nothing compared to the impact of losing her sight. The last thing she'd seen, the last thing she might *ever* see, was that monster in the room.

The monster that was still there, only a few metres away from them, somewhere in the blackness.

Paul scrambled to his feet, and so did she, and somewhere along the way she lost contact with him. She flailed, not daring to call out, not knowing which way she was facing. She heard the scratching begin again, the sound of tiny rat feet scrabbling uselessly, and a scraping noise as the thing hauled itself across the stone floor. Was it in front of her? Behind her? She couldn't tell; she was too scared. Nearby she could hear Paul shaking the torch, whacking it with his palm, cursing under his breath. That way! Yes, he must be that way!

She reached out a hand in front of her, taking a frightened step in the direction where she thought Paul was. This was a nightmare, this *had* to be, and any minute now she'd wake up and find it was all a—

Her outstretched hand brushed against something. Something hard and cold and soft and bristle-furred. Something that twisted and moved as she touched it.

Pain blazed up her forearm. She screamed and pulled back. Clutching her arm to herself. And right at that moment, the light came back, and she saw the thing in front of her, in the doorway, its flank alive with rats that scratched the air mutely.

The light was coming from behind her. She turned and saw Paul. He grabbed her and pulled her, and they ran, hurtling headlong down the corridor in the direction they'd come.

Behind them, in the darkness, the monster screeched.

3

Up the stairs and out of the dark. They ran as if the thing was on their heels, their lungs bursting, desperate to escape. Paul went ahead, Caitlyn right behind him. He climbed through the hatch into the storage room, dropped the torch and reached back for Caitlyn. She took his hand and was lifted through the crawlspace. Paul slammed the hatch behind her.

"Give me a hand," he said, not even pausing to catch his breath. He ran over to a large box, over a metre high and full of reams of printer paper. She saw what he was trying to do and went to help him. Between them, they slid it across the floor – she was shocked by the weight of all that paper – and manhandled it on top of the hatch. Paul ran back and forth, piling on a few smaller boxes full of nails and screws, a box of vice clamps, anything heavy he could find. When he couldn't pile anything else on it, he stepped back and dusted his hands. "Can't see anything getting through *that* in a hurry."

Caitlyn was trembling.

"Still, we'll need to get some stuff to reinforce it," he continued, oblivious. "No telling *how* big that'll get. Did you see how it was absorbing all those other rats? It must be kind of sucking them in, like, *adding* them. What the hell *are* these things?"

He seemed to realize he was babbling, and he looked over at her. "What's up? Hey, don't worry. We got away, right? You okay?"

She shook her head. The terror she'd felt in the tunnels was nothing compared to this. That had been sudden and sharp; this was an all-consuming, freezing dread that swallowed her whole.

"What's wrong?" he asked again, coming over to her.

She couldn't even speak. She just held out her arm to him. The sleeve of her thin woollen top was torn.

He looked down at it, took her hand and slid the sleeve up her arm.

There were three tiny parallel slashes down her forearm. The marks left by a rat's claw.

In those little lines of red were little specks of silver.

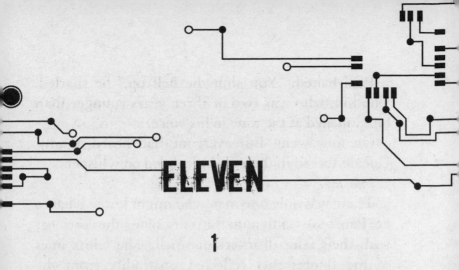

ELEVEN

1

Paul hurried down the corridor, his arm round Caitlyn, shepherding her quickly along. She was pale, her arm clutched to her body. Such a tiny little scratch, barely worth a plaster . . . but they both knew what it meant.

The other pupils were busily running this way and that, salvaging anything useful they could find and piling it up in the foyer, near the foot of a wide staircase. Some were hammering more planks over the windows. He took her past them, holding her protectively, as if he could somehow make up for not protecting her before.

And all he could think was: *this is my fault*.

Kids looked up at them as they went rushing by. One of them noticed the way Caitlyn was holding her arm.

"Hey, what's up with her?" he asked as they passed. Then, in a burst of intuition, "Did she get bit by something?"

Paul halted. "You shut the hell up," he snarled. The kid, who was two or three years younger than him, quailed at the tone in his voice.

On they went. But everyone had heard it now. Unease spread in their wake, carried on whispers.

Infected.

There was only one man who might know what to do. Paul took Caitlyn up the stairs, along the corridors with their faint disinfectant smell. The white lines of the fluorescents reflected unsteadily from the polished floor. They pushed their way through the door into the technology lab where Mr Sutton and Mark worked. Both were wearing goggles. Big plastic jars of chemicals and powders were stacked around them, along with a small pile of plastic tubes and a length of fuse. They were busy making flash bombs. Huge ones, by the look of it.

"Help her," he said.

They dropped what they were doing and hurried over. Caitlyn was trembling and frightened out of her wits, so Paul pulled back her sleeve and showed them the scratches. Already, little silver threads had clogged up the wounds and had crept a few millimetres out on to the skin.

"There was something down in the tunnels," Paul said.

"The tunnels?" Mr Sutton said. "What were you doing down the—"

"It doesn't matter!" Paul snapped impatiently.

"I've shut up the entrance, it can't get into the science block. But you need to do something about this. You *have* to!"

He heard the desperation in his voice. If he hadn't gone down that hatch, she'd never have come with him, and she'd never have been scratched. It didn't matter that he hadn't made her come. He hadn't even *wanted* her to come, particularly. But she'd followed him anyway, and now she was paying for the stupid risk he'd taken.

You knew it might be dangerous. You should have told the others, made a plan, whatever. But you had to do it all on your own, didn't you?

And now he was hoping against hope that someone could undo the thing he'd done.

"Ideas, Mark?" said Mr Sutton. He was calmly studying the wound. If he was distressed by this new turn of events, he wasn't showing it.

"I don't know. It looks too deep in to dig out. Amputate?"

Caitlyn's eyes flicked to him in horror.

"Sorry, sorry," said Mark, holding his hands up. "I just . . . I don't know. . ."

"We can't, anyway," said Mr Sutton. "We don't have the expertise or the equipment to deal with post-operation procedures. Nice try, though. What else?"

"Um . . . the camera!" said Mark suddenly. He snatched up his camera and shoved it into Paul's hands. "Keep taking photos of the wound. Every ten seconds or so. The flash will drain the battery pretty soon, but it ought to stop the wound spreading."

Paul did as he was told, thankful to be given a job. He didn't even look through the viewfinder, just pointed it at Caitlyn's outstretched arm and took the shot. The flash flickered, filling the room with a backwash of light.

"Sir!" said Mark, as another idea struck him. "Do we have a transformer? Something we can run off the mains to reduce the current?"

"In the cupboard," said Mr Sutton, and hurried off to get it.

The door swung open and Adam came storming into the lab. He looked around the room, eyes narrowed, until his gaze fixed on Caitlyn.

"You gotta get rid of her," he said, thrusting out a finger.

Caitlyn began to hitch in her breath, like she was sobbing, except that no tears came.

"Get lost, Adam," said Paul. "This isn't your business."

"She's infected! She'll turn into one of *them*!"

"I said get lost," Paul told him, his voice hardening. Anger swirled in his gut. All the fear and tension and guilt he felt came bubbling up in a tide of heat. He put down the camera and turned to face Adam.

Adam strode across the room, between the tables, coming towards them. "Give her here, then. I'll chuck her out myself, if you won't."

Paul lunged at him. He grabbed Adam by the collar, propelling him backwards. He'd meant to slam him up against a table, but Adam tripped on a stool, fell over it, and went down. Paul almost went over with him, but he just about managed to keep his balance.

"*Stop it, both of you!*" roared Mr Sutton, from the other side of the room. They'd barely heard him raise his voice before today; this was the first time they'd ever heard him really angry. "There's enough to deal with without your bloody swaggering! Behave like adults for a change!"

That cut them both. Adam struggled to his feet, kicking the stool away, puce with rage. Paul wiped the back of his hand across his mouth, his blood up. He so dearly wanted to land a fist in that stupid, ugly face, to try and beat some of the ignorance out of him. But Mr Sutton's words held him back.

"You keep your damn hands off her," he warned Adam.

"Adam," said Mr Sutton, his voice calm now. "Leave us, please. You're not helping."

Adam glared at Mr Sutton, then back at Paul. For a moment, Paul thought Adam was really going to go for him. Then he spat — actually *spat* — at Paul's feet, before stalking away towards the door.

"Paul!" warned Mr Sutton, in case Paul had any thoughts of avenging the insult. He needn't have bothered: Paul didn't intend to rise to it. He just watched Adam go, until he'd left the lab. The tension departed with him.

"Camera," Mark reminded him quietly.

Paul swore under his breath. He picked up the camera and flashed it at Caitlyn's wound again. Now the adrenaline was wearing off, his hands were shaking a little.

"You could have handled that better, Paul," said Mr Sutton, as he returned to the table with a transformer. It was a small grey metal oblong with black plastic knobs on it. It looked like the controller for the train set Paul's dad kept in the attic, back before everything went bad. Mark immediately began unscrewing the front of it.

"This might need a bit of rejigging," he said.

Paul stood there, feeling helpless, flashing the camera every so often. The silver in the wound hadn't got any worse, thankfully. He knew Caitlyn was trying to catch his eye but he couldn't look at her. He felt ashamed. Everyone else was doing what they could to fix this; Paul had only been good for getting them into trouble in the first place.

Outside, the Infected were screeching, their cries echoing across the campus. It sounded like they were calling to each other. Night had fallen. There was no trace of the sun any more.

Paul wondered if he'd ever see it again. If any of them would.

Mark had cracked open the case of the transformer

and run some wires out from it. Mr Sutton plugged it in.

"What are you going to do?" Paul asked.

"I'm going to pass a current across the wound," said Mark.

"You're going to electrocute me?" Caitlyn cried.

"Unless you want us to slice out a chunk of your arm, it's the best I can do," said Mark, his voice an irritated whine, as if he was pissed off at her for being ungrateful. He was a smart kid, but he didn't like his intelligence being questioned. "This virus, or whatever it is, it turns people into machines, right? Well, delicate circuits don't much like to be fried with electricity, do they?"

"Nor do people!" sobbed Caitlyn.

"Look, the transformer here controls the voltage. It'll be a weak shock, but it'll hurt."

"It'll kill me!"

"It won't kill you. Just trust me, alright?" he said impatiently.

Caitlyn looked around at the others, frightened. Finally her gaze found Paul, and this time he met it.

"I'll be holding on to you. If he fries you, he'll fry me too." He took her free hand and squeezed it. "We have to trust him," he said.

"Not gonna *fry* anyone," Mark muttered resentfully under his breath, but Caitlyn didn't seem to hear him. She was looking only at Paul. Paul was puzzled by what he saw there. Gratitude? Or something else?

Before he could work it out, she turned her head and gave a little nod to Mark.

"Okay," she said.

Mark put the two wires on either side of the scratches. "Ready?" he asked.

She sucked in her breath. "Ready."

Mark nodded at Mr Sutton, and he flicked the plug switch. Caitlyn's arm seized up, the muscles standing out against the skin. She shrieked. Paul clutched her hand hard, but none of the shock reached him: it was passing between the two wires, through the silver threads. They kept the current up for only a few seconds, but it seemed like an age. Finally, Mr Sutton flicked off the switch again. Caitlyn sagged, but she kept her feet. Her face was red, and she was sweating.

"One more," said Mark, with the detached manner of a doctor. "Better be sure."

Caitlyn nodded again. This time she didn't make a noise as the current flowed. When it ended, she gasped in a breath.

Her arm had gone bright red. Mr Sutton came round and studied the wound with a magnifying glass. He watched it for an agonizing minute before he drew himself to his full height and said, "It's not spreading any more. It's melted. I think we might have killed it."

"Really?" Mark said, in the tone of someone who hadn't actually expected it to work.

"I think so."

Caitlyn stared in disbelief at Mr Sutton. It was only just beginning to dawn on her: she was going to be alright. Paul felt a giddy flood of relief, and he slapped Mark on the shoulder, making him jump.

"Thank you," he said to Mark. "I don't know what to say, but ... y'know. Thank you. Sincerely. That was amazing."

Mark grinned back, ear to ear. It was a goofy sort of grin – he was an odd-looking kid – but it was the first time Paul could remember ever seeing him smile.

"No problem," he said. "Anytime."

Caitlyn burst into tears.

2

Paul found Erika on the roof.

She was at the northern edge of the science block, leaning against the waist-high railings, her back to him. Her parka was buttoned up against the night chill, and her long blonde hair blew around her shoulders restlessly. She didn't turn as he emerged through the roof access door. Either she hadn't heard him, or she didn't care.

Paul headed over to the opposite side, and poked his head through the railings. Below him, Mr Sutton's upper body was visible, sticking out of a first-floor window. The teacher twisted awkwardly so he could look up.

"Ready?" he asked.

"Throw it," said Paul.

It took a few tries before Paul caught the end of the thin cable. Each time he missed, Mr Sutton had to duck inside as it fell back towards him. When Paul finally grabbed it, he pulled it back through the railings and began walking across the roof towards the centre. Mr Sutton played out the slack, and kept doing so until Paul had made a little coiled heap on the floor.

"That's enough!" Paul shouted, and the cable stopped coming.

He scanned the roof, but there was nothing to fix the cable to that would get it high enough to make a decent antenna for the transmitter. He'd have to come back and fix a board to the side of the roof access door, and run the cable up that.

He supposed he ought to head back and get some tools, but his eye was drawn to Erika instead. She looked so alone over there. A girl like that, everyone wanted to be around her. It was somehow wrong to see her on her own.

She didn't look at him as he joined her at the barrier. She was looking north, over the flat roof of the sports hall. The moon and stars had been extinguished by the lid of cloud that lay over the valley. The only light came from below, the eerie electric-yellow glow of the campus at night, which threw mysterious shadows across the Nordic planes of her face.

Content to share the silence, Paul watched the campus. To their left, his view was blocked by the flank of the school building, rising like a crag. There were only a dozen or so Infected in sight nearby, prowling across the lawns. He wondered where the rest were. How many were there, in all? A hundred? Two hundred? Difficult to say. He had no idea how many pupils had stayed at the Academy this weekend, how many were hiding or how many were infected. He couldn't detect any sign of life in the windows of the nearby buildings. The campus had gone disturbingly quiet.

He thought about what he'd seen down in the tunnels. That rat had been absorbing the other rats, assimilating them, remaking itself into something bigger. He remembered the rats he'd seen in the basement, with the caretaker. They'd had their tails all twined together. The newly infected acted like zombies, but those rats had been smart enough to chew through a phone cable. Had they *intended* to cut them off, to prevent anyone calling for help? That was a disturbing thought.

Paul wasn't quite sure how it worked, but the Infected seemed to operate best in groups. The more of them there were, the more capable they seemed. And there were more of them all the time.

His thoughts were interrupted by the *snick* of a lighter. Erika was cradling a flame in a cupped hand, drawing on a cigarette. She blew out smoke and glanced over at him, as if noticing him for the first time. She took the cigarette from her mouth and offered it.

Paul didn't even like cigarettes, but he wasn't about to turn down an offer like that. It was the closest she'd got to being friendly since they'd met. There was a certain rueful cameraderie in it; two doomed soldiers in a trench, sharing what comforts they had.

"Didn't know you smoked," he said as he passed it back.

"No one does," she said. "And no one was ever supposed to find out. Doesn't seem to matter much now, though, does it?"

"Those things'll kill you," he said with a grin.

She snorted a little laugh, but her smile lasted only a moment before it faded, and she was maudlin again. "You know what's the worst thing?" she said. "The waste. There are kids down there who've been studying since they were old enough to think. Their whole lives, they did what they were told. Work hard, get good grades. SATs, GCSEs, A levels, all so you can go to uni, get a degree, get a career, become a productive member of society. It all seems to pile on you so fast, you don't even get a chance to think *Is this what I want? Is this what I need?*" She flicked her ash over the railing and watched it come apart in the breeze as it tumbled earthward. "Now look at them. I bet that A-star in geography will come in handy next time they're trying to rip somebody's face off."

Her voice wobbled as she reached the end of the sentence. She took another hard drag on the cigarette and passed it back to Paul.

"Hey, come on," said Paul, as he took it. "We'll get out of this. It's not the end of the world."

"The end of the world is *exactly* what it is," she snapped.

Paul sucked on the cigarette, offered it back, and when she declined, he sent it spinning away into the night. His mouth tasted like a fireplace and his throat hurt, but his face was warm and his head felt strangely light from the nicotine.

"I mean, it can't have started here," Erika said, brushing her hair away from her face. "It must have come from outside. We've seen beetles, rats, dogs . . . *people*. So how long before it infects the birds?"

"Maybe it won't," said Paul. "Maybe they'll be too heavy to fly, being metal and all."

"Fish, then. There's a river that runs right by the wall that goes all the way out to sea." She looked at him with a dull kind of acceptance in her eyes. "This isn't going to go away. This isn't something they can contain. By the time the government works out what's happening, it'll be out of their reach. You could quarantine the whole of the British Isles and it wouldn't make any difference."

"Yeah," said Paul. "I know." He'd sensed it, even if he hadn't worked it through the way she had. Things had changed for good, and they wouldn't ever go back to normal. "Just trying to make you feel better, that's all."

"Well, don't," she said, but her tone was gentle, and kind of sad. "It's the end of the world. The least we can do is be honest with one another."

Paul would have loved to be honest with her. He'd have loved to tell her everything he felt. But even the end of the world wouldn't bring *those* words out of him.

"Honest or not, we shouldn't tell the others," he said. "Some of them are only just hanging together in there."

She sighed. "I know. You're right." She turned around so that she was sitting against the railing, and folded her arms, gathering the fur collar of her parka under her chin. "Is Caitlyn okay?"

"I thought you went to see her."

"I did. She made it clear she didn't want to see me. She had some rather choice things to say, in fact."

"What's going on with you two?" Paul asked.

"She never liked me, apparently. Wasn't shy about telling me, either." Her voice was carefully level, stripped of emotion, but Paul could see how it hurt her to speak the words aloud.

"She's just saying that 'cause she's scared and angry," Paul assured her. "You don't hang out with somebody every day if you don't like them."

She gave him a sidelong glance, as if to say, *Are you really that naïve?*

"Wow," he said eventually. It was the best he could come up with. Had Caitlyn really never liked Erika all this time? He couldn't imagine the effort it would take to sustain that level of deceit.

"Like I said, it's the end of the world," said Erika, with a too-casual shrug. Tears were glittering in her eyes. "The least we can do is be honest with one another."

And right at that moment, the campus lights went out.

It happened without noise or fanfare. One moment, the scene was lit by a yellow electric glow, and the next it was lit by nothing at all. The recessed lights and lamp posts shut off. The lights in the windows went out. Even the moon and stars were hidden behind the clouds.

Darkness, everywhere. And then came the screams, high and desperate and terrified. They came faintly from a distance, and louder from the building below them.

Erika and Paul just stood where they were, the memory of light still fading in their eyes. And as their night vision came back, they saw things moving. Packs of Infected, running with purpose. Some went this way, and some went that.

And some came running towards them.

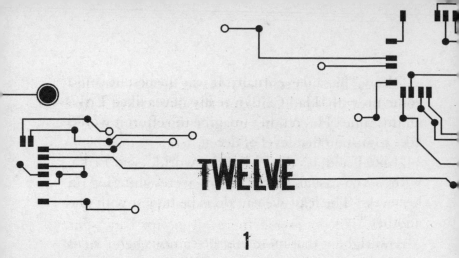

TWELVE

1

Downstairs, it was chaos.

Paul had kept hold of the torch he'd taken from the basement storage room, and he used it to guide Erika through the darkened corridors. Plenty of other kids had had the same idea. Torches were some of the most obviously useful items they'd come across while scavenging, and beams of light flashed crazily around as Mr Sutton fought to calm the panic in the foyer.

Along the corridor, Paul could see a pair of kids whacking at one of the windows with iron bars that they'd salvaged from the metalwork department. Silver fingers had curled through the gaps between the planks and were tugging at them. Paul saw four hands there, before they were knocked away.

"They're working together!" Mr Sutton cried, as he caught sight of Paul. "Attacking on all sides!"

Paul heard planks creaking as the Infected pulled at them, and suddenly he realized how feeble the barricades were. They'd been good enough to withstand the Infected an hour ago, but since then they'd got smarter, faster, and possibly stronger. And they'd learned to combine their efforts. Instead of pawing mindlessly at the obstructions, they were taking them apart.

"They're not gonna hold," Paul said to himself. Then, louder: "They're not gonna hold!"

A loud boom made them all jump. Paul spun around and shone his torch in the direction it had come from. The heavy swing doors at the main entrance were barricaded shut and boarded over, with a pole driven through the handles. As Paul watched, something slammed into them from outside, something that made the planks groan and bend and bulge. Something massive.

BOOM!

"What was that?" said a small voice at Paul's shoulder. He noticed Mark, who had a satchel full of flash bombs clutched to his chest.

Paul didn't know. He didn't *want* to know. But something had to be done. If the Infected came through that door, or got through the windows, it would soon be over. And there were too many windows for the pupils to defend them all.

No. He wouldn't let it happen. He'd only just started getting to grips with this new and changed world he found himself in. He wasn't planning on leaving it yet.

He shone his torch around the foyer. Piled on the

floor were supplies that the pupils had gathered since they'd shut themselves in the science block. Nearby was a wide staircase leading—

"Upstairs!" Paul cried. "There are only two staircases from the ground floor to the first floor. One here in the foyer, and one on the other side of the block, in the far corner. Both of them have thick double doors at the top. If we barricade them, there's no other way up!"

"We can't give up the ground floor," said Mr Sutton, but his protest was weak. He had the confused air of a man who didn't know what to do. It was the first time Paul had seen him uncertain. Mr Sutton had never been the best at enforcing discipline, preferring to outwit his pupils instead. The sudden darkness had caused him to lose control of the kids, and now he was dithering.

BOOM! The doors shook again.

"You think we can hold the ground floor if those *things* get in?" Paul cried.

Mr Sutton looked at the doors, then back at Paul. He seemed taken aback by the fierceness in Paul's voice. Paul waited a moment for a response, and when there was none, he ran out of patience.

"You three!" he said, pointing to a group of younger kids who were bunched together in a corner, frightened. "Grab up an armful of these iron rods and hand them out to anyone who doesn't have one. Everyone needs a weapon." Two kids came hurrying in from down the corridor, perhaps looking for Mr

Sutton. He recognized Freckles and Pudge. "You, and you. Take planks and nails, get up those stairs and get ready to barricade the doors at the top. Pile up anything heavy you can find. I'll be up there in a minute. Nothing gets through there, right?"

Pudge's face split into a grin. He was happy to receive a mission, possibly looking forward to the experience points he'd receive upon completion. "Right!" he said, and they got to it.

The frightened kids were watching Mr Sutton uncertainly, as if waiting for his approval. Paul didn't have time for their teacher to get his act together. "Move it!" he snapped at them, and they scampered over to the supply pile and began picking up iron bars.

BOOM!

Erika, Mark and Mr Sutton were staring at him like they didn't recognize him. Paul didn't care. Nobody was doing anything, so he'd tell them what to do. There was a certainty to it, a rightness. He was inspired.

Paul scanned the pile of supplies and spotted a dozen white plastic containers, and a few smaller glass bottles full of transparent liquid. "Is that white spirit?" he asked Mr Sutton.

"Er . . . yes. Yes, for treating wood."

Paul quickly slipped his feet from his shoes, pulled off his socks, and put his bare feet back in the shoes.

"Um. What are you doing?" asked Mark.

Paul picked up one of the bottles, unscrewed the cap and threw it away. Then he stuffed a sock into the neck of the bottle, into the liquid, leaving a length of material poking out of the end. He picked up one of several trigger-operated electric gas lighters that were used for igniting Bunsen burners, and used it. A flame sprang into life at the end of the lighter. He held it up next to the bottle.

"Molotov cocktail," he said. "Want to bet the Infected don't like being set on fire?"

"Everyone, give me your socks, bits of rag, whatever you've got," said Erika. "I'll make more of those cocktails."

"I'll hand out the flash bombs," said Mark.

"Mr Sutton. Go tell everyone. Fight them off if we can, but if the Infected get through, we fall back to the staircase on the other side of the block. We can barricade it behind us. Okay?"

"Yes," said Mr Sutton. "Er, yes, right." He seemed surprised to have his authority taken away from him, to be receiving orders instead of giving them. Then his face cleared and his expression firmed. "Yes, I'll do it."

Paul stuffed the Molotov cocktail in his coat pocket and grabbed another one, which Erika handed up to him. The sharp stink of chemicals surrounded them. The air was full of distant shrieks and screams.

BOOM! The main door rattled again. One of the planks split.

"What are *you* gonna do?" Mark asked Paul, as he hurried off up the stairs after Pudge and Freckles.

Paul nodded towards the door, and whatever was pounding on it from the other side. "I'm gonna see what I can do about *that*."

2

BOOM!

This time the impact made the floor shiver beneath Paul's feet. Freckles and Pudge paused in their task of nailing planks across the doors at the top of the staircase from the foyer. They exchanged a nervous glance, then went back to it at twice the speed.

Paul ran his torch over the doors, examining their efforts. They'd jammed a bar through the handles and run a chain around them for good measure. With the planks in place, it would be pretty hard to get through, even for a few dozen Infected. "When you're done with that, pull in the chemistry tables from the next lab and jam them in front of the doors. They weigh a ton."

"Yeah, you told us already," said Pudge, with a faint hint of annoyance. There was another boom from downstairs. "I thought you had something to do?"

Paul made a last quick check to be sure they were doing everything right, then ran off up the corridor, torch in one hand, Molotov cocktail in the other. Pudge was right to be annoyed: Paul had a job of his own to do. Why couldn't he just leave them alone to do theirs?

Because he couldn't rely on them. He couldn't rely on anyone but himself. That was the long and the short of it. But he couldn't be everywhere at once, and he had to pick his priorities. Right now that meant dealing with whatever it was that was hell-bent on smashing in the doors of the science block.

He entered the next classroom along and hurried through the tables to the far end. He reckoned himself to be right above the entrance now. The windows weren't yet barricaded on the second floor. It hadn't seemed urgent, as the Infected hadn't shown any signs that they were able to climb. He ran to the nearest one – a sash window with a grim aluminium frame – slid it upwards and stuck his head out into the night air.

The faintest glow of moonlight fought its way through the clouds and drifted down on to the darkened campus, adding a steely edge to the shadows. Though his night vision had been ruined by torchlight, Paul could make out the movement of the Infected as they scuttled and lumbered across the open spaces. He spotted them by their eyes: cold blue stars that bobbed and lurched through the blackness. And he saw how they clustered round certain buildings, like maggots at a wound.

They knew where the pupils were hiding, and they'd attacked those buildings *en masse*. This was a focused, simultaneous assault. Not the work of mindless things.

BOOM! The window frame shook. Paul looked down in time to see something recoil away from the door of the science block. Something large. He squinted into the dark.

Below him were ragged figures tugging at the boarded-up windows, gnashing their teeth in impotent savagery, clothes soaked and tattered. Most of them were more metal than flesh now, though there was still a terribly human aspect to their features. They kept something of the faces of the people they once were. Some he thought he recognized.

Then the shape lunged forward into the light again, and threw itself against the door. Paul caught his breath. This was the creature that threatened to break in the door, the leader of the assault. A brute ogre of a thing.

Mr Harrison had *grown*.

The headmaster had always been a big man, fond of intimidating people with his size and his military roar. But now he was monstrous, with great cables of metallic muscle bulging through the shreds of his clothes. He must have been seven feet tall, but he was standing in a crouch and his enormous shoulders and upper arms made him look like some grotesquely swollen hunchback. Blue eyes shone like lamps in a head made small by the size of his body.

Paul thought suddenly of the rat-thing in the

tunnels, that had absorbed the other rats around it and grown huge. Was that what had happened to the headmaster?

BOOM! Mr Harrison swung a huge fist into the science block doors. There was the sound of splintering wood and the shriek of tortured hinges. They were on the verge of breaking, and if they did, there would be nothing to stop the Infected surging in and overwhelming everyone before they could retreat.

The others needed time to get everyone upstairs and barricade the second-storey doors. Paul needed to give it to them.

With shaking hands, he held up the bottle of white spirit with his sock stuffed in the end. The spirit had soaked up through the sock by now, the fibres damp with flammable liquid. Paul touched the gas lighter to it and pulled the trigger. Flame rippled up the sock, blue and yellow and green.

He swallowed against a dry throat and leaned back out of the window. "Hey, up here!" he called, as loud as he could manage.

The ogre that had once been his headmaster looked up at him, fixing him with a sharp and soulless glare. Paul flung the Molotov cocktail down towards him. Unnerved as he was by the sight of the creature, his aim was off – but it was good enough. The bottle burst against Harrison's shoulder. One massive arm and half a leg burst into flame.

Harrison bellowed, the sound like some prehistoric beast, accompanied by that awful buzzsaw whine that underpinned the voices of the Infected. The scene was suddenly illuminated by fire. Harrison flailed and swung, knocking nearby Infected off their feet, flapping at himself in torment. He staggered away from the science block, his torn coat and trousers alight, and then with a howl he thundered away across the campus. In moments, he was only a trail of fire dwindling in the dark, heading for the lake.

Paul sat back from the window, and allowed himself a desperate grin of relief. The science block doors would hold. He'd stared into the eyes of the beast and seen it off. The reprieve would only be short, but that didn't matter. Nothing mattered. Because just for this one moment, he felt invincible.

3

"Keep 'em back! *Hit* 'em, you wimps!"

Even now, the younger pupils of Mortingham Academy were more scared of Adam than they were of the Infected. There wasn't one of them who hadn't been bullied by him, or at least learned to fear him by reputation. So when he yelled at them, they stopped backing away from the windows and did what he said. The Infected were still outside for now. Adam was in here with them.

There were three boarded-up windows in the

ground-floor classroom. Through the gaps in the planking, sharp blue eyes glowed in snarling silver faces. The Infected pulled at the boards or tried to squeeze their hands through the gaps to scratch the people inside. When they did, the three younger kids battered them with iron rods. Adam, who was stronger, wielded an old, heavy radiator pipe that he'd hacksawed off earlier. The Infected screeched as fingers and wrists were twisted and broken under the pupil's blows, but there were always more behind them, wrenching at the planks, pulling them loose.

Mr Sutton had come running through a few moments ago and breathlessly delivered the news of the fallback plan. Adam just grunted and accepted it. He wasn't much for thinking ahead. He was a creature of the moment. And right now that meant keeping these bloody things out.

He scanned the room. The furniture had been shoved against the walls. He wished they'd thought of stacking up tables and nailing them flat over the windows, but it was too late for that now. There were two torches in the room, which had been laid on a sideboard to free up the pupils' hands. They cast enough light to alleviate the darkness, but their pallid beams made sinister shadows in the gloom.

There was a cracking sound, and one of the planks came away from a window, shedding nails. Adam ran over and pulled aside the kid that was standing there. A spindly arm came thrusting between the planks and scratched at the air. The face of an Infected crammed into the gap, teeth bared. The straggly brown hair and sodden clothes told him it had once been a girl. It certainly wasn't a girl now.

Adam aimed his pipe and brought it down on the elbow, breaking the bone with a nauseating snap. The creature screeched, jaws wide, a ghoulish mockery of the person it had once been. Adam swung the pipe into its face. He felt a jarring impact up his arm, and it flew away from the window.

He picked up the loose end of the plank and shoved it back into place. "Hold this board while I nail it!" he snapped at the frightened kid who stood at his shoulder. Then he felt a thump against the plank from outside, and Infected fingers scrabbled at the wood. One of the fingers brushed against the side of his hand, chill metal against warm skin. He dropped the plank in horror, backing away, examining his hand frantically. Just one scratch from those nails and he'd turn into one of *them*. Had it broken the skin? Had it?

He put his hand into the beam of a torch. No. His hand was unmarked. Just a touch, then. Just a touch, and no more. He was appalled by how close he'd come.

By the time he turned back to the window, the Infected had wrenched the plank away, making a space big enough to crawl through. The kid was whacking at it, but he wasn't strong enough to hold it back. There was another crunch, and Adam saw that the lower plank of one of the other windows was coming free. The kids were backing off, wanting to run, held only by their fear of Adam.

And suddenly he had the sense that this was all hopeless, that there were barely enough kids to cover all the windows on the ground floor, and half of them were too young to be effective. They could slow the tide, but not hold it back.

"Get back to the windows!" he yelled. "Keep at 'em! Keep 'em out!"

He ran back to the windows and swung with all his might, smashing one of the Infected round the head as it tried to squeeze through, sending it reeling back into the night. The younger kids took courage from that, and resumed their efforts to knock away the silver fingers that spidered through the cracks.

One way or another, the Infected were coming in. It was only a matter of time. But Adam wasn't going to make it easy for them.

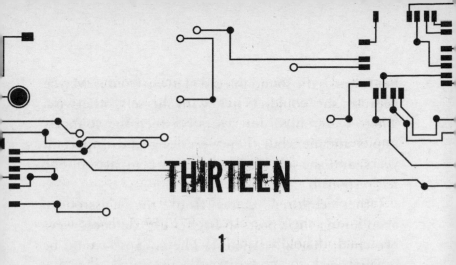

THIRTEEN

1

Erika knew when she heard the screaming that the game was up.

She came to a halt in the middle of the corridor, alone. The beam of her torch slashed the dark ahead of her, cutting across the doors of the ground-floor classrooms. A bag hung from her shoulder, mostly empty now. All but one of the Molotov cocktails had been delivered; she'd been about to head back and make more.

It dawned on her how far she was from safety. The doors above the foyer had been barricaded. The back stairs were on the other side of the building from her. If the Infected broke in now. . .

But they *had* broken in. That was what the screaming meant.

It wasn't coming from the classrooms ahead. It was coming from behind her, down the corridor, round the corner. Little voices, raw with terror. She didn't know where the courage came from that propelled

175

her towards the sound instead of away from it. Maybe because she couldn't live with herself otherwise. There were only a few years between the youngest pupils and her, but they were long and important years, and she felt like an adult in comparison. She felt responsible.

Other children came from the classrooms, abandoning their posts in fright. The defences were breached; they all sensed it. The collapse would be quick now.

"Run for the stairs!" she shouted at them as she passed. "Do as Mr Sutton told you!"

Behind them, from the classrooms, she could hear the splintering of wood as the Infected tore their way in through the barricades.

She rounded the corner and saw a pair of girls, wild with fright, backing out of a classroom. They were the screamers, their voices shrill and ear-splitting. They caught sight of her and fled senselessly, as if she were Infected herself.

"Wait!" she called after them, but they had no intention of waiting, because another pupil was stumbling after them. A boy of no more than thirteen, one hand clasped to the side of his throat, slick and wet with blood. In the other hand was a Molotov cocktail that Erika had given him only minutes before. The rag in its neck was lit. He must have been on the verge of throwing it when he was bitten.

Blood pulsed through the dam of his fingers. His

eyes met hers over the flame. They were blank, emptied out. Then he toppled, and the bottle slipped from his limp hand.

Erika staggered backwards as the corridor erupted into flame. Scorching air swept over her face. She tripped and fell as a wave of searing heat billowed past her. Her bag thumped against her body, cushioning the bottle within; somehow it didn't break. She scrambled away, one arm protecting the bottle, the other thrown across her face as she looked back. Tears were trickling down her cheeks, inspired by heat or fright, or both.

Oh no, no, there was a boy in that.

She heard footsteps. Four pupils came running round the corner. They stopped dead when they saw the fire.

"There's no way through!" she yelled at them, climbing to her feet. "Go back!"

They didn't move. They knew what was back there. The Infected. The creatures outside had already begun dismantling the abandoned defences.

"Now! Before they block us off!"

Maybe they were scared by the fierce-eyed figure silhouetted against the flames, or maybe they knew that some chance was better than none at all, but they did as she said. Erika chased after them, round the corner and back into the corridor where she'd first heard the screams.

Over the years, Erika had attended many lessons

in many classrooms all over the science block. She knew every corner of it by now. The quickest route to the stairs had been blocked by the flames, but there were other ways to get there. If they could make it in time.

There were two classrooms on their left, both with outside windows. As she ran past the first, she glanced inside. The window was a faint, ragged rectangle of moonlight. Something terrible was clambering in.

The next door was closed. She heard it open behind her as she turned the corner. She didn't look back.

Now she was in the hallway that ran along the back of the science block. The sight of pupils running away had set off the others, and all thought of defending the windows had been forgotten. Black, poisonous smoke was drifting from the open doorway of a classroom, and a hellish glow seethed within. Another Molotov cocktail thrown.

Stupid, stupid, stupid. She should have known, should have seen how dangerous it was putting fire in the hands of scared kids. The sprinkler system wouldn't work with the electricity off. They could end up retreating upstairs only to have the whole building burn down around them. Why didn't Mr Sutton think of that? Why didn't Mark or Paul think of it?

The same reason she herself didn't think of it. Everything was moving too fast. They were scared and desperate. Clear thinking was in short supply at a time like this.

Too late now. Too late to stop it. Too late to do anything but follow the plan and hope.

Most of the pupils that were bolting from the classrooms were fleeing headlong up the hallway away from her. It was the most obvious route to the stairs, which were in the far corner of the block at the angle where two corridors met. It was also the longest and most dangerous, since it ran along the outer edge of the science block, where the Infected were coming in. It would be easier and safer to cut through the classrooms and labs.

"This way!" she called, ushering passing kids towards a classroom door that she was holding open. Nobody listened to her. They were caught up in the hysteria of the retreat, pushing each other aside in their haste.

Three Year Eight girls, gawky twelve-year-olds, came running up the corridor. Behind them came one of the Infected. Perhaps it had been the same age as them once, but it had changed now, its limbs longer and thinner, fingers like claws, spiked hair sticking up and eyes glowing blue. It came lurching up the corridor with an uneven step, one hand scratching the air, head tilted to one side and howling like something damned.

Erika's hand went to her bag, and came out holding the last of her Molotov cocktails. With shaking hands she sparked her cigarette lighter and touched it to the rag. The flame sprang up alarmingly. She drew back her arm and threw it. The bottle sailed over the girls' heads and hit the Infected straight in the chest.

One moment the awful thing was there, the next there was a pillar of flame in its place. The howls changed pitch, became wild shrieks instead. It flailed onwards, staggering this way and that, a dark silhouette inside a raging inferno. For a few seconds, it seemed that even fire wouldn't stop it. But then one of its legs gave way, and it fell. It tried to lift itself from the ground, failed, and didn't try again.

Erika stared at the blazing remains of the Infected, her eyes shimmering with tears. She'd never done such violence to a living thing in her life. Now the air was thick with the sweet black stink of burning flesh and the ceiling writhed with a thin dark smoke.

She looked for the girls, but they'd gone, up the corridor and away. There was no one left now, nobody to help. The shapes moving behind the flames were not human any more. She turned tail and fled.

2

"You want some of this?" Adam roared, brandishing the length of radiator pipe. "Do you?"

Adam found nothing strange in threatening someone while retreating. He'd had dozens of fights with boys who were bigger and stronger than he was, but he'd avoided just as many. Acting scared or meek was the worst thing you could do. So you made yourself dangerous, and you backed off, and you left with your hide and your pride.

That was how it worked with people, anyway. The Infected were another matter.

There were two of them advancing up the corridor towards him. The kid they'd been chasing was behind Adam now, and still running. While everyone was fleeing for the stairs, Adam had gone the other way. He told Mr Sutton he was going to cover the retreat, make sure everyone got to safety that could.

But that wasn't the real reason at all. He just wanted to wreck some Infected.

There were certain things that Adam was deadly scared of. One time, when he had to speak at a school assembly, he was so nervous he was sick. Trying to talk to a girl he liked caused the same reaction. But when it came to fighting, things were different. Then his fear got all muddled up with his anger. He didn't feel scared in a fight. He was like a cornered animal instead. The more afraid he should have been, the more angry he got.

He should have been terrified right now. Instead, he was boiling mad.

The Infected prowled warily towards him as he backed away. They weren't used to their prey acting defiant. Or maybe they recognized him, and it made them hesitate. Maybe they still remembered how they'd feared him once.

Surely not. As Adam flashed his torch over them, he could make no connection between these twisted silver ghouls and the kids he'd once shaken down for sweets and pocket money. They were barely human any more. One of them was hunched low to the floor, the sharp metal ridges of its spine visible through the ripped remains of a shirt. The other stood ramrod straight, its head back and bent to one side. One of its hands was a deformed paw that ended in a straggle of shiny cables, as if it were midway through changing into something else, but it hadn't quite made it.

They were closing in on him now, losing their caution. Adam couldn't turn his back on them now, and they didn't look like they'd be scared off. He knew the signs. And he knew there was only one thing to do.

"Let's have you, then," he snarled. And he lunged forward and swung the pipe with all his strength.

They didn't expect an attack. The Infected with the hunched back took the full force of the strike on the side of its skull. There was a loud ring of metal on metal, and the creature slammed into the wall and went down in a heap. The second Infected lurched towards him, grabbing at his arm with its good hand. But Adam had dodged faster moves than that in his time. He pulled back, let his opponent overreach itself, and then brought the pipe down in a crushing arc on its shoulder, smashing it to the ground.

He backed off, breathing fast, cold with adrenaline. A smirk of triumph touched his lips. One, two, and they were on the floor, lying still. He'd done that. Him!

"Yeah!" he shouted at them. "How'd you like that?"

Then one of them stirred, and a moment later, the other one did too. Slowly, they lifted themselves up again. Blue glowing eyes fixed on him, and he could have sworn they had hate in them now.

"Right," he said to himself, his bravado diminishing. Then he turned and ran for it.

3

Where is she?

Paul stood on the wide staircase that led to the upper floor. Frantic kids hurried past him in the torchlight. How many now? How many hadn't made it? He hadn't even been counting. He was waiting for a sight of her. He had to know that she was safe.

But every passing second brought them nearer to the moment when they'd have to retreat up the stairs, barricade the doors and shut out the Infected. And still there was no sign of Erika.

She couldn't be one of *them*. Paul wouldn't allow the possibility. Everything else might change and turn, but not her. She was his one fixed point. If she was taken, only survival would be left.

The staircase stood at the south-west corner of the science block, at the junction of two corridors that ran off at right angles. Paul had seen to it that the windows of nearby classrooms were particularly heavily defended, so the Infected couldn't block their route to the stairs. When the attack came, the pupils fled through the building, heading for this point. But the Infected were close behind them. And Erika was not here.

Fire regulations meant that the corridors had heavy swing doors placed at intervals along their length, with narrow windows of wire mesh glass. Good thing too, because there was a dark haze gathering at ceiling height and the air stank of burning plastic and charred wood. Paul wished there was an easy way to barricade them, but unlike the doors at the top of the stairs, they had no handles to jam, and there would be no time to nail boards into place.

He saw the light of a torch beam swinging crazily in the darkness behind one of the fire doors. His hopes lifted for a moment, but then the doors swung open and Adam ran through, coughing.

"Any more back there?" Paul asked quickly.

"Just Infected," said Adam, hurrying towards the stairs. "We gotta shut the doors."

"Erika's not back," Paul heard himself say.

"Lot of kids aren't back," Adam replied as he

passed him. "Not coming back, either. At least, not how they were."

Paul looked up the stairs. He couldn't see the doors at the top, because the steps turned back on themselves as they climbed, but he knew Mr Sutton and Mark were up there waiting for him. Caitlyn, too, who'd been upstairs when the attack began. Paul would be the last one through.

"Go on," he said. "I'm gonna wait."

Adam stopped halfway up the stairs and looked back down at him. His eyes had gone narrow and piggy, a sure sign he was gearing up for a fight. Paul felt his hackles rise even before Adam opened his mouth. He couldn't stand this kid, this petty, small-minded bully. He couldn't stand anyone who tried to push people around.

"They're right behind me, I said," Adam told him. "We're not gonna have *time* to barricade the doors if we don't close 'em now."

Paul thought he could see figures moving in the dark through the windows of the fire door. "I'm gonna wait," he said again.

"And get everyone killed? No, you're bloody not!" said Adam, grabbing his arm.

The touch was the excuse he needed. Anger flared like a struck match. Paul whirled, fist clenched, ready to use it.

And then he heard her scream.

It had come from the other corridor. Before he

knew what he was doing, Paul had a flash bomb in his hand. He stuck his torch under his armpit, dug out a gas lighter he'd salvaged from the supply pile, and pulled the trigger to ignite the flame.

Running footsteps. Erika was going to be coming through the east door. He glanced at the other, the one Adam had come through, and saw blue lights in the darkness behind the glass. Eyes.

Adam had come down the stairs and was standing next him now, pipe held ready. Not getting in his way now, but supporting him, ready to take on the Infected if they came through. Paul was grateful to him for that much, at least.

He held the flame near the fuse of the flash bomb. He listened to Erika's running footsteps, and tried to hold his nerve. Timing. It was all about timing. He'd get one shot at this.

He touched the flame to the fuse and tossed it to the floor of the corridor. A second passed. Two. Three. And then it all happened at once.

Both sets of doors burst open at the same time. Through one, a half-dozen Infected poured in, a tide of limbs and teeth. Through the other came Erika, running as hard as she could. Paul saw the instant of horror on her face as she saw the group of Infected lurching into her path, but it was too late to stop herself. Their hands pawed and jaws gaped to receive her.

Then the darkness was blasted away with a loud

bang and a blinding, stuttering flash of searing light. The Infected froze at once like some grotesque tableau. Erika, shocked by the flash and the noise and still travelling at full tilt, tripped forward. She blindly kept her balance for a few more steps, then fell heavily into Paul's arms, who was there at the bottom of the stairs to catch her.

He didn't waste time on relief. He barely gave her time to find her feet before he began pulling her up the stairs. They staggered up together, Adam guarding their backs, the snarling Infected still paralysed in the dark at the bottom of the steps. At the top, Mr Sutton and Mark were waiting on either side of the doors. As soon as they were through, the doors were pushed shut, and an iron bar was rammed through the handles to secure them. Immediately, a team of kids sprang into action, putting up boards and hammering in nails.

The girls flocked to help Erika, but Paul and Adam were ignored in the frenzy of activity that followed their arrival. They went a short way down the corridor to get out of everyone's way. Paul sat down against one wall, head hung, pulling the smoky air in and out of his lungs. Adam sat against the opposite one, the radiator pipe still in one hand.

Alive, thought Paul, but he wasn't sure whether he meant himself or Erika.

And suddenly the corridor was blinking with light. Both boys looked up as the fluorescents overhead came on, flickered and stabilized. The electricity was back. The darkness was banished.

Paul met Adam's eyes across the corridor, and in that instant there was an understanding there, the shared relief of two people who'd been through something terrible and come out the other side. The knowledge of soldiers.

Then the fire alarm went off, and the sprinklers activated, drenching them. Neither Paul nor Adam moved, and neither broke the gaze. Paul saw Adam's mouth twitch at the corner. The two of them started laughing and couldn't stop.

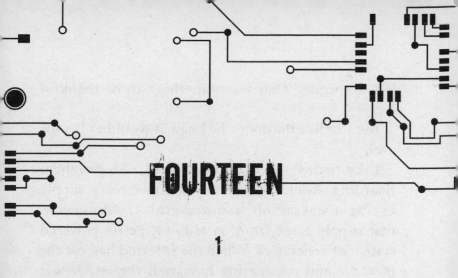

FOURTEEN

1

He could hear them out there. He could sense the weight of them, pressing on the doors.

Wanting to get in.

Mr Sutton ran his eye over the defences for the tenth time. The doors were wooden, plated with thin metal. They were barred, boarded shut, barricaded with heavy desks and braced with benches jammed against the opposite wall. The doors to the other stairway leading to the foyer were similarly secure.

It still wasn't enough.

The Infected were changing. Adapting. If another one of those hulking monstrosities came along and started pounding on the door, they'd break through eventually. And what was to stop them coming back with arms like drills, or as spidery wall-climbing things that could get up on the roof?

He glanced up at the overhead fluorescents. At least they had light. Fear spread easily without it. In their cold, institutional glare, things seemed a little less desperate. That was something to be thankful for.

But just like the doors, he knew it wouldn't last for ever.

Like many remote institutions, Mortingham Boarding Academy had its own electricity supply in case it was cut off from the grid. Unfortunately, that supply came from an ancient, petrol-powered system of generators. When the Infected had cut the power – and considering how well the attack was timed, Mr Sutton was in no doubt that they'd been responsible – the generators had taken a little time to power up and grind into life. They hadn't been needed for years, and Mr Sutton hadn't even been sure they'd work. But they did, thankfully, because this place would have burned down around them if they hadn't.

There was only one problem. The generators were housed in the basement of the school building, in locked rooms near the school's vast boiler, and there was no telling how much petrol was in the tanks. No telling how long it would last, or if the Infected would get to the generators and sabotage them first. If they could make it till dawn, he'd count them lucky. Being realistic, he reckoned they had a few hours at most. The system was only supposed to cover a short outage, and Mortingham was a big place. Across the campus, most of the lights had been left on, even in those buildings where not a single person remained.

And they were about to start draining it even more.

The doors creaked as the Infected surged against them like a tide. They were gathered there at the top of the stairwell. Their buzzsaw moans drifted through into the corridor – so near to their prey, and yet so far.

Mark knelt on the floor, busy at his new device. Something to do with resistors and transformers and a dangerous amount of electricity. Mr Sutton didn't understand it exactly, but Mark assured him that they needed it for what they wanted to do. Otherwise they'd short out the whole building.

The device was a large metal box that Mark had taken from one of the DT labs, with some parts stripped out and others put in. A thick cable trailed away from it, stripped to bare wire at the end and tied around the metal handles of the door. Nearby was a plug, waiting to be put into a socket.

Mark's idea. They were going to electrify the doors.

All his instincts as a teacher and a responsible adult told him that he should be stopping this. But those instincts belonged to a different world now. The rules had changed. Health and safety regulations were a thing of the past. Survival was all that mattered.

Mr Sutton felt useless. Impotent. He was supposed to be protecting the children, but the children were protecting themselves. The old way of things was breaking down. Without structure, without order or rules, the kids were asserting themselves, finding new ways to fit into the world. He marvelled at how adaptable they were. He wondered if adults would have managed quite so well.

A pair of pupils came hurrying from a classroom, carrying tables to be broken up and used for planks. Paul had already set the children to barricading the windows of the upper floor, had posted lookouts on the roof, and set a couple of boys to making a crude mast for the radio antenna. Good. Keeping them busy was the best way to stop them thinking. Everyone was on edge, still distressed after the last attack. At least this way they were doing something.

I should have been leading them, thought Mr Sutton. But part of him was glad that the responsibility was being taken from his shoulders. Because, deep down, he didn't think he could guide them through this. He didn't see any way out.

Mr Sutton had no wife and no children to worry about. The pupils had always been his family, an endless supply of new faces to teach and inspire and send on their way. But now he despaired, because after all these years, he believed the end was upon them. And no lesson he'd taught them would help them avoid it.

"Ready?" said Mark. It stirred him from his dark thoughts. The ginger boy was looking up at him eagerly. Mark hadn't given up. Mark still thought they could make it. So Mr Sutton put on his best encouraging face, and stepped back behind the barriers that they'd set up to stop pupils accidentally touching the barricade.

"Ready," he said.

Mark plugged in the machine and pressed the switch. The lights dimmed. There was a chorus of shrieks from the other side of the door, a frantic scrabbling of metal bodies, and then silence. Mark turned it off, and the lights brightened again.

"That ought to make them think twice about trying that door again," Mark grinned. "We should get someone to stay here and give them a shock every time they touch it."

"I'll find somebody," said Mr Sutton. "Good work, Mark."

Mark got to his feet. "Well, better make one of these for the other door too. They're pretty easy to put together. Once we've got that done, we should be able to hold them off till help comes, right?"

The hope in the boy's eyes was heartbreaking. "Yes," said Mr Sutton. "I'm sure help is already on the way."

2

"...is Radio 4, with Kate Chegwell and the evening mix..."

"...vy showers, clearing by morning, while in the west there are..."

"...expressed their disappointment at what they have called 'a travesty of justice'..."

Mark moved the pencil by a millimetre. As its tip slid across the metal surface of the razor blade, the station changed again.

"Find another news show," Erika urged.

"I'm trying," said Mark waspishly. "It's not exactly a precision instrument, you know."

The radio didn't look much like a radio at all. It was little more than a wooden board with several paper clips attached to it by thumbtacks. Thin wires ran from the paper clips to various components on the board. At one end was a cardboard tube from a roll of toilet paper, with red copper wire wrapped tightly around it. In the centre was a rectangular razor blade, the old kind that your grandfather used to shave with, which were only used nowadays by art students, and prisoners looking for something to slash their enemies with. Touching it was a small pencil, broken off to the length of an inch, with a kinked paper clip coming out of the butt end and attached to a thumbtack. It hovered over the razor like the stylus on a record player, and when Mark touched it to the metal, tinny voices came through a little speaker cone that sat on the table nearby.

Once, Caitlyn would have found it fascinating that Mark could spirit these voices out of the air with a few twists of wire, and without so much as a power supply. Now she was too scared to care.

She didn't show it, of course. She couldn't. She kept things hidden: that was her way. So she sat on the edge of a desk, and watched the others huddling round the radio in the flat laboratory light. The only person paying attention to her was Adam. He kept glancing over at her with a suspicious look in his eyes.

What are you looking at? she thought. But she knew what he was thinking. She hadn't forgotten his outburst when she'd been brought in with a scratch on her forearm.

They were all here: Mark and Erika and Adam and Paul. Mr Sutton, too. The inner circle. One teacher and the five eldest pupils, who'd somehow become the heads of the pack, whether they wanted to or not. The younger kids were busy building barricades or dealing with shock and grief in their own way. Since Mark had worked out how to electrify the doors, the Infected had learned to stay away from them, and everything had gone quiet. The pupils were taking advantage of the respite to gather themselves a little.

"*. . .been found dead in Haringay, a district of London, in what seems to be a. . .*"

"Hold it there," said Paul. The sound of his voice roused a brief flicker of interest in Caitlyn, but he wasn't talking to her.

"*. . .other news, the Prime Minister today answered questions about his policy on immigration reform, which an opposition MP recently described as. . .*"

They listened. A suicide in London. Political point-scoring in Westminster. Knife crime rising. Stock markets falling.

It was the same barrage of stories that Caitlyn had heard all her life. She'd often wondered what the point of the news was at all. As far as she could see, its only function was to make people feel frightened and helpless.

And she'd never felt so frightened and helpless as now.

"They're not saying anything," said Mark. "It's not even on the news!"

"Maybe. . ." Mr Sutton began. "Maybe they just don't know yet."

Caitlyn felt a fresh layer of unreality settle on the room. It seemed fundamentally wrong that something so dreadful could be happening to so many people, and yet the wider world wasn't even aware of it. In this day and age, it was incredible.

"How long has it been since it started?" asked Erika. "Since it spread across the academy, I mean. Three hours? If that?"

Shut up. No one wants to listen to you. Shut up.

Caitlyn knew she was being bitter and petty, but she couldn't help it. It was hard to even be in the same room as Erika now. In the heat of the moment, things had been said and done that couldn't be taken back by either of them. But she couldn't bear to be excluded, so she sat in on the group and kept a resentful silence.

"Remember they took that boy home?" said Erika. "He was bitten by a beetle. Let's say he changed at the same time as his friend. Say he started infecting people then."

"Someone would have called the police pretty quick," said Mark. "But it'd probably take them a while to get to where he was. Depending on where he lived."

"The nurse said he got picked up by his parents," Paul told them. "So they must be nearby."

"Places round here are pretty remote," said Erika. "Maybe they have a constable or something, but I'd guess forty-five minutes for the real police to arrive."

"And longer, for anyone important to get wind of it," said Paul.

"That's assuming the Infected didn't cut them off first," said Erika. "They did it to us, remember?"

Silence fell at the chilling implications of that. Maybe the Infected animals had cut the phone lines into the nearby towns. All it would take was a bunch of rats to climb some telegraph poles, gnaw through some cables.

The rats. Caitlyn felt herself shiver as she remembered the monstrous *thing* they'd seen in the tunnels. She began rubbing at her arm where she'd been scratched. Then she saw Adam staring at her, and she stopped.

"I see two possibilities," said Mr Sutton, in his slow, considered manner. "Either nobody has managed to raise the alarm to a sufficient degree to make the national media pay attention. Or somebody has, and nobody's reporting it."

"That'd be right," said Paul. "They'd suppress the information. Can't risk a national crisis. They'd make sure the media either doesn't find out or doesn't tell anyone."

"Who's *they*?" asked Adam, with a note of scornful disbelief in his voice. "The FBI or something?"

"The FBI are American, thick-arse," Paul replied. "We've got MI5."

Adam told him where he could stick his MI5.

"Boys," said Mr Sutton warningly.

"Look, let's not get into conspiracy theories yet," said Mark. He'd been uncharacteristically assertive since he discovered that his skill with electronics made him useful. "Whether it's on the news or not, someone, somewhere is going to know about this pretty soon, right? The army, the police, *someone's* going to come. We just have to hang on till then."

"Yes, that's right," said Mr Sutton, a little too quickly and eagerly.

"You alright there?" Adam asked suddenly.

When nobody replied, Caitlyn raised her head and saw that they were looking at her. She realized she was rubbing her forearm through her sleeve again, and let her hand drop away.

"I said, are you alright?" Adam asked again. His tone was nasty. He wasn't asking after her health. He was letting her know he didn't trust her.

Anything you want to tell us, Caitlyn? Anything you're hiding?

"Half the school's turned into bloodthirsty metal psychos and the world doesn't even know it's happened," she sneered. "Yeah, I'm fine. How about you?"

She jumped down from the desk and stalked out. Erika called after her, but Erika was the last person she wanted to talk to now.

She headed for the roof. It was hard to breathe, all of a sudden. She needed fresh air.

Adam. Bloody scumbag thug.

She was angry now. It was better than being terrified. Her emotions were all over the place. How was she supposed to deal with this?

She came out on to the roof, chest tight, head light. She took a deep breath of the chilly air, which was still damp and charged in the aftermath of the storm. The clouds were breaking up now. Stars shone through the gashes, and the moon peeped out now and then.

There were lookouts up here, but she ignored them. She went to the edge of the roof, unconsciously rubbing her arm again. She couldn't get it warm.

The lights were back on across the campus, and the moist grass shone in the yellow glow. There were only a few Infected in sight. She wondered where they'd all gone. Inside the buildings? She didn't know. It didn't seem important. Nothing seemed important now.

She checked no lookouts were nearby, then pulled up her sleeve.

Her forearm was covered in silver tendrils.

She let out a shuddering sigh at the sight. It had grown since she last looked. Just a little, but it had grown.

Mark's treatment hadn't killed the silver tendrils, just delayed them. Adam was right to be suspicious of her.

She was infected.

She hadn't known terror could be this way. Usually it came in sharp jags, quickly over. But this . . . this was the terror of the inevitable. This was what it must feel like finding out that you have incurable cancer. Except that with cancer, you at least knew there would be an ending. This . . . this. . .

What's going to happen to me? Will I feel it when I change? Will I still be me, trapped in a body I don't control? Will there be something else in my head, something growing there, taking me over?

She couldn't tell anyone. What could they do? She'd seen how Adam looked at her; she couldn't bear that look from Paul. They'd either throw her out of the science block for their own safety, or try to amputate her arm without anaesthetic. Both were too awful to contemplate.

It all overwhelmed her at once then, crashing in on her so hard that she teetered. And suddenly it came to her that she was standing on the edge of a roof, and that maybe there was a solution in that. She realized what she was contemplating and stepped away, shocked at herself. Madness beat its wings all around her.

No. Not wings. *Blades*.

The lookouts were shouting and pointing. She followed their gaze. Headlamps in the sky, and a red point behind where the tail rotor was. It was coming up the valley, heading towards them, its blades thumping at the air.

A helicopter.

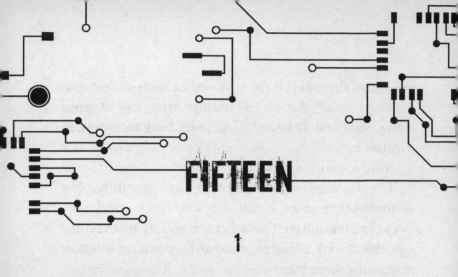

FIFTEEN

1

Something was wrong.

Paul could hear it in the sound of the engines and see it in the way the helicopter tilted and wobbled. The wind from the mountains shoved it this way and that. Judging by the direction, it must have come from the weather station on the ridge, or from the town beyond. Either way, he was amazed it had made it this far.

"Get back to your posts!" Adam roared at the kids who were cramming through the roof access door, drawn by news of the chopper. "You want those silver bastards creeping up on us while we're all staring at the sky?"

The kids in front hesitated, further jamming up the doorway. They were caught between fear of Adam and hope of rescue. But this was no rescue, Paul realized with a sinking heart. The pilot was in as much trouble as they were.

"Hey! Hey! Down here!" It was Pudge, calling to

the chopper, waving his torch about. Freckles took up the cry, and soon the whole roof was waving frantically and flashing their torches. Paul scanned the campus, checking the dorm halls and department buildings. If there were other survivors, surely they'd have been drawn out too, and they'd be making a similar racket.

He saw nothing. The school building blocked his view of the west side of the campus, but in all other directions there were no signs of life. Only the yellow stillness of the electric lights and the buzzing shrieks of the Infected.

Are we the only ones left?

The helicopter dropped suddenly, its engines rising to a high whine. A gasp went up from the roof. Their excitement faded as they saw what Paul had seen: the helicopter looked more like crashing than landing. Furthermore, it looked a lot like it was going to be crashing on *them*. Some of the pupils were reconsidering the wisdom of being up on the roof, and began to shuffle back towards the access door.

"Everybody get back! Make space!" said Mr Sutton, catching on at last. "Go downstairs, you'll do no good standing here gawking."

"Go on, get moving!" Adam bellowed, glad to act as the enforcer once more. This time the kids listened.

Paul kept his eyes on the helicopter. He could make out its shape now, lit by the moon above and the campus below. It was medium sized, with sliding side doors, the kind of craft used for mountain rescue missions or troop drops in a jungle. How many of them could a chopper like that carry? Six? Eight at most?

Six or eight, it wouldn't matter how many, if the pilot couldn't bring her down safely.

The helicopter dropped again, and slid sideways as it was pushed by the wind. A cry of alarm went up from the kids still on the roof. It was losing height too fast. It wasn't going to make it to them.

Then it veered, and Paul saw the pilot's intention. They weren't going to try to land it on the science block. Instead they were heading for the wide, smooth expanse of the sports hall roof.

The helicopter swung in the air, caught in a crosswind, its tail sweeping around. Paul held his breath as it dropped lower, the pilot wrestling with the clumsy craft. He found himself willing them down, and was surprised by how much he suddenly cared about the plight of the unseen stranger – or strangers – inside.

Come on! Come on! You can make it!

The chopper touched down with a rattling thump, and the engine cut out with a bang. Paul let out a breath. For a minute, there was only the descending whine of rotors and the *whup-whup-whup* of the slowing blades. And then there was silence.

Mark came up beside him and stared down at the wide expanse of open ground between the science block and the sports hall, where several Infected still roamed aimlessly. Then he raised his head, looked at the helicopter, and scratched the back of his neck.

"Well," he said. "That's kind of inconvenient."

"Someone's coming out," said Mr Sutton.

The light was just enough to see two people emerge from the craft. Two men, by the looks of it. One of them wore a lab coat and looked like a scientist; the other wore the helmet and fatigues of a pilot. The pilot leaned on the scientist's shoulder, and he was limping badly as he got out.

"Hey!" Adam yelled at them, hands cupped to his mouth. "Oi! You alright over there?"

They waved their hands and shouted something back, but the wind took their words and carried them away.

"I said, are you alright?" Adam roared, loud enough to dislodge a lung. But it was still no good: their replies were lost. They were too far away, and the wind was blowing in the wrong direction.

The pilot seemed to realize there was no point in shouting. He hobbled back into the helicopter. After a moment, the headlights began to flash intermittently. Three long flashes, then three short, then three more long, followed by a pause. After that, it would begin again.

"What's he doing?" Adam asked.

"It's Morse code," said Mark.

"Three long, three short, three long," said Paul. "SOS. Save our souls."

"It means 'Help'," Mark added, for Adam's benefit.

It took Adam a moment to catch up with everyone else. When he did, he threw his arms up in the air. "Save our souls?" he cried. "That's bloody great, that is. I thought *they* were supposed to rescue *us*?"

2

"Are you sure about this?" Mr Sutton asked, for the third time.

"Course I'm sure," said Paul, not sure at all. He stuffed another flash bomb in his satchel. "I said I'd do it, didn't I?"

Mr Sutton looked at him a long time with those sad, droopy eyes of his, until Paul began to feel uncomfortable under his gaze. Paul could tell the teacher didn't want to be endangering one of his pupils; it went against everything he believed. But he also knew that beneath that calm appearance, Mr Sutton was as scared as the rest of them, and he didn't want to go out there alone.

"Look, it's got to be done, hasn't it?" Paul snapped, as if Mr Sutton had tried to dissuade him. "They'll never get to us without flash bombs, not with the pilot's leg the way it is. So someone needs to go over there." He looked out of the window at the sports hall, its curves sleek in the dark. "Anyway, they might be able to help us. If they came from outside, they might know what's going on. And there could be stuff in that chopper, even if it can't fly."

Mr Sutton didn't say anything more.

Mark readied the escape ladder for them. They'd found it in a wall-mounted case with the legend "BREAK IN CASE OF EMERGENCY" printed on the glass. Adam had accepted the invitation with glee. It came in a bundle that could be attached to a window sill and unrolled into a plastic-fibre rope ladder. Paul presumed it was there so people could climb to safety in case a fire blocked their route downstairs. With all the Molotov cocktails they'd thrown about earlier, they'd come pretty close to needing it.

Caitlyn had protested when they told her about the plan, then become upset and left after Paul had volunteered. Paul didn't really understand why, but then he often didn't understand girls. Erika had gone to check on supplies. Paul found himself wishing she were here now.

Is it because of her? he asked himself. *Is she why I'm doing this?*

A detonation echoed through the night, making the window shake in its frame. A clamour followed in its wake: pots clattering, whistles blowing, shouts and taunts.

"They've started," Mark said quietly.

The Infected that were roaming the open ground

between the science block and the sports hall lifted their heads at the noise coming from the other side of the building. One by one, and then all together, they started running towards it. Another bang went off: a home-made firework, courtesy of Mark.

After a short time, the way to the sports hall was clear. To the right was the wall that bordered the campus grounds, to the left was the school building. They glimpsed other Infected running in the distance, but nothing nearby. It was as safe as it was going to get.

"Ready?" Paul asked Mr Sutton, when he didn't appear to be making a move.

Mr Sutton drew a deep breath to steady his nerves, and nodded. "Adam. You're in charge till we get back, okay?"

Adam grinned. "Right."

Paul was surprised. *Him?* He didn't think that was a good idea at all. He glanced at Mark, but Mark just looked relieved that Mr Sutton hadn't picked him.

Mr Sutton caught the look on Paul's face. "Anything you want to say, Paul?"

Adam stared at him, a challenge in those piggy eyes, as if daring him to protest.

But all Paul said was, "Good luck."

Mr Sutton tossed the escape ladder out. It unspooled from the window sill and thumped on to the grass.

Better make sure we come back alive, thought Paul.

Because they won't stand a chance with that goon in charge.

And then there was nothing left but to go for it.

3

Paul dropped off the end of the ladder and was running the moment his feet hit the lawn. His senses screamed danger. The air was loaded with threat. It was fear such as he hadn't felt since he was a child, the fear of the empty house at night, where monsters lurked in every nook. But then it had been the dark he was afraid of: now it was the light, the yellow glow from the lamp posts, exposing him. Only by going forward could he stop himself going back.

It wasn't far, really. A few hundred metres. You could sprint it in a minute at full pelt, and Paul had always been a fast runner. Mr Sutton was ahead of him, and for a guy in his thirties, he could move at a fair old clip too. They ran full out, looking in every direction, Paul's head jarring on his neck as he fought to cover every angle. No telling where one of the Infected might come from. No telling how fast it might be, what it would look like.

Panting breath, the dull impact of their shoes on the turf, iron bars swinging as their arms pumped. Behind them, the noise of the fireworks. The kids were making a hell of a racket back there. That was good. But the Infected weren't all stupid. How long before one of them worked out what was going on? Did they think like human beings any more? Or were they more like smart animals, incapable of understanding deception?

I hope that's true. I hope they've already got as smart as they're getting. Because if they get much smarter, we're all dead meat.

Dead meat, or worse. Live machinery.

Paul didn't want to think about it. Not for the first time, he asked himself why he'd volunteered for this ordeal. But the answer was always the same. He couldn't just do nothing. And he just didn't believe that anyone was going to rescue them. The world had already proved its cruelty to him by taking his parents: his faith in miracles was all out.

So make your own damn miracles.

Halfway there now, without cover, without anywhere to hide. Further to go back than to go onwards. He abandoned himself to chance, the way a soldier did when they ran on to a battlefield, not knowing if the next bullet would take them down, or their neighbour. At any moment he expected to hear an accusing screech, to see blue eyes glowing in the shadows of a nearby building.

This time, chance was kind.

He slammed up against the side of the sports hall, hugging its sheet-metal walls and the shadow they provided. Mr Sutton came staggering up a few moments later – Paul had overtaken him on the way. Both of them were momentarily exhausted; terror had driven them hard.

But they'd crossed the divide. And nothing had come for them.

Paul looked back at the science block. The distance didn't seem half as far now. The building looked small, an ugly island, its lower windows gaping, shattered boards like rotten teeth. Mark was watching from upstairs. He'd already drawn up the ladder, and was standing guard.

Mark. Mark, who'd built the weapons they used, and the radio. Mark who'd electrified the doors to keep the Infected out. Strange how quickly they'd all come to rely on him. A few hours ago they'd hardly have noticed he was there.

"You okay?" he whispered at Mr Sutton. Mr Sutton, doubled over and leaning on his knees, just about managed to give a thumbs up.

The front doors were too exposed, so they crept along the back of the hall, where they were screened from sight by the campus wall to their right. They found a fire door, which couldn't be opened from outside. Nearby, a window looked in to a small office area for the staff. Paul, not wanting to be outside a moment longer than necessary, hefted the iron bar he was carrying and smashed the glass in.

"Vandal," Mr Sutton said. Paul grinned.

They climbed inside, taking care not to cut

themselves. The lights were out in the room, and it was chilly and full of shadows, but Paul felt immediately safer now that he was out of the open.

"The sports hall would have been locked up by dinnertime, right?" he whispered.

"Right," said Mr Sutton.

"So there shouldn't have been anyone in here when it all happened. And there would be no reason for any Infected to try and get inside."

"Let's just keep an eye out anyway, hmm?"

Paul remembered the rats in the basement, the caretaker's screams, Caitlyn crying as Mark electrified her arm. A chill ran through him. Nowhere was safe. He had to remember that. One little slip, one careless moment, and it would be over.

He opened the door to the office and peered out into the corridor. Nothing moved. The building was silent, the echoing hush of a leisure centre. The main lights were off, but dim night lights cast a faint yellow glow, providing enough illumination to see by but not enough to drive away the dark.

Paul was conscious of the need to hurry. The distraction caused by the kids in the science block wouldn't last for ever. They followed the corridor towards the stairs, listening out for movement.

They hadn't gone far when they came up against a pair of doors, barring progress along the corridor. When Paul tried them, they were locked. They looked too thick to break through.

"We can cut through the swimming pool," Mr Sutton suggested.

Paul nodded. His nerves were taut. He knew there was no reason why any Infected would be in here, but it didn't stop him thinking they were going to jump out of every doorway. The silence pushed in on him.

"Sir? Why'd you put Adam in charge?" he said, as they backtracked and went up a new corridor. He needed to talk, to break the quiet a little.

"Who would you have picked?" Mr Sutton asked.

Paul thought about it. Who was there? People might listen to Mark, but they wouldn't take orders from him, and he didn't want to be a leader anyway. Erika? Well, she had a smart head on her shoulders, but he was yet to be convinced that she was any good in a crisis. Caitlyn was a mess at the moment. All the rest were too young.

"I suppose you're right," he said. "But Adam . . . I mean, people will do what he says 'cause they're afraid of him, but he's not all that bright, is he?"

"He's been very brave, though."

"Dunno if bravery and being too dumb to realize you're in danger is quite the same thing, sir."

"Now come on, Paul. I expect a bit more from you than that."

Paul felt vaguely ashamed. He thought about how Adam had gone out in the rain to round up everyone into the science block, how he bullied the kids into staying at their posts and fighting the Infected, how he'd covered their retreat upstairs. And he remembered how Adam had stood with him on the stairway when he was waiting for Erika.

"Yeah," he said eventually. "He's done alright, hasn't he?"

They reached a pair of solid doors that led to the swim hall. Paul could smell the chlorine from the pool beyond. He pushed them open a crack and peered through.

The hall was full of whispers and the echo of lapping water. Underwater lights cast blurred ripples on the ceiling. He could see no sign that it was occupied, so he went in. Mr Sutton followed.

It was a large hall for competitive swimming, with tiered benches along one side and lanes marked out in the pool. They walked along the edge of the pool towards the other side.

"You know who I would have left in charge?" said Mr Sutton. "You."

Paul frowned.

"When the Infected attacked us, you were the one who got everybody organized," the teacher continued. "You didn't try to do it all on your own. You got everyone working together." He paused. "That's what a leader does."

Paul was beginning to feel uncomfortable at the way the conversation was going. He didn't see himself as any kind of leader. He'd just been frustrated with Mr Sutton's indecisiveness.

"We all have to trust each other now," said Mr Sutton, quietly enough that it seemed he was talking to himself. "Rely on each other. Even Adam. We're going to need one another to survive."

The words settled like a weight on Paul. He knew the teacher was right, and yet the thought of it scared him. He'd relied on people before. He'd put his faith in his parents, trusting them to come back each time they went away. How could he do that again?

A loud scraping noise rang through the swimming hall, a screech of metal, like a bucket being dragged briefly along the floor.

Paul's blood froze. They looked over in the direction it had come from. On the other side of the pool, there was a corridor that led to the changing rooms.

"Nobody has the keys to this place, right?" he said quietly. "Nobody that might have, I don't know, hid in here after dinner?"

"No pupils, but ... well, there are the PE teachers. . . I suppose Mrs Fowler might have. . ."

Paul swore under his breath. "Come on," he said, and they hurried to the door at the far end of the hall. As they slipped through, Paul looked back. In the dim yellow glow of the night lights, he caught a glimpse of something. Something that was crawling slowly up the corridor from the changing rooms towards the pool.

He shut the door. He didn't want to see any more.

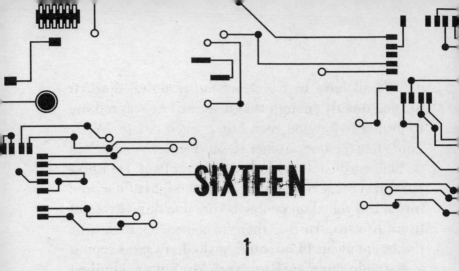

SIXTEEN

1

The roof of the sports hall was reached by a ladder and a hatch, and they got there without seeing another sign of the Infected. Once, Paul would have thanked whoever might be listening for that good fortune. These days, given the evidence, he suspected that nobody was listening at all.

He pushed open the hatch and popped his head through. The first thing he saw was a shadowy figure that was about to bring a wrench down on his skull.

"Whoa! Whoa! Wait!" he cried, holding his arm up to fend off the blow.

The pilot lowered the wrench a little, but he was still half-cocked for a swing. With his helmet off, Paul could see a long, deeply lined face with a short grizzly beard.

"You been bitten? Scratched? Any of those things touched you?" he demanded in a gravelly voice.

"No!" Paul said irritably, as anger overtook fright. "Now put that bloody thing down, unless you want us to leave you here." After the risk they'd taken to run over from the science block, he'd expected a friendlier reception.

"Put it down, Carson," said a quiet voice. Paul turned his head and saw the scientist standing nearby. He was a black silhouette with yellow rectangles for eyes: his glasses, reflecting the light from the campus.

The pilot grunted and backed away, keeping a wary distance as Paul and Mr Sutton climbed through and on to the roof.

"I hope you'll pardon our rather nervous welcome," said the scientist. He stepped closer, though not too close. He was a small man with greying hair at the sides of his head and none on top, and he wore a lab coat. "My name's Radley. We've had a somewhat harrowing day."

"I should think we all have," said Mr Sutton.

Paul looked past Carson at the helicopter. Carson caught his thought. "That ain't going anywhere right now," he said.

Paul's faint hope dwindled. "What about a radio? You got something we can call for help on?"

Carson and Radley exchanged a glance. Paul spotted it, and wondered at its meaning.

"Radio's out," said Carson.

"We should get moving," said Mr Sutton. "The pupils have set up a distraction, but the Infected won't stay distracted for ever."

"You want us to come back with you?" Radley asked in surprise.

"You'd rather stay here?" Paul said. "There, we've got weapons. If they come for you here, you don't have a chance. And there's at least one of them in the building somewhere."

He saw how that news concerned them. They thought for a moment. "Carson can't run," the scientist said.

"Turned my ankle," Carson grunted. "Hurts like a sonofabitch."

"Well, then he'll hobble," said Paul. "But we're not sticking around. So if you want to come with us, grab anything useful from the chopper and get moving!"

2

Caitlyn stood at a window in a deserted classroom, looking out through the gaps between hastily nailed-up planks of wood. She'd left the lights off to suit her mood. The crashing of metal objects echoed through the corridors of the science block, the defiant yells of twelve- and thirteen-year-olds, the occasional blast of a dangerously potent firework. From the far side of the building, the hungry wails and howls of the Infected drifted up into the air, where they were dashed away by the wind.

Madness. Madness all around her. Madness inside her, too. The world had taken on the surreal tint of a nightmare. Only a few hours ago, everything had been so ... so *normal*. And so had she. A normal girl living in her normal world: Caitlyn the Unexceptional.

How quickly things had changed.

All that wasted time. God, the days, the months, the *years* she'd let slip by. Ingratiating herself with the strong and the popular, manoeuvring herself to make sure she was on the winning side. Worrying about what people thought instead of worrying about herself.

No wonder she was always second best. How could you grow when you planted yourself in someone else's shadow? She wanted Paul to see her for who she was, but she didn't even show it to her best friends.

I just wanted to be somebody, she thought. *I wanted to be me*.

But she'd spent her days on games, stupid games, and none of it mattered any more. Not now.

She clutched her arm. It felt heavy and cold. She'd found a pair of black rubber gloves in a lab and put them on, because the creeping silver tendrils had made their way past her wrist now. It was a pitiful attempt to disguise what was happening to her, but she had no better ideas. She hadn't dared look beneath her sleeve since the helicopter landed. If she didn't look, it wouldn't get worse.

But it *was* worse. She could tell. This was what it felt like when you changed. This chill, sparkling feeling, followed by the numbness, like when you leaned on an arm too long and it went dead. It had happened rapidly to the other kids, sweeping through them in one swift conquest, taking them over in minutes. For Caitlyn, there was no such mercy. It seeped into her like rot, and turned her inch by inch.

And when it reached her brain, what then? Would that, too, go cold and numb? Or would something even more terrible happen?

She stared through the gaps between the planks. Out there, on the roof of the sports hall, she could see Paul and Mr Sutton and the strangers. They were climbing down through the hatch into the building. In a few minutes, if all was well, they'd come running back towards the science block.

He had to make it back. He had to. Because she had to tell him something. She had to tell him how she felt. And it didn't matter that he didn't love her back. It didn't matter that it was all too late. What mattered was that she said those words. Because she refused to pretend any more. And she wanted him to know her, before the end. She wasn't going to waste another second.

God, how could she think so calmly? Why wasn't she wild, flailing about crazily and raging at her fate?

Because it wouldn't do any good. She was infected. It was over.

She heard the door to the classroom open behind

her. She didn't turn. She knew who it would be. He'd come for her.

"Alright, Caitlyn?" said Adam.

She felt a wave of disgust at the sound of his voice. "Get lost," she told him.

He ignored her and wandered into the room. She heard the door close behind him, and turned away from the window. He stood there in the darkness. Slats of yellow light from outside lined his face and broad body. He was holding the radiator pipe in one hand.

She was afraid of him, always had been. Afraid of his stupid, unthinking, brutal nature, afraid of the way he might lurch into violence at any moment. And she hated him, like she hated Erika. How was it fair that they'd escaped the fate she was condemned to?

"You cold or something?" Adam asked.

"Huh?"

"The gloves. What you wearing gloves for?" he said, in a tone that suggested he knew *exactly* what she was wearing gloves for. Why did he bother with those sly intimidations? They both knew what he was going to do next.

"What do you want?" she asked him anyway.

"I want to take a peek at that cut you've got. See if it's healing up okay."

"It's fine," she spat. "Thanks for your concern."

"Think I'll take a look anyway," he said, stepping closer.

She darted to one side, but he was quicker. He grabbed her by the shoulder, shoved her hard up against the wall. The impact was enough to bring tears to her eyes. He pinned her there with the iron bar pressed across her breastbone, and yanked back her sleeve hard enough to rip her cardigan.

Silver. Her whole arm was covered in a mesh of silver.

He shoved himself away from her, fear and anger in his own eyes now. He kept the radiator pipe pointed at her, keeping her at a distance, staring at her accusingly. She sobbed, shocked by his attack, dazzled by the pain.

"Don't," she said, and was ashamed of herself for begging him. "Don't tell them."

"*Infected!*" Adam yelled over his shoulder. "We've got Infected in here!" And he raised his pipe as if to hit her.

Caitlyn cringed away and slipped to the floor, cowering there. She was crying in earnest now.

"*Infected!*" Adam shouted, this time right at her, and she thought he *was* going to hit her then, to bring that pipe down on her skull, and part of her hoped he'd do it. There were running footsteps coming along the corridor, and two more boys ran in, with iron bars and Molotov cocktails in their hands. They stared at her there, amazed by what they saw, not knowing what to do. Then their eyes were drawn by the silver glint on her arm, and they understood, and their expressions changed. She knew what they were thinking then, and the horror of it made her cry all the harder.

Monster. Outcast.

Infected.

3

Paul pushed open the door of the swim hall, and looked through.

Nothing moved, and everything moved. The restless play of light on the ceiling from the pool lamps made the whole hall alive. The drip and lap of water rang in the empty space.

Paul waited. He searched out every hiding place he could see. The shadows under the benches. Behind the lifeguard chair. The corridors to the changing rooms, where he'd last seen the *thing* that might once have been Mrs Fowler. No matter how hard he looked, he couldn't be sure.

"I think it's gone," he whispered.

He pushed the door open, and they hurried into the room, Carson with his arm round Radley's shoulder, hopping as fast as he could go. Paul took the lead, iron bar held ready, head turning this way and that to seek out danger. The shifting patterns of light from the water confused his vision.

Don't be here. Don't be here.

They passed along the side of the pool, following

its length to the far end of the hall, trying not to make a noise. And miraculous though it seemed, nothing emerged to threaten them. They reached the far door, opened it, and found the corridor on the other side equally deserted.

It was only as Paul was closing the door behind him that he thought he heard a splash from the pool. But when he looked back into the hall, he couldn't see what had made it.

They retraced their steps to the office where Paul and Mr Sutton had broken in. At the back of the sports hall there was only a narrow corridor of lawn with the campus wall on one side and the hall on the other. It was sheltered from sight, and out of the way. Paul checked the coast was clear outside, and they helped Carson through the window.

They could still hear the distant hue and cry from the science block as they crept up to the corner of the sports hall and faced the expanse of open ground that lay between them and safety. It would be a lot longer on the way back, now they had to slow to Carson's speed.

He checked the way ahead. There were a few Infected running past the staff garage, over by the driveway. He thought he saw something moving near the fountain further down the drive, but that was some distance away. Considering how many pupils had been on campus, and how many had presumably turned, there weren't very many Infected around.

So where were they? And what were they doing?

Well, for now, he wasn't going to look a gift horse in the mouth. He waved at Mark, who was standing vigilantly at the window with the rolled-up fire ladder. Mark spotted him and beckoned frantically.

Paul looked back at the others. "Let's do it," he said.

And they were off. Except this time there was no frantic sprint, no shoes pounding the turf and lungs bursting as their legs ate up the distance. Carson travelled in jolting hops, his arm across Radley's shoulders like a man in a three-legged race. Mr Sutton went ahead of them, and Paul brought up the rear, but they couldn't move much faster than a jog without leaving the pilot behind.

On the way over, time had stretched to impossible lengths, turning a minute into ten. On the way back, it was worse. Paul had to resist the urge to bolt for safety. He didn't even know why he stopped himself. What did he owe Carson, after all? The man was all but useless if the helicopter didn't work.

And yet he wouldn't let himself abandon the pilot. Not the scientist, either. It didn't matter how useful or useless they were, it was because they were in it together. All of them: the teachers, the pupils, and these newcomers. And whether he liked them or not, it didn't matter. He might not have chosen them as companions, but there they were.

Mr Sutton was right. They needed each other to survive. And Carson needed them right now.

He saw a group of Infected nearby, running in the other direction. They didn't look over, didn't see. There was a flash of movement in a lower window of the science block, something passing across the shattered hole left by the broken planks. Whatever it was, it didn't spot them. By then they were halfway, and Paul was beginning to wonder how much longer their luck could possibly hold.

The answer came a few seconds later, with a blood-curdling screech.

An Infected came racing towards them from around the west side of the sports hall, where a path ran between that building and the main body of the school. Though it had once been small, its limbs and fingers were long and thin, giving it the look of some hideous goblin. There was little that was human in its face any more: its nose had virtually disappeared; its mouth had widened and filled with fangs. Its hair had turned to filaments, hanging limply round its head. It moved with the flexibility of an animal, but there was no flesh visible now: tongue and tendons, joints and eyes, all were silver.

"Move it!" Paul screamed at Carson, as he dug in his satchel for a flash bomb.

But they were already going as fast as they could. And right at that moment, another Infected appeared, coming from round the side of the science block. Rushing to cut them off.

Paul clicked the gas lighter, trying to make a flame,

but it wouldn't work when he was running so he was forced to halt. He clicked again, but it stubbornly refused to catch until the third time. By then he was panicking, and when he raised his head the Infected was closer than he'd imagined. He lobbed the flash bomb out on to the lawn and ran at full speed to catch up with the others.

A few moments later, the bomb went off with a bang, stunning the scene with a flicker of artificial lightning. Both of the Infected froze; the one ahead of them tumbled to the ground, tripped by its own momentum.

"Keep going!" he yelled at Radley and Carson, who'd slowed at the sight of the Infected in their path. He shoved them onwards, past Mr Sutton, who was struggling to light a Molotov cocktail. Paul looked back at the frozen creature that had been chasing after him –

– and the creature burst into motion again, flailing at the air, screeching, as if it had never paused.

No, no, that's too fast, it wore off too fast!

The flash bombs weren't working so well now. The Infected were adapting.

Paul swung the iron bar in his hand, and caught the creature hard on the side of the neck with a loud ring of metal on metal. It went rolling to the ground, long limbs tangling like a killed spider. But it wasn't dead: only stunned. He'd bought them a few seconds at best.

A *whump* of flame and a wave of hot air brought his attention to the other Infected, but that one was out of the game now. Mr Sutton had thrown his Molotov cocktail and burned it where it lay. It tried to get to its feet, but the fire consumed it, and its efforts didn't last for long.

Mark let down the ladder; it unrolled and thumped to the ground. Carson and Radley were almost there now. Three more Infected came rushing in a group from the direction of the lake. It seemed they all knew now, whether by the cry or some other, more insidious form of mental communication. They were flocking.

The Infected that Paul had hit was trying to get up. Paul smashed it over the head again. He couldn't kill it, but he could buy them the seconds they needed.

Radley pushed off Carson and climbed up the ladder ahead of him. The pilot clambered after, more slowly. Mr Sutton yelled at Paul to get moving. Paul obeyed, having delayed as long as he dared. A glance at the oncoming Infected told him that they were too far away to intercept them before they got to the ladder.

We're going to make it!

But then he saw movement in the shadow of the school building. Something huge. A hunched shape that slunk into the light

The dog. Except much, much bigger.

"Oh, hell," he muttered, and ran.

It broke into a lope and then a sprint, rushing across the lawn towards them. When Paul had last seen it, it had been unusually big, but not freakish. Now it was more like the prehistoric mammals he'd seen depicted as models in the glass cases of a museum. It must have been nine feet long and five feet at the shoulder, a monster of armour and sinew with jaws like industrial machinery. It had warped and swollen into a thing of primal savagery, future and past all crushed together, raw instinct cased in cold metal.

Mr Sutton had seen it too, and backed away towards the ladder. Radley was already at the top, clambering over the sill. Carson was struggling up behind. Paul had time for a flash of anger at the scientist, who'd left his companion stranded while he saved his own skin. Then he saw the horde of Infected come pouring round the side of the science block building.

The distraction had finally failed. The Infected were alerted. They were coming.

There was a blinding flash, and the horde stopped, some of them clattering into each other and tipping to the ground. It was a flash bomb, thrown by Mark from the window. Paul hadn't even seen it coming, and it dazzled him too. He kept running anyway, blinking the glare from his eyes. Mr Sutton was shouting at him. "Go on, Paul! Go on!"

But what about you? Paul thought. It wasn't enough

to slow him. He was too frightened, too scared of the beast bearing down on them and the horde closing in. There was no way to fight them now. His bravado had disappeared. And there was Mr Sutton urging him on to the ladder and not even a second to waste on argument. So he launched himself at the ladder and scrambled up it as fast as his legs and hands would take him, following the pilot, who was being pulled inside by Mark.

Then the horde were in motion again. They vaulted over the fallen and raced towards Mr Sutton. Mr Sutton grabbed on to the bottom of the ladder and began yanking himself up, and as Paul got one knee up on the sill he looked back and saw that the horde was still too far away, that Mark's flash bomb had bought Mr Sutton the seconds he needed to get to safety. And Mr Sutton knew it too. As he looked up and met Paul's gaze, those sad eyes were full of hope.

Then there was a blur of silver beneath him, and a tearing sound. The ladder was wrenched sideways, and Paul almost fell, but Carson grabbed his arms and hauled him inside with one huge tug.

Paul collapsed on the floor on the other side of the sill, his breath shuddering. Mark was staring out of the window, his eyes wide. Paul waited, and waited . . . but Mr Sutton didn't come.

"The dog?" he asked quietly.

Nobody replied. Paul felt a numbness spread through his body, killing all feeling. It had happened again. Just like his parents, it happened again. One minute here, the next . . . gone.

"Pull up the ladder," he said.

"There's not much ladder left," said Carson, who was also looking out.

Mark began to say something, but then he started crying instead. Radley stood nearby, mopping his brow with his sleeve, looking awkward.

Paul got to his feet. He could hear the baying of the Infected outside. Mr Sutton was gone. That was all there was to it. They'd lost him.

He looked from the pilot to the scientist and back again. "You two had better be worth it," he said, and he walked out of the room.

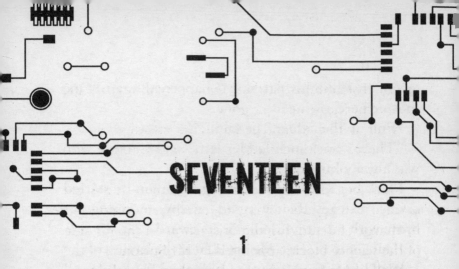

SEVENTEEN

1

Paul only made it a short way down the corridor before his legs went weak, and he had to lean against the wall to prevent himself from sliding to the ground.

Mr Sutton. He's gone. Just like that. Damn it, what do we do now?

He barely had a moment to recover before he heard footsteps, and saw a Year Ten coming purposefully towards him. He recognized him by his emo fringe: a kid Mr Sutton had called Johnny. Paul stood away from the wall and steadied himself.

"Did you get 'em? The men from the chopper? Who are they?" Johnny asked.

"We're gonna find out," he heard himself say. That calm voice couldn't possibly have been his.

"Where's Mr S?" asked Johnny, looking past him.

The lights overhead dimmed and flickered. They both looked up. Were the generators running out already? Was it just a stutter in the supply? Or had the Infected gone after the generators the way they'd gone after the power lines?

After a few seconds, the lights steadied again. Their eyes met, and each knew what the other did. Time was running out.

Paul looked over the kid in front of him. He seemed like he was holding together well. He'd been in charge of arranging the distraction on the far side of the science block, appointed by Mr Sutton.

Well, if Mr Sutton trusted him, then Paul did too.

"Listen, here's what I want you to do. You did a great job causing a distraction, but now we need everyone back at their posts. Lookouts on the roof, people on the windows, and somebody watching the doors to the stairs in case the Infected try another push. Somebody responsible, who can give 'em a jolt of electricity if necessary. Think you can organize all that?"

Johnny regarded him from behind the black shield of his hair. "Sure," he said. "I'm on it."

"Soon as there's news, I'll let everyone know," said Paul.

"Right," said Johnny, and turned to go.

Paul closed his eyes in relief. If Johnny had noticed that Paul had avoided answering his question about Mr Sutton, he didn't show it. And that was good. Right now he needed everyone busy, everyone involved with a task. That way, they might not notice Mr Sutton wasn't around. He'd have to tell them the teacher was dead eventually, but he wanted to put it off for as long as he could. Hope was all they had at the moment.

Johnny stopped in the corridor, as if struck by a thought. He looked back over his shoulder. "Hey," he said. "You might not have heard. You know that girl who got scratched? Caitlyn something?"

Paul felt his stomach sink. "What about her?"

2

Adam had locked her up in the staff room.

Paul hurried down the corridors, face flushed, skin hot. The world seemed to be closing in on him, pressing on his chest so it was hard to breathe, reducing his vision to a narrow tunnel. He didn't know if he was furious or grief-stricken or both. He'd barely had time to register his own brush with death, and the loss of Mr Sutton. Now there was this. The shocked numbness he felt a few moments ago had been swept aside by the news that Caitlyn was still infected.

His fault. His responsibility.

And Adam! Damn it, Adam! Adam had suspected, the way he suspected everyone. He'd waited till Paul was out of the way, and then he'd gone to get her.

How had he done it? Paul would lay bets he hadn't been gentle. Did he threaten her, drag her away down the corridor? Did he tie her hands? He thought of

Caitlyn, scared and crying, and he wanted to drive his fist into Adam's stupid ignorant face and beat him until . . . until. . .

Fury swamped him then, making him light-headed. He slammed himself up against the side of the corridor, drew his hand back into a fist, ready to smash his knuckles into the cold stone. He wanted to hit something, anything, *everything*. A cry of inarticulate rage forced its way out past gritted teeth.

I killed her. I led her down into that basement. I didn't make her follow, but some part of me knew she would. I led her down, and she got infected, and all because I wouldn't wait for the others. Because I wanted to do it all myself.

Something moved; a scuff of shoe on stone, a gasp of breath. He turned his head and saw a Year Seven, an eleven-year-old boy in an outsize cagoule, standing transfixed and terrified in the doorway of a nearby classroom. It took Paul a moment to realize what he was frightened of.

Me. He's frightened of me.

The rage drained out of him. He took in a long, shaky breath and let it out. Then he unclenched his fist and stood away from the wall.

The kid was still staring at him, wide-eyed. Paul opened his mouth to say something, to reassure him that he hadn't gone psycho. But the boy turned tail and ran, the frantic clatter of his shoes echoing away up the corridor.

Paul stood there, amazed by the kid's reaction. Frightened of *him*? Ridiculous. What, did that kid really think Paul was going to get violent? That was the kind of thing that Adam would do. And he wasn't like Adam. He wasn't *anything* like Adam.

Are you sure?

Paul caught himself. He remembered fighting with Adam down at the lake, and later when they were trying to treat Caitlyn's infection. Both had been fights he himself started. He recalled his surly attitude with Mr Sutton, when Mr Sutton had asked whether he'd told anyone about his parents. He'd ignored Mr Harrison's instructions to stay in his dorm, and because of that, Mr Harrison followed him out into the rain and got clawed by the same dog that later took Mr Sutton. He'd gone blundering down into the tunnels without thinking, and Caitlyn had paid the price for that.

All of those sounded like just the kind of things Adam would do.

He'd always thought of himself as better than Adam, smarter, more capable. But his efforts to do everything on his own had just got people hurt. Adam might have had a clumsy way of doing things, but he'd done a lot less harm than Paul since the Infected first appeared. He might be a loudmouth bully, but he'd been out there working tirelessly to defend everybody this whole time, and he was certainly strong and brave.

Adam hadn't changed. The world had changed. That morning he was a good-for-nothing thug; by evening he was something else. He didn't fit into the old world, but he fit the new one. Perhaps better than Paul did.

You know what? You're no better than him. And Mr Sutton was right: he's all you've got left. Him and Mark and Erika. You might not like it, but there it is. And we all need each other now.

Another confrontation with Adam was the last thing he wanted right now, but it needed to be done. He took a few deep, steady breaths. Then he pushed his hair back from his face, crushed all the grief and anger way down inside him, and composed himself.

Time to do this. And this time, I'm gonna do it right.

3

Adam was waiting for him.

He stood guard before the staff room door, radiator pipe clutched in one meaty hand. Paul could see he was geared up for a fight. His small eyes narrowed and his shoulders tensed the moment he caught sight of Paul approaching.

Of course he expects a fight. That's all anybody ever gives him. The ones who aren't afraid of him, anyway.

"Stay back. You ain't letting her out," said Adam, pointing the pipe at him.

Paul held up his hands. "I just want to talk to her."

"Don't think so," Adam smirked. He held up a ring of keys. "Door stays locked."

Paul felt anger rise in him again, boiling up like acid in his stomach. Didn't Adam realize that his aggressive manner made *others* aggressive in response? He fought to hold it down.

"Listen," he said. "I don't want to let her out. I just want to say sorry to her, or ... I don't know, *something*." He squeezed his eyes shut. It was almost physically painful to say the words he needed to, but he forced them out anyway. "Came to apologize to you too. I've been acting like a ... well, you know. We've not exactly seen eye to eye, have we?"

Adam didn't say anything to that. He just watched him, suspecting a trick.

"You did the right thing," Paul said, motioning towards the staff room door. *Even if you did it in the wrong way, even if you probably scared the hell out of her.* "None of us saw what was happening. Me ... I just wanted to believe she was okay. We all wanted that. So we didn't check on her, we just figured. . ." He shrugged. "But she's infected. You spotted it. Who knows what would have happened if you hadn't?"

Adam seemed confused. He wasn't used to people being reasonable with him, or paying him compliments. "It's too dangerous having her out with the others," he said. "I mean, what if she turned suddenly? Can't keep an eye on her every second. What if she scratched someone, like by accident or something?"

"Right," said Paul. "Exactly."

"It's like in the movies, you know?" said Adam. "Someone gets infected, like a zombie or whatever, and everyone knows they're gonna change, but they have to wait until just the moment they turn before they . . . you know . . . kill 'em."

"Which we're *not* gonna do to Caitlyn," Paul said, chilled.

"Not as long as she stays in there," Adam said offhandedly. "Anyway, you know how it is. They leave it till the last moment, then suddenly the infected one turns zombie and bites someone else, and then you've got two dead people instead of one."

"This isn't like the movies. . ." Paul said, but it was too quiet and Adam didn't hear him.

"Problem in them films is that everyone's too nice. Times like this . . . this is when being nice is being stupid."

Paul felt like he ought to disagree, but when he tried, he found that he couldn't. "Reckon that's true," he said. "This is life or death. *Nice* doesn't come into it."

Adam gave him a grudging nod. All the hostility had gone out of him. *Is this all it took, all along?* Paul thought. *He just wanted someone to treat him like he wasn't an idiot?*

There was an awkward moment when neither knew exactly how to proceed. Then Adam waved at him vaguely and said, "You get the people off the chopper?"

"Yeah."

"What about Sutton?"

Paul's expression told him everything he needed to know. Adam tutted.

"Liked him," Adam said regretfully. He scratched the back of his neck and sized up Paul. "He left you in charge, right?"

Paul thought for a moment. Technically Mr Sutton never actually said that, but Paul had the sense that the role was being offered to him. That Adam had decided not to oppose it. Maybe he just liked to be the enforcer more than he liked to be in charge. Or maybe he just didn't feel the need to fight Paul on everything any more.

"Yeah," Paul said. It was a small lie, but it was simpler that way. "You okay with that?"

Adam shrugged. "You act like an arsehole, I'll bloody deck you."

"I'll do what I can. No promises, though."

Adam thumbed at the door. "You want to talk to her?"

"I should."

"I can go in with you if you want. Make sure she doesn't try anything."

Paul shook his head. "I'll talk through the door."

"I'll get out your way, then," said Adam. "You want the keys in case?"

"Keep 'em," he said. "I might be tempted to let her

out otherwise."

Adam nodded and pocketed them. "Sometimes being nice is being stupid," he said again.

"Why don't you go find Mark and the people we brought over from the chopper? See what they're up to. I'll be with you in a few minutes. Then we can find out if that pair were worth saving."

"Gotcha," said Adam. He gave Paul a comradely slap on the arm on his way by, then went walking off up the corridor, swinging the length of radiator pipe loosely in his hand. Paul watched him go.

Bloody hell, thought Paul. *I think I just made a friend.*

Then he turned back to the staff room door, and whatever was behind it.

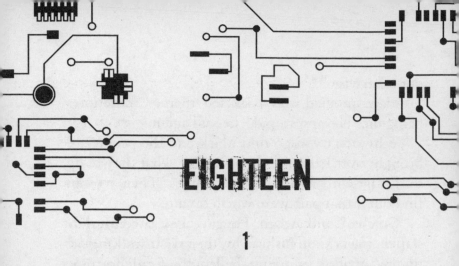

EIGHTEEN

1

"...*don't know what to do. He says he loves me, but he...*"

"*...stock markets had rallied by end of closing...*"

"*...rid of persistent animal smells with Carpet-Rite!...*"

Mark moved the pencil another millimetre along the razor blade, tuning his improvised radio. He found a late-night chat show.

"It's like it isn't happening," he said, his voice heavy with despair.

"Oh, it's happening," Erika said. She wiped her reddened eyes and stared angrily across the lab, where the scientist and the pilot sat murmuring to each other. "And *they* know all about it."

The scientist looked up at her momentarily, then resumed his conversation.

Erika brushed her hair back behind her ear, sniffed, and straightened. It annoyed her that she was crying; it made her anger less effective. Mr Sutton had died for these two. Kind Mr Sutton, replaced by two strangers who muttered between themselves, plotting. They were adults, used to being in charge. They didn't answer to kids.

She could tell they knew about the Infected. By their secrecy, she could tell. And that meant they were part of what was happening to Caitlyn.

New tears threatened at the thought. Even after the cruel things Caitlyn had said to her, Erika couldn't throw away their friendship. *She* had thought they were friends, even if Caitlyn hadn't. And anyway, it was just something she'd said when she was upset. Just words, pitched to hurt. She didn't mean them.

Probably.

Erika had gone to see Caitlyn after she found out what had happened. But when Caitlyn had heard her arguing with Adam outside the staff room door, she shrieked at Erika to go away.

It wasn't what she said that made Erika leave. It was the sound of her voice. The thin, buzzing sound, like an overloaded microphone, barely detectable beneath the words. The machine voice of the Infected.

Erika had left then, overcome with horror. She dared not imagine what Caitlyn was going through behind that door, what transformations were occurring, but her mind kept returning to it like a tongue probing at a painful tooth.

Caitlyn. Oh, Caitlyn.

Erika was disgusted at herself. Where was her strength now? Where was the fortitude she'd promised? She'd tried to prove herself, to make herself useful, but what good had she done? Mark had given them weapons and inventions. Paul had saved them all when the Infected attacked the science block. Even Adam, standing silently in the corner, had shown more value than her.

She'd told herself that she was more than just a pretty face and a set of grades. But she hadn't done a thing to justify it yet.

The door opened and Paul came in. He closed the door behind him and leaned against it, head hung. He looked older than his years; she saw the weariness in him.

"How is she?" Erika asked.

"She wouldn't speak to me," Paul said quietly. "She just cried."

Erika felt her throat tighten up again. She forced down the tears. *No more crying*.

Paul raised his head and surveyed the room. "Only we six know that Mr Sutton is dead. I'd like to keep it that way."

Mark looked down hard at the radio, and nodded. Mr Sutton's death had shaken him. Of all of them, he was the one who knew the teacher best.

Paul walked over to them. Adam fell into step with him. Mark sat dejectedly fiddling with the radio. Erika was perched on the edge of the desk.

Consciously or unconciously, she notice how they gathered together. The four pupils on one side of the lab. The adults on the other. Wariness and distrust between them.

Us against them, she thought. *Just like always.*

"I think it's time you told us what you were doing flying a helicopter down the valley in the middle of the night," Paul told them.

Carson looked expectantly at Radley. Radley adjusted his glasses and coughed. After a moment, Carson gave the scientist a little shove. "If you ain't gonna tell them, I will," he said.

Radley threw up his hands in despair. "We came from the weather station!" he said.

"It ain't no weather station," Carson snarled. Radley glared at him. "What?" said Carson. "You think the Official Secrets Act is gonna help us now?"

"I knew it," Erika said. "You're part of this, aren't you?"

"Whatever you've got, you need to tell us," said Paul firmly. "We're all in this together now. If we want to have any hope of getting out of here—"

"There *is* no hope!" Radley cried. He was up on his feet now, huffing and puffing round the lab. "It's *everywhere*!"

His words fell into silence.

"*What's* everywhere?" said Paul.

2

"Carson and I, we work for a company called Loriston Biotech," Radley told them. "You won't have heard of us. We're one of several companies contracted by the Ministry of Defence to research certain technologies that the public are better off not knowing about. Public companies have to answer to ethics committees and all that palaver. A company like Loriston Biotech doesn't answer to anyone."

"And what were you making?" Paul prompted.

"Weapons," said Radley. "Biological weapons."

That hung in the air between them for a time.

"Have any of you ever heard of nanomachines?" Radley asked.

"I have," said Mark, but he seemed too dejected to elaborate.

"In layman's terms, nanomachines are minuscule robots, smaller than you can see. But as small as they are, they can be programmed to do miraculous things. They can seek out a cancer in the body and destroy it. They can detect wounds and heal them at an incredible rate. Some of us dreamed of a day when you could inject a patient with a serum full of nanomachines and they would repair internal injuries without the need for surgery, or rebuild an eye, or fix a damaged brain. That's what they were *meant* to be used for.

"But the Ministry of Defence wanted a weapon,

and Loriston Biotech wanted to give them one. It was meant to be a plague, a *nanoplague*, something we could drop on an enemy city and watch as the population turned against itself. We crossed the rabies virus with the nanomachines, made it more robust, more targeted. Instead of days, it took just minutes to turn a man into a maniac. And after twelve hours, once they'd bitten or killed everyone nearby, the infected would just drop dead. That was the idea."

"The Infected," said Adam." That's what we call 'em, too."

Erika was glaring at Radley, her eyes full of scorn. "Jesus," she breathed. "You people."

Radley ignored her. "The nanos were designed to be able to communicate with each other, so as to coordinate the invasion of a body. An individual nanomachine is about as smart as a rock. A few million of them, all networked and acting together, they're smart enough to make decisions. A few billion, they're maybe as clever as a housefly. A few *trillion...*"

Mark looked up from his radio. "You crossed them with a virus and they replicated like a virus."

Radley adjusted his glasses. Carson was looking down at the floor, past his newly splinted ankle, face scrunched up, shaking his head in disgust. The pilot was no friend to the scientist either, it seemed.

"We didn't know what we had at first," said Radley. "You see, the nanos aren't capable of building a networked intelligence from scratch; it's just too complex. They need a framework, which they then take over gradually. A brain. It wasn't till we injected it into rabbits that we realized what the nanos could do."At first they simply fought each other, like we wanted. Killing or infecting the others. But the survivors didn't die like they were supposed to. The nanos kept them alive instead. So we waited and watched to see what would happen. And the nanos began to *evolve*."

The eager glimmer in his eye made Erika angry again. "And you didn't think to stop it then?"

"We thought we were safe!" he snapped. "We'd built in a failsafe, a weak spot. We made them light-sensitive. Sudden bright light made the nanos overload, shut down the network, paralysed them completely. We had strobe lights set up to take them out if it got out of hand."

"Strobes? Flickering light?" asked Mark. "We've been using flash bombs, camera flashes. . ."

"The lightning messes them up too," said Paul. "But it only works for a few seconds."

"Yes, yes, they worked their way around it," said Radley, waving a hand at the air. "They work their way around *everything*, that's the point! Give them enough time, they'll remedy any weakness, overcome any obstacle."

Adam snorted. "Well, aren't you scientists a clever lot?"

Erika had caught the tone in Radley's voice. That

glimmer was back in his eye. "You *admire* them, don't you?" she said. "They're killing people, they're killing *everyone* . . . and you admire them."

The scientist rounded on her, about to deliver a dismissive reply. He'd had just about enough of the insolence of this bunch of fifteen-year-olds: she saw it on his face. But then he saw the hostile expressions of the people in the room, and shut his mouth. They might have been younger than him, but he was alone here. Not even Carson was on his side.

"Well," he said. "I see how it is. Shall I go on, or do you want to lynch me now?"

"Why don't you finish, and we'll let you know?" Paul said.

"It wasn't my idea! I was just part of a team!"

Paul waved away his protests. "Look, mate, we don't have much time. In case you haven't noticed, we're surrounded by the things *you* let out. The generators probably have an hour or two of juice left, and after that we're going to lose the electricity. Right now that's the only thing stopping the Infected from smashing through the stairway doors and getting up here. So can the self-pity and tell us something useful."

Radley seemed flustered at being addressed in such a way. He huffed in irritation, crossed his arms, adjusted his glasses again, and finally settled back to his story.

"The rabbits died in the end," he said. "The nanos couldn't keep them alive for ever. So we introduced the evolved nanovirus into a colony of monkeys. What we saw was incredible. The nanovirus tried a new strategy this time. It began to change them, rebuilding them at a molecular level. They weren't trying to hurt their hosts, they were *improving* them. Rewiring the body, turning the raw materials into some kind of metal that was beyond anything our best engineers could manufacture.

"We identified four main stages of infection. In the first stage, the host is enraged, virtually mindless. It is uncoordinated and slow, because the nanos are settling into its system, learning the environment. It exists only to spread the virus to others."

"That's what it was like, at the start," said Mark quietly. "Then they got faster."

Radley gave him an impatient look. "By the second phase, the host *is* faster, and capable of planning and rudimentary thought. The nanos have better control of the body by then. More importantly, it's capable of networking with its fellows. The hosts are all part of a network, but it only works if they're in close proximity. That's how they think, by sharing the information load. Take an infected host away from its companions and it becomes stupid again."

"The more there are, the smarter they get," said Paul.

"Up to a point," said Radley. "After a while, the network reaches its limit. Its like . . . well, it's like when millions of people call each other on their mobile phones at midnight on New Year's Day.

Too many connections, everything gets jammed up. Messages don't get through. The system can't manage it. By that point, they're about as smart as a seven- or eight-year-old child, but they can't get any smarter." He coughed. "At least until they get to stage three."

3

Carson grimaced. "Scientists," he said. "You never can say something in ten words when you can say it in fifty instead."

Radley gave him a scathing look over the rims of his glasses. "Stage three," he said firmly, "is metamorphosis. Once the nanos have taken over their hosts, they begin to change them into specialized forms. They're rather like ants in a colony: they do whatever needs to be done for the good of the group. But the nanos can't make something out of nothing. They need raw materials. We saw some of the hosts sacrificing themselves, monkeys *absorbing* other monkeys, combining their raw materials so they could grow."

"I saw that," said Paul. "Down in the tunnels." He felt a creeping dread at the memory. "There was this . . . massive *rat* which had absorbed all the others. . ."

The tunnels. Maybe they could have used the tunnels, if they could have worked out some way to deal with the creature that had infected Caitlyn. But there was no sense thinking about it now. To reach the tunnels they'd have to go downstairs, and that would be suicide.

"During this phase, one of the hosts – in the monkeys it was the dominant male – becomes a being which we called the Alpha Carrier," said Radley. "The Alpha Carrier absorbs the majority of the available hosts and becomes . . . well, sort of like the queen ant. It becomes a communal brain for the whole group, a hub for sorting information. The Alpha Carrier removes the limits on the network. Do you see? They hit a problem and they work their way around it. The Alpha Carrier lets them become smarter than we'd previously imagined they could be. We found out just how smart today."

"When they got out," said Paul.

Radley looked helpless. "I don't know how they did it. I was working outside the security zone when the alarm went off. By then they'd already cut our communications. They *planned* it somehow. The secure zone was sealed, but they were already—"

He faltered for a moment, and for the first time Paul heard real doubt in his voice.

"We had to purge the secure area, destroy the Alpha Carrier," he said. "There were still people in there. People who hadn't been infected. . ."

Nobody said a word. Radley adjusted his glasses and frowned, as if irritated by something.

"Anyway, we learned one thing. Once they evolve an Alpha Carrier, they come to rely on it heavily.

The whole network depends on it. Taking out that particular organism threw them right back, turned them stupid again, sent them wild. But it was too late by then. With the lockdown protocol in place, people couldn't get out of the compound. We were trapped in there with the Infected. We were—"

He stopped again, frowned, adjusted his glasses once more. Every time he threatened to get emotional, he did the same thing. A moment to regain control.

Carson took up the story. "We were trapped in that place most of the day," he said. "Hiding, holding out, fighting when we had to. There were six of us in our little group at five o'clock this afternoon. Only me and him made it to the landing pad. The mechanics had been working on my bird, maintenance and that. Thought they were finished up, but it turns out they weren't."

"Can it be fixed?" Paul asked.

"Maybe," said Carson. "I had a look at it while we were up on that roof. Couple of the spark plugs are misfiring. That's what brought us down. Easy to sort out if I had the parts, but we ain't gettin' airborne till I do."

"So you just need new spark plugs?" asked Mark, perking up.

"Reckon so," said Carson.

Mark looked about the room, his face suddenly alight. "Can't we just pull some out of a car engine?"

Carson dug in the pocket of his flight overalls and

pulled out a spark plug. It was a few centimetres long, and looked like a long, thick bolt with a nut around its middle, one end tipped with white plastic. "Two of these ought to do it. More if you can get 'em." He tossed it to Mark, who caught it in the air. "Gotta be the right gauge, though, or they won't fit."

"There's, like, two dozen cars in the staff garage. Surely *one* of them will have the right gauge?" Mark was excited now.

Carson shrugged. "Possible. Ain't likely, though. Helicopter engines and car engines ain't all that similar."

"But it's a chance!" Mark said, looking at Paul for backup.

"It's a chance," Paul agreed. *A slim chance, but a chance.*

Erika was watching Radley, who was slumped against a desk, dejected. "You told us there wasn't any hope," she said. "What did you mean?"

He raised his head. "I mean this virus is already out. There's nowhere you can fly to. There's no way they can stop it. You'll buy yourselves a few days, a month, a year if you're lucky. But it'll find you in the end. All you've got to look forward to is chaos. Governments crumbling, cities consumed in the crisis." He sighed and deflated. "Today is the first day of the end of the world."

Paul's eyes went to Erika. She looked back at him. The news didn't faze her; she'd guessed it from the start. This wouldn't end with them as grateful rescuees wrapped in blankets, surrounded by paramedics and police. If they somehow managed to escape, it would only be the beginning. There'd be no more waking up in soft beds and heading downstairs for breakfast, no more hot showers, no more Facebook or sports days, no more weather reports or chocolate bars, no more central heating, no more supermarkets or mail-order or anything like that.

The world was going to change. Not just their world, but the *whole* world. They couldn't outrun that. All that was left was for each of them to decide how they were going to face it.

She knew all that, and she'd accepted it. Paul saw a strength in her then that he hadn't seen before.

"Gather everyone," he said. "Five minutes. Up on the roof."

"Right," said Adam. He got up and left without another word.

"What . . . er . . . what are you gonna do?" asked Mark nervously.

Paul was still holding Erika's eyes. "It's the end of the world," he said. "The least we can do is be honest with each other."

A smile touched the corner of her lips. Paul kept that memory with him when he left the room.

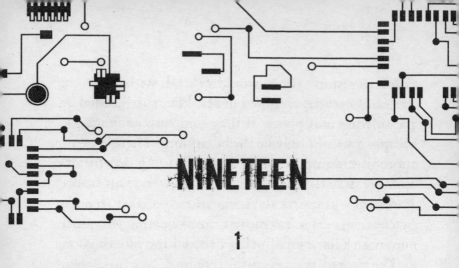

NINETEEN

1

Nineteen of us left? Is that all? That's not even a classroom's worth.

The wind whipped around Paul. His coat rustled and flapped. The clouds overhead had gone, and the moon sat fat and bright, low to the horizon. Behind the assembled pupils, the school building rose like a black cliff, punctured by windows that glowed with a deceptively inviting light.

But he was sure there was nothing alive within. Not now.

The school was dead. The traditions and structures it represented were gone. If Radley was right, soon other schools would go the same way, along with banks, governments, armies, police. Economies would tumble, religions would fall and rise. He couldn't imagine what the world to come would look like, but he knew one thing:

He wanted to be there to see it.

Many of the younger pupils were sobbing and

sniffling. Somehow they already knew about Mr Sutton. Or maybe they guessed when they saw he wasn't here. They weren't grieving for him, though: he was well liked, but not that much. They were crying because they were frightened, because they'd looked up to adults their whole lives and now the adults they knew were gone. All that were left were two strangers: a scientist with cold, watery eyes and a pilot with a hard face. Neither showed any inclination to take charge.

Those who weren't crying had their eyes on Paul. He felt exposed beneath their gazes. He'd chosen the roof so the lookouts could still keep an eye on the Infected, but there was barely any sign of them around the campus now. Where had they got to? He didn't know. He hoped it was a good sign, but he doubted it.

The silence was becoming agonizing, so he spoke.

"I suppose most of you know who I am," he said. The wind took his words, and he could see kids at the back leaning forward as they strained to hear. He raised his voice. "I'm Paul Camber. Year Eleven."

It was a bad start. He sounded weak and uncertain. Blood heated his face.

Do better.

"I've been at Mortingham Academy since the start of this year," he said. "I didn't want to come here. Never imagined finding myself in a boarding school in the middle of nowhere."

There was puzzlement on the faces of his audience. He took a deep breath. *Now or never.*

"You know, once I had a pretty good idea of how life was going to go. I had good friends, I was doing well at school, Mum and Dad had a bit of money between them. We didn't want for much. I didn't know what I was going to do when I left school but hell, who really does, right?"

He faltered. He had their attention now, even the ones who'd been crying, but it was mostly because they had no idea where he was going with this. Erika's eyes had softened with pity and disappointment. He was dying up there, and she knew it. That hurt him, and drove him onwards.

"Then one day, everything changed. My folks. . . Man, I loved my folks, they were the best. I mean, they were still parents, right? They still drove me crazy, but. . ."

He felt a lump gathering in his throat. Tears threatening. *Not now,* he thought, and willed them back. *Not now. I need to speak.*

Damn, this was harder than he thought.

"Well, one day I got a call from South America. They'd gone on holiday there, the first holiday they'd had on their own since I was born. I said I'd rather stay at a friend's. Three weeks in summer without Mum and Dad on your back, you know how it is. The guy on the other end, I don't know how he had my mobile number . . . he wanted to talk to my aunt but

I guess they couldn't . . . y'know, they couldn't reach her and . . . and I *knew*, right away, the moment I answered the phone. Before they even said anything, I knew."

He sucked in his breath through his teeth. His chest hurt. His eyes glistened.

"They were in some twin-engine piece of crap and it went down over the rainforest. They never even found it. Plane just disappeared, no bodies, nothing. Swallowed up." His voice broke then. He took a moment to bring himself under control again. "I never saw them again. Never heard their voices, except on some stupid home videos. I mean, they were just *wiped out of existence*. And all that stuff about people living on in memory, how they're still alive if they're not forgotten, that doesn't mean a damn thing because they're not *there*!"

He felt suddenly angry. Furious. He'd never spoken about this before, not to the counsellors, not to anyone. It all came out of him like he was retching up something vile.

"So they sent me to my aunt and uncle's, right? But they had their own lives, they didn't have kids, never wanted them. They didn't need a screwed-up teenager on their hands. They tried their best, and I tried *my* best, but in the end none of us could deal with it. So they sent me here. Here, to Mortingham bloody Academy, where I could be out of everyone's way. Where I wouldn't be a *problem* any more."

His audience was fixed on him, hanging on his story. With his anger came a surge of confidence. Suddenly, he knew what he was doing. The words came easily now. Honesty always did.

"I know what it's like to lose the ones you love! I know what it's like when the world turns upside down! I've been there. But I'm *still here*! And all of you are still here! Yes, we've lost Mr Sutton. Many of you have lost friends today. And I know you want to curl up and die, but you *can't*! Because you're not alone, because there are other kids who need you right now, just like you need them. We're the ones who've made it through this far, and we're the ones who have to carry on. Because if all of us stick close, if we hang on to each other, we *can* get out of here. And we'll get out *together*!"

His throat hurt and his chest heaved by the time he was done. Maybe he could have worded it better, but that didn't matter. The feeling was what was important, not the words. He *meant* it. He blazed with the passion of his message. Because he knew what it was to face your grief alone, to turn away every helping hand, to armour yourself in a protective shell and never trust a soul. And he was done with all that now.

"Now listen up!" he said. "Here's what we're gonna do. As long as the generators keep going, we ought to be able to keep the Infected out. That means they need refuelling. And that means somebody's going to have to go into the basement of the school building and fill them up. This is the most important part of the plan, so I'm putting the best man on the job." He looked up. "Adam?"

Adam looked faintly startled.

"Adam, no one can beat the hell out of the Infected like you can." There was a ripple of laughter at that. "Will you handle this part of the mission?"

The eyes of the crowd turned to him. For a moment, his eyes narrowed and turned suspicious, suspecting a joke. Then, when he saw that Paul meant it, his expression changed, went firm with determination and pride.

"Yeah," he said. "Alright. I will."

"Now, as for me, I'll be heading for the staff garage, where I'm going to try to salvage some parts." He pointed to where the helicopter sat in the moonlight, over on the sports centre roof. "Mr Carson over there thinks he can repair the chopper if we get him what he needs, and I'm gonna make sure he gets it."

This was news to most of them. Excited whispers ran through the crowd. He saw Freckles and Pudge exchange a thrilled glance at the prospect of getting the helicopter in the air again.

"I'll go with you," said a small voice. Paul's eyes found Mark at the edge of the crowd, holding up one thin arm. "Well, the pilot's crocked, isn't he, with that ankle? And there's no one else I'd trust to get the right gauge of spark plug."

"Nice one, Mark," said Paul. "Glad to have you along."

Adam grinned and clapped Mark on the shoulder, hard enough to make him yelp.

"I'll go and all," said another voice. Paul spotted him. Johnny, of the emo fringe. Paul didn't know him well, but he'd proved himself to be a steady and reliable sort.

"Great," said Paul. "You're in." He turned his attention back to the crowd. "Now I need someone to run this place till we get back. To organize the lookouts, keep an eye on the defences, make sure the Infected are kept out. Erika, would you take charge?"

She held his gaze for a long while, her ice-blue eyes showing nothing. He didn't know if she was mad at him, or grateful, or neither.

"Yes," she said. "I'll do that."

"Alright," said Paul, raising his voice again. "If we can keep the generator running, we can keep the Infected out. If we can get the chopper in the air, we can go for help. You all have your part to play. Look out for one another and we'll get through this. Now, back to your posts."

They dispersed with a new purpose in their step, animated and chatty, their tears briefly forgotten. Paul let out a long, shaky breath and walked through the scattering crowd towards where the older kids and adults had gathered in a group. As he approached,

Carson grunted and gave him a wry smile.

"Good job, son," he said. "Heck, *I'd* follow you after that little show."

"All we've got is a plan," Paul said. "Now we've got to make it work."

2

Preparations were made.

There was an air of feverish excitement in the science block. No longer were they defending or simply reacting to events, they were *doing* something. Taking control. Even the most distressed were buoyed by that feeling.

Erika had to admit, Paul had been impressive up there. It was a far cry from the angry boy who'd been scrapping with Adam by the lakeside that morning. These past hours had changed him. Or perhaps they'd simply turned him back into the person he'd always been.

"Carson's the important one," Paul was saying to her as they walked down the corridor. "Without him, that helicopter's useless, and we're done for. If anything happens, you need to get Carson to the helicopter."

"Alright," she said.

"Keep someone posted on the doors, ready to electrify them if the Infected attack. Keep the bursts short, though. We don't have much juice. And you could—"

"Paul," she said firmly. "I can handle it."

Paul gave her a sheepish glance. "Sorry."

They walked a few steps in silence.

"Why did you pick me to stay behind?" she asked. "Tell me it's not because you wanted to keep me safe."

A fleeting expression of guilt crossed his face. *Thought so*. She felt herself become irritated. Still getting treated like a princess.

"What if I'd volunteered to go with you?" she said, and some of the annoyance bled into her voice.

"I'd have taken you," he said. Then, with a little anger of his own: "But you didn't, did you?"

That was fair enough. She might have wanted to prove herself, to earn her place like everyone else, but she hadn't wanted it enough to go out there into the dark.

"Look," said Paul. "You're smart. The girls look up to you. Half the boys fancy you. That means they'll do what you say. You're the best one for the job, that's all."

It made sense, but she didn't believe that was the real reason. "I want one thing straight," she said. "I don't need protecting. I don't need saving. I don't want special treatment. You gave me a job, and I'll do it. But I just want to be clear, okay?"

Paul shrugged. "Fine. Just make sure everyone's here when I get back."

"*If* you get back," she said, and regretted it

immediately. It had just slipped out.

He stopped, and she stopped with him. They were alone in the corridor beneath the unsteady fluorescent strip lights. Paul looked troubled, as if what she'd just said had struck a chord in him somewhere.

He took a breath, steadying himself. "I gotta say something. Might be my last chance."

But she saw what he was going to say. She'd seen that expression on a lot of boys in the past. So she touched his arm gently, and gave a small shake of her head.

"Don't," she said.

He deflated a little.

"You're a good guy, Paul. You're just . . . I dunno." She gave him a helpless look. "You're not my type?" she suggested, as if any explanation would be good enough.

He gave a little laugh. "Least we can do is be honest with each other, huh?"

"Least we can do," she agreed.

He thought about that for a moment, then drew himself up, as if putting the moment behind him. "Well, then," he said. "Let's go see Caitlyn."

3

Paul felt surprisingly light of heart after what Erika had said. It was actually kind of a relief to have that burden lifted from him. Rather than a rejection, it seemed like a problem that had been taken care of.

He'd done all he could, and now he knew: she didn't want him. Maybe he'd secretly hoped that would be the case. Maybe he wasn't ready for that kind of closeness yet, and preferred to adore her from afar, without the complications.

For whatever reason, he didn't feel ashamed. He was glad he'd cleared the air. Now he could get on with the business at hand.

You got what you wanted, Mr Sutton. Everyone's looking to me now. Hope I don't let you down.

His thoughts turned to Caitlyn again. He needed to make one last check on her. Maybe she'd talk to them this time, maybe she wouldn't. But it felt wrong to leave without some sort of goodbye. And some sort of apology. It might have been Adam who locked her up in the staff room, but it was Paul's fault she was in there at all.

When they reached the staff room there was a pupil outside the door, guarding it.

"I put someone on the door with instructions to come get us in case she got violent," said Erika.

"That was good thinking," said Paul.

"Well, duh."

Paul smiled at her. He deserved that.

They approached the girl, a bright-eyed thirteen-year-old, who was dancing from foot to foot restlessly. An iron bar rested against the wall near her, but she looked scarcely capable of using it.

"She's not made a sound," the girl reported. "Not

since I've been here."

Paul knocked on the door. "Caitlyn? Are you there? It's Paul."

There was no reply. Paul closed his eyes. He couldn't imagine what she was going through in there. Had she turned, like Mr Harrison had turned? Or was she still Caitlyn, still frightened, watching the threads of silver as they crept relentlessly up her arm towards her head?

It was cruel to lock her up in there. Barbaric. She needed comfort and support, and they treated her like a prisoner.

But what else could they do?

He knocked on the door again. "Caitlyn? Please talk to me."

He listened. Nothing. No sobbing, no movement. Except. . .

He looked down. The hem of his trousers stirred in the breeze that slipped beneath the door.

"You feel that?" he asked Erika.

Erika frowned, not understanding.

"Something's wrong," he said. He banged on the door again. "Caitlyn? Are you alright?"

Still no response. Only the sound of papers rustling, teased by the wind.

"Give me the key," he said to the girl.

"Paul, you're not going in there!" Erika cried.

Paul took the key from the girl's outstretched hand and picked up the iron bar that had been lying against the wall.

"What if you let her out?" Erika demanded.

Paul gave her a long look of disbelief. "It's *Caitlyn*," he said.

"Is it?" she replied.

That stopped him. Yes, he knew the danger. Yes, she might be waiting in there for a chance to get out. But he couldn't just leave her in that room, her condition unknown. He owed her enough not to leave her forgotten.

Sometimes being nice is being stupid. He heard Adam's voice, warning him.

But he still put the key in the lock.

Erika stepped back from the door. The girl went further, running off up the corridor.

Paul pushed the door open a crack. Through the gap he could see the staff room. It was bleak and functional: easy-clean IKEA sofas, a cheap plastic clock on the wall, a cluttered kitchen unit. A wind was blowing around the room. Sheets of paper curled and flapped along the floor.

Nothing else moved.

He pushed the door open further. The room was starkly lit from above. He could see half of it now, and still no sign of Caitlyn.

Is she behind the door? That's where I'd be. Waiting.

The thought frightened him, and he shoved the door open hard, hoping to catch her by surprise. But the door only hit the wall, and now the whole of the staff room was revealed to him.

The room, and the open window, through which the wind was blowing.

He scanned the room cautiously, wary of a trick. But all the sofas were against the wall, and there were no nooks to hide in.

"She's gone," he said.

"Are you sure?" asked Erika from behind him.

Paul checked again and then, inspired by an irrational worry, he looked up, in case she was clinging to the ceiling like a spider.

"I'm sure."

Erika came up to his shoulder. Only when she'd checked the room herself did she dare to enter. By then Paul had gone to the window and was looking out. There were no handholds on the wall.

"She jumped," he said.

"Is she . . . down there?" Erika asked quietly.

He shook his head. "No. She's out there. With them."

Then Erika started to sob, and he put his arms around her, and this time she let him.

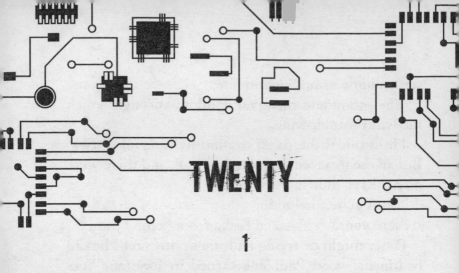

TWENTY

1

"Where'd they all go?"

Mark looked out of the open window on the west side of the science block, Paul and Adam to either side of him. Before them lay an expanse of lawn, wet and churned with footprints. Paths lit by recessed yellow lights led away towards the the school building, black and hulking in the night. Closer by, they could see the low rectangular structure that housed the parking garage.

Of the Infected, there was not a sign.

"This is weird," said Paul.

"Maybe they all left?" Pudge suggested. He was crowded up with Freckles at the other window. They'd volunteered to look after the ladder: someone needed to raise it after they were gone and lower it on their return. It didn't take two people to do the job, but the pair were inseparable.

"I doubt we're that lucky," said Johnny, who was leaning against the wall nearby.

"Could be a trap," Adam muttered, ever suspicious.

"They're up to *something*," Paul said.

"Yeah, but what?"

This from Freckles. The question hung in the air.

"Lookouts haven't seen anything for a while," said Paul. "And there's been no noise from downstairs, either." He listened to the quiet. "They're not calling to each other."

"They might be trying to lure us out," said Mark.

"Maybe," said Paul. He turned to Johnny. "You want to go with Adam? Two and two would make more sense."

Johnny gave a little shake of his head. "You need me for the cars." He pulled a wire coat hanger from his satchel and showed it to them.

Mark twigged first. "You know how to break into a car?"

"World's most forgetful parents," said Johnny. "You wouldn't believe how many times they locked their keys in. I'm pretty good at breaking into houses too, for that matter."

Adam shrugged. "One of us or ten of us, doesn't make much difference. Less likely to get caught if it's just me."

"There's at least one of them down there," said Paul. "The caretaker." Something passed across his face then, a flicker in his eyes. Fear? Guilt? Mark couldn't tell. "And a bunch of rats too. Unless they've found their way out by now."

Adam gave a grunt of acknowledgement. "Might be one in the garage as well," he said. "Me and Sutton left it locked up in his car, but whether it's still in there..." He tailed off and stared out of the window. "Gotta try, though, don't we?"

He was right. Trap or not, the way was clear. They couldn't afford to pass up the opportunity simply because it might be too good to be true. The alternative was to do nothing, and that would be worse.

"Let's go," said Paul.

Freckles and Pudge set up the escape ladder. It was torn off partway down – the sight of that ragged end brought back memories of the immense dog that had snatched Mr Sutton away – but by playing it out to its full length, it reached far enough.

Mark was terrified, of course, but he was also enjoying himself in a strange way. There was something warming in this camaraderie. He was so used to being on the outside, being ignored, that the feeling of being part of a team made him absurdly happy. They listened to him. They accepted him. And he felt brave, for what might have been the first time in his life.

He remembered how he'd been earlier that morning, how desperate he must have seemed. Lying about Adam to save Paul's skin. The humiliating way he'd tried to make friends with Paul in DT class. He could never have imagined that by the end of the day they'd be companions, united by something far more atrocious than classroom politics.

And if tomorrow the world went back to the way it had been? What then? Would they still talk to him? Would they greet him in the corridors, pat him on the back, good old Mark with his great ideas? Probably not. But he wasn't worried about that, because the world *wasn't* going back. And a little part of him was glad of it. In his own way, he'd been as badly suited to the previous one as Adam had.

"Ready?" Paul asked the group. They nodded grimly. Each carried satchels full of flash bombs and Molotov cocktails, and they all had iron bars to bludgeon away the enemy, except Adam, who carried his trusty length of radiator pipe. Mark had also brought a small selection of socket wrenches for removing the spark plugs.

Paul went first, followed by Adam, and then Johnny. Mark watched out of the window, expecting to see a horde of Infected swarming out of the shadows the moment their feet touched the ground. It didn't happen.

On his own, Mark might never have mustered the courage to move when it was his turn. But he was driven on by the group. He couldn't chicken out in front of the others. So he went, out of the window and down the flexible ladder, the rungs twisting and unsteady beneath his feet.

When he reached the gravel he looked about

quickly, searching for signs of movement that the others might have missed. Paul and Johnny were peering carefully through the windows of the science block to look for any Infected on the ground floor. By their expressions, they saw none there either.

They hurried away from the science block, preferring the darkened lawn to the lighted paths. The moon was their enemy now, bathing the campus in silver, exposing them. Their shoes squelched on the turf as they ran. Mark clutched his iron bar hard enough to make his knuckles hurt.

Where are they? What are they doing?

And still the Infected didn't show.

According to plan, they split up as soon as they'd got enough distance between themselves and the science block. Adam broke off and headed for the school building. Paul, Mark and Johnny continued on to the parking garage.

There was an electronic gate on the far side of the garage, which faced on to the drive, so the cars could get in. The teachers had key fobs to activate it, but it was impossible to open without one. Instead, they were heading for the smaller door at the side of the building, used for getting in and out on foot. Normally it was locked, but Adam had the key, which he'd held on to from his last visit. He didn't think he'd locked it on the way out last time, but he'd given it to them just in case.

The door came ever closer. Was it actually possible

they were going to make it? Mark, as was his way, had only thought ahead as far as getting there. By keeping everything in compartments, making the world into a mental flow chart, he kept the crisis small enough to cope with.

Where did they go?

Breathless, they reached the metal door at the side of the garage. Paul spared a glance towards Adam, who'd almost reached the school building by now. Mark scanned his surroundings one last time as Johnny tried the door. Many of the windows he saw across the campus were lit up, but many were dark. Were there glowing blue eyes fixed on him even now, watching from some hidden vantage?

They didn't even need the key in the end. The door wasn't locked. Johnny pushed it open and they went inside.

2

Mark could barely believe it. Had they really made that run across open lawn without encountering a single Infected? It didn't seem possible.

Maybe the creatures really *had* gone. Maybe they'd got everyone they were going to get, and they'd decided that the last few holdouts were more trouble than they were worth. Maybe they'd headed off for easier targets, out into the valley, out towards the town.

Maybe.

Before them lay the narrow concrete length of the garage, grim and grey beneath the buzzing fluorescent lights. The shadowed bays to either side provided a dozen hiding places.

They stood there by the door for what seemed like a long time, waiting for something to happen. Nothing did.

"Come on," Paul said eventually. "Let's get searching. Keep an eye out for that Infected kid. He's in here somewhere."

"You mean split up?" Mark squeaked.

"Don't be daft, this isn't *Scooby Doo*."

Johnny chuckled at that, and Mark cracked a smile of relief. He wouldn't have liked to face this threatening emptiness alone.

They headed to the nearest car. Johnny checked it over while the others kept a lookout.

"We want to keep this quiet," he said. "No alarms. This one's old, it should be alright."

He pulled out the wire coat hanger and untwisted it so it was straight. Then he slipped it between the driver's side window and the rubber seal. He moved it around for a few moments, then pulled sharply. There was a soft thump as the car unlocked.

Mark couldn't help a thrill of terror at being part of a crime. He supposed it didn't matter any more, but he still felt guilty. Johnny opened the car, reached inside and pulled the release lever under the dashboard. Once the bonnet was up, Mark unscrewed a spark plug from the engine with a socket wrench. He held it up and compared it to the one he had.

No good.

Johnny was already at work on the next car, but he was having more trouble with that one. Paul was standing with him. Mark walked over to a nearby parking bay which would give him a good view of the garage, in case anything was sneaking up. There was a car there, half in the shadow of the bay wall. As he approached, his eye caught the faint shine of something inside.

He frowned. Maybe it was a key, or a weapon, or something else which might help them. He bent down to peer in through the passenger-side window, shading his eyes from the electric light.

A screaming silver face slammed against the glass.

Mark yelled, stumbling backwards to bump heavily into the wall of the parking bay. He scrabbled along the stone barrier, fighting to get further away from the thrashing horror in the car that battered the windows and shook the seats. Then he was seized by the arm, and Paul pulled him sideways and out of the bay. He tripped to the floor and lay there, manic with shock.

Paul and Johnny approached the car warily. The Infected was making a heck of a racket, its buzzsaw shrieks echoing off the walls, but when it didn't come out after them, Mark realized it was stuck in there.

After a few moments to collect himself, he got to his feet and joined the others.

"Well," said Johnny. "Looks like you found him."

The Infected within was small, and its ghoulishly distorted face bore little trace of the boy it had once been. Now it was just a thing, a monster of sinew and silver. It scratched stupidly at the windscreen, trying to get to them, snarling like an animal.

"All it has to do is unlock the door," said Johnny.

"It's not smart enough," said Paul. He turned to Mark. "What did Radley say? They're only smart in groups?"

Mark just about managed to squeak a "Yes" from a throat that had gone suddenly dry.

"I suppose this one got left on its own. Maybe the concrete walls are too thick for it to connect with its mates."

"I reckon we don't need to worry about making noise any more, then," said Johnny. He tossed away the coat hanger and brandished the iron bar he'd been carrying for defence. "Route one it is." He smashed the window of a nearby car, reached in and popped the bonnet.

They left the Infected in the car while they searched. It was hard on Mark's nerves, hearing the creature screeching away in the background, but at least that meant they knew where it was. If it went quiet, *that* was when he'd worry.

Occasionally they set off an alarm on one of the

newer models, but Mark worked out how to disable them quickly enough once they had the bonnet up. He fretted about the noise attracting the Infected, but if they heard, they made no sign. He just had to hope that wherever they'd gone, they'd gone for good.

They checked car after car, but none had the kind of spark plug they needed for the helicopter.

His earlier optimism began to feel foolish. Had he been clutching at straws the whole time? What had Carson said? *Ain't likely. Helicopter engines and car engines ain't all that similar.* What if this didn't work? What if they *couldn't* fix the chopper?

Suddenly, the mental flow chart he'd been relying on had come to a dead end.

Faster and faster he searched the cars, leaving their bonnets open and their guts gaping. He unscrewed spark plug after spark plug, then flung them over his shoulder in disgust.

"Not right! Not right! Not *right*!"

"Hey," said Paul, laying a hand on his arm to still him. "Hey, it's okay. Look, it was a long shot, and we had to try something. Might be that the Infected have left anyway, right?" Paul was trying and failing to hide the disappointment in his own voice. "So we head back to the science block, and if Adam refills those generators then we'll be safe till morning, I reckon. Help's gotta come by then, right?"

"No!" Mark shouted. "No, I don't want to go back

there! We have to get *out* of this place, don't you get it? We have to—"

The lights went out. The words died in his throat.

For a few seconds they stood there, not daring to move, frozen in the pitch darkness of the windowless garage.

Then the shrieking began. Not just a single voice. A dozen, two dozen, *more*, rising from all over the campus like the hunting cry of a wolf pack.

The Infected hadn't gone. They'd been hiding. Waiting.

Until now.

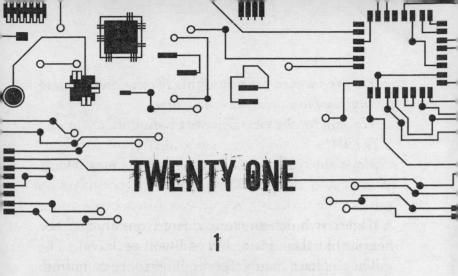

TWENTY ONE

1

"They're coming!" screamed the lookout, as she hurried down the stairs from the roof. "They're coming from *everywhere*!"

Erika had been on her way to check the defences on the western side of the science block when the lights went out. She'd felt the hand of dread then, as she stood stock-still, waiting for her eyes to adjust because she hadn't thought to bring a torch with her. When she heard the rising shrieks from all over the campus, she'd known what was coming, and yet some small part of her had clung to hope. The hope that whatever terror was about to occur would pass them by.

The lookout's warning put paid to that.

BOOM!

She jumped at the sound, which came from a nearby corridor. It took her a moment to recognize it. Something had pounded on the door to the stairwell. Something that made the stout barricade of benches and tables shift and groan.

They're out there, she thought. *They've been waiting just outside those doors the whole time.*

Waiting for the electricity to be shut off.

BOOM!

Move, she told herself, but she didn't know where. What could she do? How could she possibly stop this?

Children burst screaming from classrooms. She heard smashing glass and splintering wood. The sound of a flash bomb; dazzling light flickering from a classroom down the corridor.

Indecision gripped her. Paul had left her in charge, but there was no way to fight against those things, no way to repel a concerted assault. She backed up the corridor, blinking away the after-image of the flash bomb, and looked into another classroom in time to see something moving beyond the window. A shadow, glimpsed through the gaps between the boards.

They're climbing up the walls!

A claw swept into the classroom, smashing through glass and wood, tearing a way inside. The owner was long-limbed and spindly, a ragged thatch of filaments hanging over an inhuman face, two cold eyes burning in the darkness. Its fingers were long and sharp, hag's claws, and as it came clambering in, it moved like some horrifying insect.

Erika barely even knew she had the Molotov cocktail in her hand until she'd lit it. The flame that ran up the rag focused her. It drew the attention of the Infected too. The creature screeched as it saw her, gathered itself, and leaped through the air, covering the length of the room in one bound.

But the bottle of white spirit had already left Erika's hand. She threw herself aside, the creature and the bottle met in mid-air, and a fiery bundle of limbs came crashing into the hallway, right at the spot where Erika had been standing. She scrambled away up the corridor as the thing thrashed and squealed, but the flames had it now, and there was nothing it could do to save itself. It finally slumped in a heap, its blazing body blocking the corridor, cutting Erika off from the growing chaos on the other side.

The kids . . . oh no, the kids. . .

BOOM!

She heard the cracking of wood as the doors to the stairwell began to give way, but she still didn't know what to do, where to run, because they were coming from below and all around and they were even on the *roof* now. She could hear them up there.

No way out.

Paul's words came to her then. *Carson's the important one. Without him, that helicopter's useless, and we're done for. If anything happens, you need to get Carson to the helicopter.*

She fixed on that idea. She didn't know how she could get him out. She didn't know how she could get *anyone* out, not even herself. But she couldn't just stand here. She had a task, and that was all she had to cling to.

She turned from the flames and ran, back towards the room where she'd last seen the pilot and the scientist. As she went, the screams of the younger pupils echoed after her, and her vision blurred with tears.

2

Too late, Adam thought. *I'm too late.*

He'd made it to the basement without coming across any sign of them. Paul had told him about the press-switches that turned on the lights, but Adam hadn't needed them. He had his torch in one hand, the radiator pipe in the other. If that caretaker showed his face, he'd get a clubbing like he'd never forget.

After a little searching, he'd found a faded plastic sign pointing the way to the generator room, and followed it. The dark didn't bother him much. He'd faced too many real threats in his life to be scared of imaginary ones. As he slipped through the corridors, he heard the hum and rattle of the generators, getting louder and louder as he closed in on them.

And he heard when they shuddered and stopped.

There was a terrible quiet left in their wake. Distantly, he heard a faint chorus of wild screeching, coming from the campus above. And behind him, somewhere down the corridor, he heard the dragging of metallic feet.

Adrenaline flooded him, gearing him up to fight or run. He swore under his breath. He could hear other movement now, soft shuffles and scrapes that had previously been masked by the sound of the generators. In the labyrinth of corridors it was hard to tell where they came from, or how far away they were. He shone his torch this way and that, in case anything was sneaking up on him. Nothing.

Then his torch beam fell on a sign on the wall in front of him. Another plastic arrow, pointing the way to the generator room.

Going back was no good. There were Infected in that direction, and anyway, with the science block defenceless, he wasn't sure what he'd be going back to. But at least he might be able to get those generators running again. Turn on the lights, maybe get the electricity back on the barricades. Give everyone a fighting chance.

He'd been entrusted with a job. An important job. Not told to, not made to, but *entrusted*. Because he was the best man to do it. And he was going to get it done.

He headed off down the corridor. His torch would give him away to any Infected nearby, but that couldn't be helped. He'd rather face them head-on in the light than get pounced on in the dark.

Reaching a corner, he shone his light around. There

was no sign of movement, only another corridor lined with doors. He hurried onwards, and was halfway along it when something caught his eye. He aimed his torch at the foot of one of the doors.

A ruined padlock lay on the ground. It looked like it had been chewed through. He raised the beam of the torch. The door was made of flaking metal, and hung slightly ajar. A rectangular patch, lighter than the rest, showed where there had once been a sign. Scrawled in its place in permanent marker were the words: GENERATOR ROOM.

They got in. They killed the power on purpose, timed it to match their attack, just like last time. Clever bastards.

Probably they'd already sabotaged the generators by now. Or maybe they'd simply switched them off. Either way, he'd come too far to go back.

He reached out carefully, pushed the door open, and shone the torch inside.

With a scream, the caretaker lunged into the light.

3

Carson and Radley were in the lab where Erika had left them. Radley had crushed himself into a corner; Carson was beating an Infected over the head with an iron bar as it tried to climb through the window. As she burst in, the creature fell off the sill with a shriek.

"You have to get us out of here!" Radley yelled at

Carson, as the pilot retreated from the window, out of breath from his savage exertions.

"Get us *where?*" the pilot cried.

Radley ignored him and turned on Erika. "They've evolved, don't you see? I told you they would! Climbers! They're specializing!"

"You shut your goddamn mouth a minute!" Carson barked at him, pointing the bar threateningly in Radley's direction. Once the scientist had clammed up, he turned to Erika. "Is there a way out of here?"

Erika was choked up with fright, and the words wouldn't come. "I can't ... I don't... They're *everywhere!*" she managed at last.

She felt herself on the verge of hysteria. Some part of her was aware enough to be ashamed of herself, but she couldn't help it.

"Hey." Carson held out his free hand, fingers splayed, his rough voice softening as if he was gentling a skittish horse. "Calm down a moment. Take a breath."

She swallowed and nodded. Took a little of his calm for herself.

"Now think," he said. "We gotta get out of here. What's the safest way?"

Safest? There was no safest way. The Infected were coming from every direction.

Except maybe one.

"The back," she said, her eyes widening in realization. "The science block is open on three sides, but at the back there's only the campus wall. If the Infected are coming at us from all over the campus—"

"They won't be coming from that direction," Carson finished.

"You want to go out *there*? Outside?" Radley shrilled.

"You want to stay, be my guest," said Carson. He turned his gaze to Erika. "Lead on."

4

The hallways were filling with smoke. Mad silhouettes flitted across fiery doorways, like capering demons from some medieval nightmare.

"Out the back!" Erika screamed to anyone within earshot, and immediately began to cough. She seized a frantic pupil and shoved him in the direction he needed to go. "That way! Out the windows!"

Radley pushed past her. Carson's arm was across his shoulders; the pilot was limping as fast as he was able with his twisted ankle. Erika looked about for more kids. There had to be more. She couldn't just leave them; she was supposed to look after them.

But they were lost, somewhere in the smoke and the screams and the fire, and she didn't know where they were.

BOOM! And this time there came the grinding of splintered wood after the impact, a massive slow sound like a ship's prow ploughing into a dock. The barricade was being bulldozed aside. Somewhere out of sight, the doors to the back stairs had been driven open, and the Infected were swarming through.

No time left. No way she could save anyone else. But she could try to save the pilot.

They burst into a classroom, darker than the firelit corridor. Moonlight slid through the gaps between the planks that covered the windows. Those windows faced on to the back of the science block, and they were unbroken. The Infected hadn't come in this way.

Carson left Radley to close the door, limped to the window and began prising the planks with the iron bar in his hands. Erika ran to help, tugging them away as he loosened them.

Escape was hopeless, she knew that. Even if they got outside, it would be out of the frying pan and into the fire. In the open, with Infected everywhere, they'd be caught in seconds. But she wouldn't stop, she wouldn't lie down and accept her fate. She'd struggle till the end, because that was all she had left.

"Hurry up!" Radley snapped at them. He opened the door a crack and peered outside. "Hurry up, they're coming!"

Carson swore at him under his breath. With a wrench, the last plank fell away. He smashed the window, cleared the jagged glass from the frame, and looked out. Erika looked out with him.

At the back of the science block, a sunken path ran round the exterior of the building. On the other side, the ground rose a metre, a slope topped with a thick row of bushes, separating the path from a narrow strip of lawn. Beyond that was the wall.

And in that slender corridor between building and wall, there were no Infected to be seen.

"Go!" said Carson, his eyes glimmering fiercely in the moonlight. "I'm coming right after."

Erika didn't argue. She climbed up on to the window sill. The drop looked scary, but if she hung off with her fingers, it wouldn't be so bad. Two metres or so, that was all. She shuffled herself round so she was kneeling on the sill, facing into the room, and got ready to lower herself.

"Hurry *up!*" Radley said again, and then the door exploded inwards and a huge hand reached in and seized him by the leg. The scientist screamed as he was pulled out into the hall. But he only screamed for a moment.

Something dark dipped its misshapen head and glared in through the doorway with round blue eyes. Its dreadful gaze caused Erika to lose her balance on the sill. She slipped backwards, fell through the air, panic bursting across her senses.

She landed on her back in the bushes with a flurry of vicious scratches. But the bushes were soft, and raised higher than the path, so they cradled her as she hit and nothing was broken in the impact. She was still looking up at the window when Carson launched himself out. He flailed clumsily in the air before landing in the bushes next to her with a grunt of pain.

Her senses locked back into place and she could move again. Suddenly she knew what she had to do. She clambered to her feet, grabbed Carson's hand and hauled him out of the leaves. He suppressed a yell as his ankle came down.

"Under the bushes!" she gasped. "Get under the bushes!"

It took him a moment to understand her, but when he did, he scrambled to obey. The bushes were thick, but they were set widely enough to push through, and there was space underneath. They crammed themselves in where they could, hiding like children from the horrors of the night.

When they were in as far as they could go, they stopped, and there they lay cocooned in the cold damp tangle of leaf and branch, chests heaving. They listened to the sound of their breathing and the dreadful shrieks of the Infected as they went to work on the children left behind.

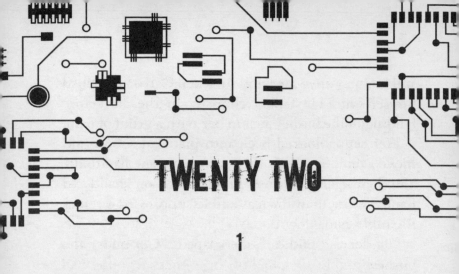

TWENTY TWO

1

The science block was burning.

The metal door of the parking garage had been opened a crack, and Paul's eye stared through the gap, flames reflected in its moist surface. His breathing was ragged with emotion. He watched transfixed, disbelieving, as the last of his hope died.

Fire glowed and flickered behind smashed windows. Poisonous smoke seeped and twisted into the night sky, or hung around the building in a filthy haze. In the light of the blaze, there were silhouettes, moving behind the windows like some depraved Victorian shadow play. Great hunched monstrosities; spindly clawed things; fat-bellied, waddling lumberers; four-legged creatures that ran back and forth with the restless energy of the crazed. The Infected raced across the roof, clambered up the walls, storming the building.

He pulled the door shut before any of the Infected could notice him. He'd seen enough anyway. There was no way anyone was getting out of that. All those kids, taken.

Erika, taken.

A great gaping ache of loss swelled in his belly. He locked the door with the key Adam had given him, slumped against it and slid down to sit dejectedly on the floor. Mark was standing nearby, awkward, unsure what to do or say. The wan light from his torch barely held off the darkness. Johnny was elsewhere. He'd walked off once the screaming had begun, knowing what it meant. He didn't want to come and see for himself what was happening. He wanted to be alone. Paul knew how he felt.

"Is it bad?" Mark asked.

Paul could only nod. The science block, lost. The fact that the electricity had died meant that Adam hadn't made it to the generator room. Likely he'd already joined the army of the enemy.

That left Paul and Mark and Johnny. Three left, against the world.

I failed, Paul thought. *It's over*.

He was supposed to lead them. Wasn't that the task he'd taken on? He'd persuaded them to trust him, to put their safety in his hands. And look at them now.

All those kids. His responsibility. Damn it, he should have known. He should have known not to care about them. At least when he was alone, nothing could hurt him like this.

The Infected kid in the car was shrieking. An

endless, maddening wail, echoing from the blackness beyond the torchlight.

"Shut up!" he screamed at it. "Shut your bloody mouth!"

It ignored him and carried on. Mark stared at him, wide-eyed, frightened.

"What are we gonna do?" he asked.

"What are you asking *me* for?" Paul cried. "Who do you think got us into this?"

Mark recoiled from him, wounded by the anger in his voice. "I just . . . I thought. . ." he stammered. Then he hung his head. Tears gathered in his eyes.

Paul hadn't realized it was possible to feel worse than he already did. He bit his lip and grimaced at himself.

"Sorry," he muttered.

"S'alright," Mark muttered back.

They were silent for a time, listening to the screeches from outside and inside. He could hear Johnny shuffling on the lower level, his shoes scuffing concrete as he wandered aimlessly, disconsolate. After a short while, Mark sat down next to Paul, his back to the metal door.

"What are we gonna do?" he said again.

"Stay here, I suppose," said Paul. "Wait."

"Wait for what?"

Paul shrugged.

Mark looked at him. "Are you giving up?"

Paul shrugged again.

Mark stared ahead into the middle distance. Suddenly he sniffed, and began to cry.

"I don't want to die," he whispered hoarsely.

Paul felt tears prickle at his own eyes. "Nor do I," he said. "I was only just working out how to live."

Mark sniffed again. "It's not fair."

"What ever is?"

Paul would have liked to offer him some kind of comfort, but he didn't have any to give. It *wasn't* fair. It wasn't fair that he'd done his best and failed. It wasn't fair that Erika had gone out of the world. It wasn't fair that his parents had died. It wasn't fair that the world was going to end because a bunch of scientists built a weapon they couldn't control, all so the government might win another one-sided war. A lot of things weren't fair.

But you kept going anyway.

He felt a small flicker of defiance ignite inside him. He knew this feeling, this despair, this black damp shroud settling on his soul. He'd felt it before, a year ago, when he picked up the phone and heard a voice from South America asking how to get in touch with his aunt. He'd hugged the darkness to him like a blanket then, he'd burrowed into it and hid until it set solid around him, a scabbed shield to protect him from the world.

But he knew now that the darkness was no friend to him. It didn't want to protect him, it wanted to keep him to itself. And just when he'd begun to fight free of it, it came at him again, hoping to drag him back.

No. No, he wouldn't. What was that whole speech he made on the roof about, if not this? If he caved in now, how spectacularly hollow those words would sound. He remembered how he'd felt when he'd spoken them. They'd come easily because they felt right, they felt *true*. Because he hadn't really been speaking to his audience at all. He'd been speaking to himself.

We have to look out for one another, he thought. Well, there were still two kids here to look out for. He listened to Mark's sobs and felt ashamed, and he took strength from that shame. Johnny might be able to stand on his own, but Mark wouldn't make it out there without help. Mark needed him. They all needed each other.

And what about Adam? Adam, whom he'd sent down to the basement, where the caretaker might still be lurking. Didn't he owe it to Adam to at least go looking? Even if the thought of going down there turned his guts to water, shouldn't he try?

And suddenly it hit him. The caretaker. A memory flashed into his mind, of the caretaker leading him through a long hall on their way to the basement. A hall with seven glass display cases. The Osbourne Gallery, they called it, though it was more popularly known as the Hall of Show-Offs. It was where the work of the Academy's most famous ex-pupils was displayed. He remembered a model of a molecule, he remembered a book. . .

And he remembered an engine.

"Hey," he said, and hit Mark's arm with the back of his hand. Mark jerked out of his sorrow. "What about that engine they've got in the Hall of Show-Offs?"

Mark looked bewildered for a moment, and then his face cleared. "It's a light aircraft engine."

"Well? Isn't that closer to a helicopter's engine than a car's?"

Mark seemed confused by the sudden note of encouragement in Paul's voice. "What are you saying?"

"I'm saying that engine might have the kind of spark plugs we need!"

Mark wiped his nose with the back of his hand. "But we don't have a pilot."

"We don't know that. I told Erika, I said, 'Whatever happens, you've got to get that pilot to the chopper'."

"But she's gone . . . they're all gone. How could anyone get out?"

"I don't know. But she's smart, isn't she? Why do you think I left her in charge? If anyone could do it, she could."

Paul wasn't entirely sure he believed his own words, but just saying them made it all seem possible. Maybe she *was* out there somewhere.

"I dunno. . ." said Mark, unconvinced.

"Well, either way it's better than staying here till

our torches run out," Paul said, getting to his feet. "Honestly, I'm gonna go nuts if I have to sit here listening to that thing in the car screeching for much longer."

Mark cracked a faint smile at that. "Are you totally crazy?"

"What else have you got to do right now?"

"We could wait," Mark suggested.

"Wait for what?"

Mark chuckled ruefully as he heard his own words thrown back at him. "Yeah, I suppose you're right," he said. "Nobody's coming, are they?"

"You heard Radley. Everyone's gonna be way too busy to worry about us."

Mark sighed. The shadows were deep on his face in the torchlight. He held out his hand. Paul grabbed it and pulled him to his feet.

"What makes you think Erika even did what you said? I mean, she might have just run for it."

Paul thought about that for a moment. "I guess I just trust her," he said. Then he turned away and hollered into the dark. "Hey, Johnny! Get up here! We got a plan!"

2

Erika didn't dare to move.

The Infected were close, so close. She could hear them prowling nearby. Sometimes she caught a glimpse of them through a gap in the bushes. They slunk along the lawn, or dropped from the walls of the burning science block and thumped away down the path. The air reeked of smoke and the stench of chemicals. Her throat tickled and she wanted to cough, but she swallowed hard and held it down.

The attackers were deserting the building now, climbing through the windows and hurrying away. Some were carrying bundles: children, newly infected and clumsy, who would otherwise perish in the flames before their change was complete. They treated their burdens with appalling tenderness, like mothers with their young.

Even monsters care for their own. The thought came clearly through the paralysing haze of fright that trapped her, trembling, where she hid.

Carson was crammed up under the bushes alongside her, close enough that she could smell his musty flight suit and the sour tang of dried sweat. His eyes darted about and he started at every movement. He was as scared as she was, though he was doing his best not to show it.

She reached out and grasped his hand. She wanted to comfort him, and she needed comforting herself. His rough, calloused fingers closed over hers, and their eyes met.

How are we going to get out of this?

Terrifying as their situation was, she could think more clearly now than when the Infected had first attacked. She'd become accustomed to the fear, and now it sharpened her thoughts instead of muddling them. Survival instinct had taken over.

Come on, Erika. You're supposed to be so smart. Figure it out.

Leaving the bushes was out of the question at the moment – there were still too many Infected nearby – but if the opportunity came, she had to be ready. She peered out between the leaves.

Now that the lights were out, the campus was much darker than before. Could the Infected see in the dark any better than humans? She didn't know. The moonlight was too strong to offer much concealment anyway.

But the moon cast a shadow like the sun.

She shifted her head so she could see out across the narrow lawn to the wall. The moon was above and behind it somewhere, throwing shadow towards them. Between the smoke-haze and the darkness, the area at the base of the wall was as black as pitch.

"Carson," she whispered. She nodded towards the wall. Carson looked across and saw what she meant. "Carson, I have to get you to the sports hall, to the chopper. That's what Paul asked me to do if anything went wrong."

"I can't run," he said.

"Then you can lean on me."

Carson suppressed a cough. They were too near the burning building; Erika could feel the heat of it on her skin. They couldn't stay here much longer, and Carson knew it. She saw it on his face.

Finally, he nodded. "Alright," he muttered. "When?"

When indeed. She judged that most of the Infected had left the science block by now, as she hadn't seen any pass their hiding place in a while. But her view was restricted by the leaves. There could be an Infected lurking nearby and she wouldn't see it until she emerged.

"Hey," said Carson, tilting his head attentively. "Listen."

She listened, and she heard. It was a familiar sound in the Lake District during the day. A sound like gathering thunder, slow-motion explosions in the sky.

Jets.

Hope surged inside her. Jets! The air force had scrambled! At last, someone had alerted the armed forces. Now surely rescue must come. The army would be here soon, and the Infected would be driven back, and—

The look on Carson's face stemmed her excitement. Why wasn't *he* excited? He looked grimmer than ever.

The jets roared closer, passed overhead and went south, off down the valley.

"They must have seen the fire!" she whispered. "They must ha—"

She was interrupted by an enormous detonation, a great deep wave of sound that rolled along the valley from the south. As one, the Infected *screeched*, a deafening buzzsaw cacophony, shrill with feedback. Erika clapped her hands over her ears. The sound of their outrage was unbearable.

"Come on," said Carson, tugging her. "If there's any time, it's now."

They scrambled out from under the bushes, on to the raised lawn at the back of the science block. Mercifully there were no Infected close by. Twenty metres separated them from the wall, ten of them in shadow so deep it was like ink. Carson threw his arm over Erika's shoulder and they hurried across the lawn and pressed themselves against the bricks.

Now she could see what had caused the commotion. Down the valley, high up on a ridge, flames rose into the night. The weather station – no, the *biological weapons facility* – had been obliterated.

There could have been people in there. People like Carson and Radley.

And then she knew why Carson had looked so grim at the sound of the jets. The infection was far too dangerous to risk a rescue at ground level. This was how they'd handle it: purge it, destroy everything, and hope that nothing got out.

"And that's why we didn't call for help on the chopper radio," Carson muttered. "Best hope they don't come back to 'rescue' us."

There would be no help from the armed forces. No help from anyone. If they were getting out, they'd have to do it themselves.

The Infected that she could see beyond the science block were in a frenzy. They all ran in one direction: south, towards the main gate, towards the weather station. There must have been plenty of Infected still inside when the missiles hit. Enough that their deaths were felt even this far away.

Good, she thought bitterly. *See how it feels*.

She pulled on Carson and they got moving, hurrying along the base of the wall, sticking to the deep shadow. The sports hall was not far, and it backed up against the wall in the same way the science block did. The Infected all had their eyes fixed on the burning weather station, and they howled and screeched and ran like mad things. None of them saw two furtive figures heading in the other direction, hugging the wall like mice scampering along a skirting board. None of them saw those figures slip out of the shadow and climb in to the sports hall through the same window Paul had smashed a short while earlier.

There were a hundred of them out there, but none of them saw.

None of them, except one.

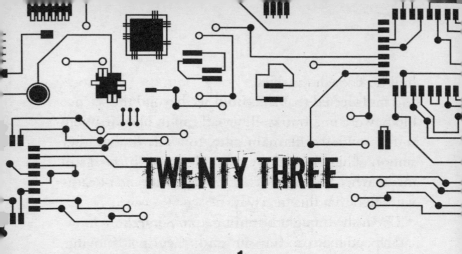

TWENTY THREE

1

"Go!" said Paul, and they ran.

The night screeched and sawed with the jagged cries of the Infected. The creatures lurched and leapt, blue eyes fixed on the flaming ruin of the weather station, high on the ridge in the distance.

Paul didn't know the source of their distress. He'd been inside when the jets had done their work, and even now the parking garage blocked his view of the south end of the campus where the Infected were gathering to rage and lament. All he knew was that there were none to be seen on the short run between the garage and the school building, and it was a chance he wasn't about to pass up.

Johnny and Mark ran with him, flash bombs and Molotovs ready. Some way away they saw a half-dozen Infected, but they were all heading south, and none so much as turned their heads. Paul heard a long howl from somewhere near the lake, and with a chill he knew it must have come from the monstrous dog that had taken Mr Sutton.

They'd come out ready for a fight. The idea was to throw down flash bombs and escape into the school while the enemy were paralysed. To their amazement, they didn't need to. The Infected were so distracted that they reached the school unseen.

The heavy main doors hung ajar. Something large had ripped them open at some point during the night. They slipped inside and into the foyer, where they leaned against the wall and caught their breath.

"What's happened out there?" Johnny whispered.

"Whatever it was, it really stirred them up," said Mark.

"I thought they were machines? Machines don't get *angry*."

"They're not *just* machines. They started as humans, remember?"

"Yeah," said Johnny. "Been trying to forget that."

Paul slipped across the foyer and peered carefully down a corridor. In contrast to the bare and modern interior of the science block, the school was old, with arched doorways and groined ceilings and stone moulding on the walls. With only the moonlight through the windows to see by, it was a chill place, cloaked thick with shadows.

"This way," he whispered.

They crept down the corridor. From outside they could hear the shrieks of the Infected, where once there would have been the shouts of kids playing at lunch break. From within, they heard nothing.

"You think the Infected are all outside?" Mark asked, as they passed the doorway into yet another empty classroom.

Paul didn't reply. He remembered the last time the Infected had all seemed to disappear. Then, they'd simply been waiting for the right time to attack. He wouldn't underestimate them again.

They stopped at every corner, every doorway, to check for signs of the Infected. All they found was a ripped blazer, a discarded shoe, an overturned chair. The Infected had been through here, but apparently they hadn't stayed.

"I really don't like this," Johnny muttered. "I'd almost rather we saw a couple of them. At least we'd know where they were then."

Paul knew the feeling. The tension was agonizing. He kept a flash bomb in one hand and a gas lighter in the other, waiting for the moment when he'd hear a screech and something awful would lunge from the shadows.

That moment had still not come by the time they reached the Hall of Show-Offs.

2

The long hallway stretched away from them, seven glass display cases evenly spaced down the centre.

Paul saw the engine immediately, but he stopped and checked again before he entered. This whole thing still didn't feel right.

They gathered round the engine in the gloom. It had been kept in pristine condition, every part polished and looking new. Paul read the plaque by moonlight.

XR-300 Engine for Light Aircraft. A revolutionary design offering fuel efficiency 9% greater than other models of the time. Designed by J. Harvey Ostermann.

"Well, J. Harvey Ostermann," Paul muttered. "I hope to hell you used the right sort of spark plug."

Mark was examining the glass case. There was a lock securing it to the base. "How do we get in?"

"Stand back," said Johnny, pulling out the iron bar from his belt and raising it, ready to swing. When they stared at him in amazement, he said, "What? Anyone got a better idea?"

"The noise," Mark said.

"There's nobody to hear," Johnny replied.

"Wait," Paul said. "No sense taking chances." He slipped off his coat and laid it over the display case. It wasn't big enough to cover it entirely. "Give me your coats," he said. "We can muffle the sound."

They laid their coats over the display case, and between them they covered it up. Mark and Paul held them in place while Johnny took aim with the bar.

"Let go when he hits it," Paul told Mark.

"That was kind of the plan," Mark replied, deadpan.

Johnny swung, and the glass smashed. Paul and Mark jumped back, wary of cutting themselves, but the case was made of tempered glass for safety, so it smashed into small granular chunks instead of sharp shards. Those that weren't swaddled by the coats scattered across the floor with a hissing sound.

Paul waited anxiously, listening for sounds of the Infected. All in all, the sound of breaking glass had been as quiet as Paul could have hoped, and unlikely to be heard from more than a few rooms away. But that was still too loud for Paul's liking.

Yet still no Infected came.

"Let's do this, huh?" said Johnny. "I hate this place."

They pulled their coats off the engine and dropped them to the floor. Paul and Johnny kept an eye on the doorways while Mark unscrewed one of the spark plugs. He pulled it free and held it up to the moonlight, turning it round till he found the markings that indicated what gauge it was.

He checked it against the one from the chopper. Then he checked it again.

"Well?" Paul demanded, when he could stand it no longer.

"It's good," Mark said with a note of disbelief in his voice. "It's the right one."

"You're kidding," said Paul.

Mark shook his head.

"You mean we can actually fix the chopper?" Johnny asked.

A grin broke out on Mark's face. "I think so," he said. "You were right, Paul."

Johnny whistled softly. "Never thought it'd work," he said. "Guess we've really got a shot now, huh?"

Paul marvelled at the spark plug in Mark's hand. Yes, they really had a shot. Wild hope had become real hope. And if this part of the plan had worked, was it too much to believe that the rest had worked too? Didn't he owe it to Erika to trust that she had done her part and got Carson to the helicopter?

"Get all the spark plugs out of that thing," he said urgently. "Get yourselves back to the helicopter."

"Where are *you* going?"

"I'll catch you up. I've got to look for Adam."

"You're not serious," said Mark flatly.

"I sent him down there," Paul replied. "Into that basement. What if it was you?"

"If it was me, I'd be infected by now, just like Adam is."

"He's right," Johnny told Paul. "Getting yourself killed won't help him."

Paul opened his mouth to argue, then closed it again. Adam's words came back to him. *Sometimes being nice is being stupid*. It was just the kind of thing he'd been warned against. Risking his life on some dumb notion of heroism, when there probably wasn't even any point to it.

He shook his head. "You're right. Come on."

They stripped out the spark plugs with the socket wrench, taking them all in case they needed spares. When they were done, Johnny and Mark made to hurry off. But Paul was still dragging behind, looking off in the direction of the basement. It didn't feel right. Didn't feel right at all.

"Let's *go!*" Johnny said through gritted teeth. "You're gonna get us *all* caught and then *none* of us will get out of here!"

"Yeah," said Paul, quietly. "Yeah." And he picked up the pace and followed them.

Clank-clank-clank!

Paul stopped and spun towards the noise. The others froze.

Clank . . . clank . . . clank. . .

The sounds came slower this time. Paul looked around the room. Nothing moved. The three of them stood tense with their weapons ready, waiting for the inevitable attack.

Clank-clank-clank!

Faster again, the same as the first time. This time Paul zeroed in on the source.

"The pipes," he said. "It's coming from the pipes."

Set inconspiciously in recesses in the wall were several sturdy iron radiators, painted black. Thick pipes fed them water through the floorboards.

Clank-clank-clank! Clank . . . clank . . . clank. . . Clank-clank-clank!

A rhythm. An unmistakable rhythm, made by hitting something against the pipes elsewhere in the building. Paul had heard that prisoners sometimes communicated this way between cells. The pipes carried sound: you could hear it all the way through the cell block.

Clank-clank-clank! Clank … clank … clank… Clank-clank-clank!

Three short. Three long. Three short. Morse code. *SOS.*

"It's Adam," said Paul slowly. Then, excited, "It's Adam! He's still alive."

"It's a trap!" Mark blurted.

Johnny raised an eyebrow at Paul, the only one visible behind his hair. "He could be right, y'know. They're smart enough."

Paul thought about that. There was no doubting that they could be right. But he couldn't be sure, either.

"Go on," he said to them. "Get to the chopper and fix the engine. I'll catch you up."

"Tell me you're not actually going down there," said Mark, aghast.

"Got to," said Paul.

"It's *Adam*!" Mark said. "What do you owe Adam? He's a stupid, violent bully and he's not *worth* it!"

Paul was surprised by the anger in Mark's response. "You'd rather leave him there?" he asked.

"Yes! Rather him than you!" he said. "Look,

look, I figured it out. The tunnels! Remember the tunnels? That's why the Infected disappeared off the campus. They've been down there in the tunnels, travelling between the buildings, up to who knows what. And where do all the tunnels lead to? The *basement*! They're not up here because they're *down there*!"

"Why else would Adam need help, if not something to do with the Infected?" Johnny added.

"He's not even down there! Or if he is, he's not Adam any more! They're luring you!" Mark cried.

"Either way." Johnny shrugged. "Infected in the basement."

It was tempting, so tempting to just turn away then. They had what they needed to escape. There was almost certainly going to be Infected if Paul chose to go after Adam, and there was a very good possibility that Adam wasn't there at all, or was past saving. And what *did* he owe that kid, anyway? Adam had been the closest thing he had to an enemy at Mortingham. Paul had despised him for exactly the same reasons Mark did.

But that was then, and this was now, and they only had each other to rely on. If Paul let him down, what kind of leader would he be? What kind of ally? What kind of friend?

Sometimes being nice is being stupid. Well, then he'd be stupid. Because if the new world started here, it wouldn't start like this.

"No one gets left behind," he said. "Get going. I'll see you on the roof of the sports hall."

Before they could argue, he left, his footsteps tapping away along the polished floor. Heading for the basement, and whatever waited there.

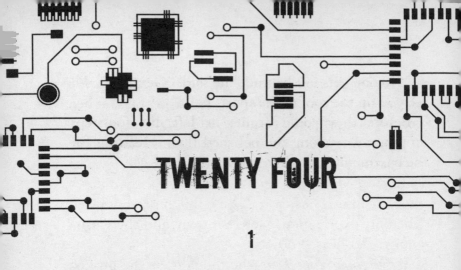

TWENTY FOUR

1

We're going to make it, thought Erika. *We're going to make it. We will.*

She kept saying it to herself, over and over, pounding it into her mind. She needed to believe. She felt like every last drop of courage had been used up, and there was nothing more in her. It was only by constant reassurance that she could continue putting one foot in front of the other.

They'd escaped the science block. They'd slipped through the horde, across open ground, and they'd made it to the sports hall. All it would have taken was for one Infected to spot them, and it would have been over. But they'd rolled the dice and won.

But all those kids, left behind. All those kids.

You couldn't save them, she told herself. *But you saved one man. And he might be able to save whoever's left*.

But who *was* left? Paul, Mark, Adam and Johnny – where were they now? Had they suffered the same fate as the kids in the science block? Did it even matter if she got Carson to the helicopter, when nobody else might be coming?

Yes, it mattered. Because Erika would have done her part. All her life, she'd fought hard to live up to other people's expectations. Now, when nobody expected much of her at all, she fought even harder. The only expectations were her own, and she wasn't going to let herself down.

We're going to make it, she thought, as she pushed open the door to the swim hall.

2

Drip. Drip. Drip.

The swim hall was painted silver. A row of huge windows, high up on the east wall, let in the moonlight from outside. The swimming pool was on their left, water lapping gently against the sides. To their right were tiered benches for spectators. Hollow echoes chased each other round the room, bouncing off the tiles.

Drip. Drip. Drip.

She put away the lighter in her hand and let her eyes adjust to the moonlight. In contrast to the terrifyingly dark corridors that led them here, the swim hall was a relief. Neither of them had torches, so they'd been forced to use the cigarette lighter to navigate until now. But Erika had learned to fear open spaces, and the

315

swim hall was uncomfortably open. If there was something in here, it could come at them from any direction.

But there's nothing in here, she told herself.

"Are we going?" Carson murmured. He was carrying a fire extinguisher in one hand, which he'd liberated from a wall bracket to serve as a weapon. His other arm was slung over Erika's shoulders. The weight of him was tiring, but she could bear it. She was stronger than she looked.

All that netball was good for something, I suppose.

They moved out into the swim hall, following the route that led between the benches and the pool, heading for the door on the far side. Erika's gaze roamed restlessly, searching for danger. She wanted to run, to sprint across this awful empty space and get back to the confining safety of the corridors. But Carson couldn't run, so she couldn't either.

Step by steady step they went, dreading to hear the sound of something moving, creeping up behind them, the screech of an Infected just before it attacked.

There's nothing here, she told herself. *There's nothing here*.

But there was.

It was the water that warned her. A splash too loud to put down to the stirring of the pool. Something had broken the surface.

At the far end, at the near corner, there was a face above the water. Blue eyes shining.

Erika came to a halt with a lurch. The creature was between them and the exit. The urge to flee was overwhelming. But if she did, she'd be leaving Carson to his fate, and she hadn't brought him this far to abandon him now.

She'd thought she was out of courage, but it turned out she wasn't quite yet.

It slunk out of the water, never taking its eyes from them. This one looked as if it had started out as an adult, one of the female staff, although beyond that it was impossible to tell who. Locked inside the sports hall alone, it had evolved, altering itself to its environment: the swimming pool. Its hands were clawed and webbed, splayed into spiked fans of silver. A thin dorsal ridge ran from its neck down its back, and when it climbed on to the poolside it dragged a tail after it, tipped with a rudderlike fin for steering.

It stood there dripping like some drowned ghoul in the moonlight, and it never took its eyes from them.

Drip. Drip. Drip.

"Back away," Erika whispered. "I've got a flash bomb. Once it's stunned, hit it with the fire extinguisher."

Carson gave a small grunt of acknowledgement. The Infected watched them, crouched low, its tail flipping restlessly on the wet tiles. Erika reached into her satchel and drew out her last flash bomb and the cigarette lighter.

Carefully, moving slowly so as not to alarm the

creature, she rolled her thumb over the flint wheel to spark a flame.

Snik!

As if that was the trigger, the creature burst forward with a scream, racing towards them on all fours, moving in great loping bounds. Erika panicked, working the flint wheel frantically.

Snik! Snik!

A flame appeared at last, but too late. The creature jumped at her, and Carson pulled her out of the way, down and to the side. The flash bomb and lighter spilled from her hands as she fell in a heap on top of the pilot.

The Infected's leap took it past Erika, but it landed with inhuman agility, already set to spring back at them. They scrambled to untangle themselves, but in their struggles they tangled again. They were defenceless, helpless to avoid the next attack.

Erika shut her eyes as the creature bunched to spring.

A shriek. A crash of metal on metal. Water splattered her cheek.

She opened her eyes again, and the creature was gone.

They got up, breathless with disbelief. The swimming pool was churning. Shapes thrashed within it, hidden by dark waves and spray. There were things fighting in the water. Mechanical screams echoed round the swim hall.

Then there was a loud crack, and all at once the thrashing stopped.

Erika and Carson stared at the swimming pool, which was still swilling back and forth in the aftermath of the conflict. Floating on the surface, face down, was the Infected that had attacked them. As they watched, it sank beneath the surface, and was lost to sight. There was no sign of whatever had killed it.

"Come on," Erika whispered, recovering her wits. "We have to go."

The flash bomb had skidded near to the edge of the pool when she dropped it. She didn't dare retrieve it. Instead, she snatched up the lighter that had fallen by her feet. Carson threw his arm over her shoulder, and she propelled him as fast as she was able towards the door at the far end of the swim hall.

They'd barely gone three steps before the water blasted up in a geyser of spray, and a shadowy figure leapt out, landing directly in their path.

It was an Infected, there was no doubt of that. But this one was different to the others. It was . . . *incomplete*, somehow. One blue eye glared through the long hair that hung in sodden strings across its face, but the other was not blue. It was a *human* eye, mottled with silver but still human. One of its arms was metal, disproportionately long, fingers tapered to grotesque points. The other was that of a girl, though partly covered with plates and mesh.

Its face had distorted from the original, but its features hadn't been entirely wiped away. Erika knew the ridge of that brow. She knew that sharp nose. She knew that eye.

"Caitlyn?" she managed, through a throat closing up with tears.

The creature's good eye flicked to her and fixed there. It stood hunched, curled in on itself, twisted by the change being wreaked on it.

"Caitlyn?" she whispered again. "Caitlyn, it's you. You saved us."

It stood there for long seconds, regarding her. Then it drew in air. When it spoke, it was like the tortured mechanical wheeze of an old synthesizer.

SAVE. . . YOU? it said. It seemed to think about that for a moment. Then its lip curled into a snarl and its eyes narrowed hatefully.

KILL YOU!

3

Rage.

Caitlyn had never felt anything like it. Wild, primal, overwhelming. It filled her veins with bubbling fire, swept away grief and regret. Some faint part of her knew that this rage was not hers, that it was given to her by the microscopic invaders that were slowly transforming her into something else. But that part was drowned out in the deafening roar of pure, undiluted fury that rang through all the chambers of her mind.

And all of it was focused on Erika.

enemyenemyenemy

After Caitlyn had jumped from the window of the staff room, she'd headed for a nearby dorm hall. Even before she set off, she'd known it was deserted. She sensed it. Whispers in her subconscious, the wordless knowledge of the network, transmitted through the tendrils of silver that were working their way into her brain.

She'd still been human enough to be terrified of the Infected at that time. But several of them spotted her, and they paid her no mind. That was when she knew. She was one of *them* now.

She'd holed up in a dorm room and cried to herself for a while, but it hadn't done any good. The infection continued its insidious crawl through her body. Mark had tried to destroy it with electricity, but he'd only damaged the strange machinery that was taking her over. Instead of changing her in minutes, it took hours.

At some point she stopped being scared. It was as if someone had reached into her mind and turned a dial down. Her fear simply faded out, and the tears dried in the one eye that was still capable of producing them.

They did that. They stopped me being afraid, she thought, and she was almost grateful.

She'd known the Infected assault was coming, in the same way she'd known the dorm hall was empty. She considered warning the lookouts, but in the end did nothing. By then one arm had turned to metal, and the numbness was being replaced by something else: new nerves coming on line, giving her control. While the Infected were pouring into the science block, she sat there in the window, half her face silver, and stared fascinated at her new hand as she flexed and unflexed her fingers.

She was aware of the distress of the other Infected, the ache of loss as so many of their brethren were exterminated by the jets. But she was only loosely connected to their network, so she herself only felt a vague unease, not enough to bother her. She was still at her window when two figures slipped out of the bushes behind the science block and headed for the sports hall.

Caitlyn's mismatched vision made it difficult to see well, as the signal from her mechanical eye fought to marry up with her human sight. But she looked closer, and she saw, and her thoughts turned black and smouldered.

Erika, alive. It had to be Erika. She was just that kind of girl. Born lucky, born smart and talented and oh-so-beautiful. Why did *she* get to survive? Of all people, why her? Everything was so *easy* for that girl. It was like the whole world bent to accommodate her, as if life itself bowed down to lay its cape in her path.

She always won, she always came out on top. It wasn't fair. It wasn't *fair*!

The rage had come then. The rage that filled her with an overwhelming urge to bite and scratch and kill, made her dizzy with bloodlust. It filled her, tormented her, twisted her thoughts to murder.

Erika. Erika. Erika.

And she went out to find her.

4

"Caitlyn," Erika said, her voice trembling a little. "Caitlyn, don't."

But the thing that looked like Caitlyn didn't seem to hear her. She came closer, slowly, creeping towards her like a predator. There was an animal savagery on her face, a wild hate in her eye.

Erika backed away, but Caitlyn kept on coming.

"Hey!" Carson called. He was standing to the side, propping himself up with one hand on the raised benches, hopping backwards on his good leg. In his other hand was the fire extinguisher. "Hey! Not her! Me!"

Caitlyn paid no attention. It was like he wasn't even there.

Erika's mind raced. *She wants to kill me. She's going to try and kill me. If she so much as scratches me, I'll turn into one of them.*

The flash bomb. It was the only weapon she had.

She dared not turn to look at it, for fear of giving her plan away, but she knew where it lay. Near the edge of the pool. Not far, but too far to get to before Caitlyn was upon her. The cigarette lighter was still clutched in her hand. What if it didn't light first time? What if the fuse of the flash bomb was wet? What if, what if?

"Hey, you ugly heap of scrap! Here!"

At the word *ugly*, Caitlyn's head snapped round to face the pilot. She glared at him balefully, a snarl on her face. Carson blanched and hopped back another step.

The moment Caitlyn's attention was drawn away, Erika leaped for the flash bomb. Caitlyn's head snapped back towards her, and she screeched. But Erika had already gone down to her knees, scooping the flash bomb up from the tiles, bringing the lighter up to the fuse with her other hand.

Snik!

The flame caught first time, the fuse fizzed into life, and Caitlyn sprang at her with a howl. Erika threw herself sideways, trying to dodge. She only half managed it, and was off-balance when Caitlyn caught her a glancing blow with her shoulder. She staggered and crashed painfully into the tiered benches that faced the pool. The flash bomb was knocked from her hand and skittered away. Caitlyn skidded, turned, and came at Erika again, not giving her even a moment to recover. Erika saw her coming, but by then it was too late to do anything about it. She braced herself and—

An explosive *hiss* sounded by her ear. Caitlyn screeched as Carson unleashed the fire extinguisher in her face, a pressurized blast of carbon dioxide that sent her flailing back. In moments they were all consumed by a cloud of white gas that swelled to surround them. By the time Carson let his hand off the trigger, Erika could barely see.

She cast around frantically, searching through the fog. Where was Caitlyn? Where was the flash bomb, its fuse still burning? But Carson grabbed her arm and tugged her, and she went with him, heading for the door on the far side of the swim hall. The cloud was dissipating fast, fading into the moonlit dark, but when it disappeared they saw that Caitlyn had disappeared with it. As they fled, they looked frantically this way and that, desperate to catch sight of Caitlyn before she came at them again.

They didn't look the right way.

Caitlyn leapt off the top tier of the benches, and dropped catlike in front of them. Erika had only time to scream as Caitlyn swung a clawed metal hand at her face.

BANG! The world went white again, but this time it was the dazzling white of the flash bomb. For an instant, Erika was blind. She blinked frantically to clear her eyes, crushed them closed, opened them again.

Caitlyn was frozen in front of her, jaws agape,

sharp fingers centimetres from Erika's face.

Then there was a loud ring of metal as Carson swung the fire extinguisher into Caitlyn's ribs with all his might, swatting her aside. She smashed limply into the benches. Erika screamed again, a small scream because there was still enough of Caitlyn in that creature to make her baulk at hurting her.

Carson had no such attachment. He slung his arm over Erika's shoulder and propelled her onwards towards the exit. They ran-hop-dragged themselves as fast as they could, the door coming closer and closer until they shoved it open and were through, into the corridor, and—

They were suddenly thrown forward as Caitlyn leaped through the open door and smashed into Carson from behind. Shoved across the corridor, they collided with the far wall. Carson hit head first, and went limp. Erika staggered away, barely keeping her feet as the weight of Carson slid off her. She whirled, trying to find Caitlyn; but Caitlyn found her instead. Erika was seized by the throat and slammed against the wall hard enough to drive the breath from her body.

She hung there, gasping, feet scrabbling uselessly against the floor. She couldn't get any air into her lungs. The impact had winded her, and Caitlyn's metal hand was round her neck, her long sharp fingers driven into the wall on either side. She couldn't breathe, couldn't breathe, and what if

Caitlyn had scratched her, what if she'd made even the tiniest *scratch*?

Caitlyn brought her face closer to Erika's. In the corridor it was almost pitch dark, but the moonlight from the swim hall limned her Infected features. Erika's vision blurred with tears of fright. This mechanical parody, this vile fusion of metal and flesh, this patchwork monster – she couldn't bear to look at it, but she couldn't turn away.

Carson was not stirring. He was out cold, or worse. There was only Erika and Caitlyn. The world had shrunk to the distance between their faces.

Caitlyn bared her teeth.

"Caitlyn," Erika tried to say, but she still couldn't draw in the air, and it just came out as a whooping sound. "Caitlyn."

Caitlyn hissed, tilting her head slowly from side to side as if examining every angle of Erika's face. *So this is you. You're not much.*

Erika tried again, and this time the breath came, and she sucked it in and screamed, "Caitlyn! It's Erika! I'm your *friend*!"

The creature's human eye tightened a little, the brow twitched. Puzzlement. Recognition, perhaps.

"Caitlyn!" Erika panted desperately. "You remember? You remember how we used to hang out at breaktime? You remember how I'd always pick you for my team at netball? When you, me, and Soraya used to go into town and laugh ourselves sick?"

And there *was* something in Caitlyn's face now, she saw it. Something like regret. Whatever this creature was, there was still some of Caitlyn in there.

"Please," Erika begged through her tears. "Please, I'm your friend. I was always your friend, no matter what you thought of me." She swallowed. "What did I ever do to make you hate me so much?"

Caitlyn's face fell. Her mottled gaze flicked from one of Erika's eyes to the other, as if trying to see inside her head. And then the eye began to swim, and a single tear spilled free from the lid, and raced down her cheek.

"Caitlyn. . ." Erika whispered.

Then the hand was gone from her throat, wrenched violently from the wall. There was a fast movement in the darkness, and Caitlyn crashed through the swing doors, back into the swim hall, and was gone.

Erika stood dazed in the silence that was left in her wake. Automatically, her fingers went to her throat, searching for blood, a scratch, a graze even.

Nothing. There was nothing. The skin was unbroken. She was not infected.

She slid down the wall, and hugged her knees, and began to cry like she'd never cried before.

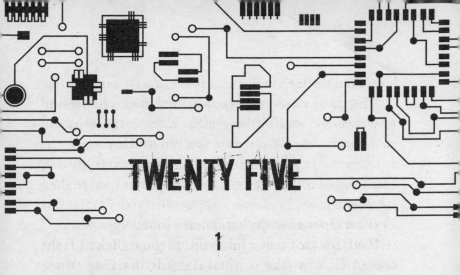

TWENTY FIVE

1

Paul pushed open the door to the basement, and saw only darkness inside.

Last time he'd been through here, the stairs down had been brightly lit. Now, the moonlight seemed to stop at the threshold, showing nothing of what was within.

From below, he heard a faint screech, muffled and made distant by the stone.

He felt in his satchel. His fingers found a flash bomb, a Molotov cocktail, a lighter and a torch. They were his only weapons apart from the iron bar in his hand.

What are you doing, Paul? he asked himself. *You don't need to go down there.*

He heard the *clank-clank-clank* again, resonating through the pipes. Adam's cry for help. *SOS.* Paul thought about clanking back, but he didn't dare. If it wasn't Adam making those sounds, he didn't want to warn them he was coming.

He took a deep breath, let it out, and headed down. The dark closed in around him. The only sound now was the scuff of his shoes on the steps, too loud in his ears. He didn't dare use his torch in case the Infected saw the light. Instead, he was forced to go by feel and memory. But memory threw up more than he wanted.

What if the caretaker's still down here somewhere?

Paul felt a fresh chill run through him at the thought. Was the caretaker still walking these corridors, or had he found his way out through the tunnels? And along with the caretaker and the rats, it was hard not to think of Billy McCarthy, the boy who'd died down here. The caretaker had told him about Billy, trying to give him a fright. At the time it had been a bit of fun at Paul's expense, and Paul had scoffed at it. But in the dark Paul's imagination threw up visions of Billy's ghost. Would he be down here, his eyes glittering from his hiding place in the air ducts, waiting to reach out a hand and snatch him as he passed? Paul had to stop and take more deep breaths to calm himself. The urge to turn on the torch was almost overwhelming.

It's just a story, that's all. A stupid school legend. There are worse things to worry about than ghosts.

Once he had himself under control again, he headed to the bottom of the stairs, feeling his way down, step by uncertain step. His hand found the corner of a corridor; it led both ways, he remembered.

He craned his head out, hoping to see something he could fix on, but the small orange guide lights had gone out when the electricity had died. How long was the corridor, anyway? Hard to say. In this total blackness, he'd lost his sense of where things were.

You have to risk it, he told himself. He took out his torch, muffled the end with his hand and turned it on. His palm glowed pink-red and white where the light shone into it. In the faint glow that spilled out, he could see the corridor.

Empty. Bare brick walls, plastic warning signs, thick pipes along the wall. It seemed smaller and narrower than he'd pictured, less threatening somehow.

Once Paul had the dimensions fixed in his mind, he switched off the torch again. In the dark, he made his way down the corridor, his fingertips brushing over rough brick and smooth doors that led to rooms he'd never been to. He walked to the corner, looked round, listened.

Another shriek, the cry of one of the Infected, echoing through the maze of corridors in the basement. But it didn't sound like it was nearby. He listened again, and when there was no further sound he dared his torch once more. Once he'd glimpsed the corridor, he turned it off again and crept forward.

In this manner Paul made his slow way deeper into the basement. Occasionally he heard the steady *clank-clank-clank* ringing through the pipes, but it was hard to tell where it was coming from. He wondered if the Infected had realized what it was, if they'd understood that this rhythmic noise was being made by a human. They'd shown animal cunning and problem-solving abilities, but he hoped they weren't capable of that kind of subtlety.

Assuming it wasn't the Infected making the noise themselves, of course.

With every step his journey seemed more hopeless. He had no idea where Adam was, and searching in the dark was virtually impossible. And yet, the knowledge that Adam could be nearby, just around the next corner, kept Paul going on.

And then, gradually, he became aware that he could see. Only a little, only the vaguest of outlines, but he could *see*. And that meant light was coming from somewhere. Paul stopped still and let his eyes adjust for a moment. In the gloom, he could just about make out a grate propped up against the wall, and a large, dark rectangular gap in the wall next to it.

"Billy," the caretaker said. *"I keep fixing it, he keeps taking it off."*

The air duct without a grate. Paul knew where he was now. This was where the caretaker had begun winding him up about the ghost.

He headed onwards, towards the source of the light. It was a faint blue glow, coming from round the corner. He crept up and looked.

The corridor beyond was empty, but from behind one of the doors, a cold blue light shone. The door was ajar, and the illumination leaked out through the gap between the door and the jamb. It was faint, but to Paul's thirsty eyes it seemed bright in the darkness.

He knew that door. He remembered the caretaker standing there, gleefully recounting the story of Billy McCarthy's death. He remembered the old copper sign it bore: DANGER.

"Can't go in there. That's the boiler room. Behind that door is the whole heating system for the entire building. Great big Victorian gas-fired monster, takes up half the basement, pretty much."

There came a great groaning, clashing sound from within, as if a junk heap had suddenly shifted and part of it had collapsed. Then silence, but for half-imagined noises of movement on the edge of his hearing.

Danger or not, Paul had to find out what was going on in there. He stepped out into the corridor.

Something screeched, terrifyingly close. He ran back into cover an instant before one of the Infected turned in to the corridor at the far end. It walked awkwardly on its hands and feet, but its limbs were skinny and its body bulbous, like a spider. Six eyes shone from a tiny round head, above a fringe of waving metal filaments that took the place of its mouth.

Paul drew himself back behind the corner,

horrified. The more time went on, the more the Infected changed, and the less human they were. It was like the nanomachines were experimenting with their hosts, trying different shapes to see what worked. That thing was a mistake, an abomination: he wanted to burn it with a Molotov cocktail on principle.

But the Infected was making its wobbling way up the corridor, and he had to retreat. He headed back into the dark as fast as he could, but he'd barely gone twenty metres when he heard another noise. The scuffing of footsteps. Slow, shambling footsteps, coming towards him from the other direction.

Panic seized him. He couldn't go back, and he couldn't go forward. He was trapped, and in seconds one of the Infected would come round the corner and see him. He tried the door next to him, and found it locked.

Don't let them find me, he thought. *Don't let them find me*. He fumbled in his satchel, but all his weapons seemed so inadequate now. Maybe if he lit a flash bomb he could try and run for it, maybe, but—

Something grabbed his leg. There was the soft scraping of a grate.

Billy McCarthy!

Paul looked down in terror, and just for a moment he saw two black eyes shining balefully in the dark, the face of a boy staring up at him from the open air duct. His heart leapt into his throat.

But there was nobody there. His trouser leg had snagged on the edge of the grate that was propped against the wall. And now he saw the way out, Billy McCarthy's way, and ghost or not, it was better than the alternative. Paul quickly unhooked his trouser leg from the grate, crouched down and scrambled into the air duct. Once inside, he held his breath and went still.

Footsteps in the corridor. The duct was uncomfortably cramped, but he could just about turn his head to see behind him. Warped metal legs passed before the duct entrance. Then another set of legs went by in the other direction, feet dragging. In the blue light, Paul saw caretaker's overalls.

He let out his breath quietly, then turned back to look ahead. All that lay before him was darkness.

He swallowed down his fear, and began to crawl.

2

Blind and confined, Paul forged onwards, shuffling on his knees and feeling ahead with his hands. The metal sides of the duct bumped against his shoulders and back. He was not claustrophobic, but he was scared nonetheless. He couldn't forget what he'd seen a moment ago, when he'd glimpsed the boy's face looking up at him.

You didn't see anything. You imagined it. You're frightened to all hell and it was dark and you imagined it.

But as he groped his way forward, he dreaded

the moment when his hand would touch something other than metal. The cold flesh of a dead boy, eyes glittering, teeth bared.

Finally, when he'd turned a corner and then another, he could bear it no longer. He muffled the torch with his hand and prepared to turn it on.

And what if, when he did, the boy was there, crouching in the duct, mere centimetres from his face?

You. Didn't. See. Anything.

He turned on the torch. The empty expanse of the air duct stretched away before him. He let out a long, shaky breath.

Adam, you better be grateful when I find you, he thought.

He crawled along the duct until he came to a junction that split three ways. Choosing a direction at random, he set off down it.

Clank-clank-clank.

He stopped. Listened.

Clank . . . clank . . . clank. . .

"Other way," he muttered to himself.

Clank-clank-clank.

He backed up to the junction and headed towards the sound. It was easier in the ducts to pinpoint the noise. Whenever he came to a junction he stopped and waited for Adam to send out his SOS again. Progress was slow, but at last it felt like progress. He was getting closer.

Paul shuffled round a corner, and saw light up ahead. Torchlight. Quickly he turned off his own torch.

Clank-clank-clank.

Much louder now. He shuffled up to the corner, and saw a short length of duct that led to a sturdy iron grate at the end. The light was coming from the room beyond. He slid towards it on his belly, quiet as he could, and looked through.

Clank . . . clank . . . clank. . .

And there, in a small room with walls of bare brick and a metal door, was Adam. He was grubby and sweaty and dishevelled, kneeling in the glow of a torch that lay on the floor. With the length of radiator pipe that he carried as a weapon, he was whacking at another, bigger pipe that ran through the room along the base of the wall before disappearing into the ceiling.

Clank-clank-clank.

"You called?" Paul said through the grate. Adam jumped so violently that he dropped the pipe. He looked about, eyes wild, trying to locate the source of the voice.

Paul started to laugh. He couldn't help it. He was giddy with relief at finding Adam. It meant that they could soon go back, and get out of this awful place. "Down here," he said.

Adam found him at last, and scowled. Paul remembered how he hated to be laughed at, and fought to compose himself, but that only made it worse.

"You should see your face," he said, and cracked up.

And then Adam began to chuckle too, and then to laugh, and then he put a finger over his lips and *shushed* at Paul, even though it was Adam himself who was making the most noise. They laughed at each other in silence, their shoulders shaking with suppressed mirth.

"You scared the piss out of me," Adam chortled, wiping his eyes.

Damn, it was good to laugh. "You stuck in there?" Paul asked.

"I wouldn't have been banging on that bloody pipe for half an hour if I wasn't," he said, rolling his aching shoulder. "Found your caretaker, by the way. Jumped out at me." He picked up the pipe again and swung it in the air. "Soon wished he hadn't."

Paul grinned. "You're not scratched? Bitten?"

"Nah. Ran too fast. At first it was like there were hardly any Infected around, then suddenly they started coming out of everywhere." He motioned towards the metal door. "There was a key sticking out of the door on the outside, so I nicked it and hid in here, locked it from the inside. I think they saw me, but once they'd tried the door a few times, they just left it alone. They're still out there – I hear 'em moving about. But it's like they're not bothered about me as long as I stay put. Like I'm not worth the effort." He scratched his jaw. "Kind of insulting, when you think about it."

Paul put his fingers through the bars and gave the grate a shove. It didn't move.

"Tried that," said Adam. "It's bolted right in to the wall, and I can't get the nuts off with my fingers. I need a wrench. Or a blowtorch, if you got one handy."

Paul cursed under his breath. "Alright," he said. "Sit tight. I'll see what I can do."

"I'm not going anywhere," said Adam, sitting against the pipe with a sigh. "Least it's warm here. The heating's still running, you know? Must be all gas."

"That's great," said Paul, not interested at all. "Back in a bit."

"Hey," said Adam. He picked up his torch and waved it. "Hurry, eh? Not much battery left."

3

Paul backed up the duct to the junction and headed off another way. If the ducts came out into one room, they'd come out in another.

He explored several more routes. Each time they ended in a grate with a darkened, empty room beyond. When he shone his light through, he saw rooms with wiring boxes on the wall, or half-full of storage gear. But even if he'd seen what he needed in there, he couldn't get through the grates.

How can I get Adam a wrench if I need a wrench to get into the room?

He carried on looking. Maybe he'd find another loose grate. He had to do *something*.

Presently, he saw light again, and turned off his torch. This time it was not torchlight, however. It was the same cold blue light he'd seen shining from behind the boiler room door.

There must be a grate into the boiler room, he thought. *There are bound to be tools in there.*

As he approached, he heard the sound of metal shifting on metal again, a vast sound like a scrapheap collapsing. The same noise he'd heard outside the door of the boiler room. He waited till it had stopped and crept carefully up to the grate.

His breath caught in his throat as he saw what was beyond.

When the caretaker said the boiler room took up half the basement, he hadn't been exaggerating. Paul couldn't even see to the far wall due to the thin fog of steam that hung in the air. Massive black iron tanks loomed out of the blue haze; thick riveted pipes ran between them. Paul felt heat on his face, and heard the grumble of flames as the ancient boilers heated water. It was sweltering in there. Though the chamber was wide, the vaulted ceiling was low, supported by rows of rough brick pillars. Between the heat and the mist and the cramped space cluttered with dark and clattering machinery, the place had an infernal feel to it.

And where there was hell, there were demons.

The Infected were here. A hundred of them, maybe more. They crowded the floor of the boiler room, swarming between the tanks and pipes, sometimes clambering over each other like ants in a nest. Here in the depths of the school, they'd changed, and Paul stared astonished at the variety of monstrous forms that moved in the mist and shadow. Long-necked creatures on crooked, spindly legs; spined things that lumbered; waddling, gnashing, toadlike beasts; stealthy, slinking figures with tongues like whips, feeling along the floor ahead of them.

And everywhere, eyes. Eyes like lamps, the eyes of a hundred Infected, all shining with that cold blue light. Together, they made the room bright: the source of the glow that had drawn Paul to this spot.

He heard the collapsing-metal sound again. Just at the edge of his vision, a huge shadow moved in the blue mist. He'd thought it was a water tank at first.

It wasn't.

The creature was enormous. So large that its humped back pressed against the ceiling of the boiler room. He saw one colossal arm move, dislodging pieces of metal with a great screech and clatter. The nearby Infected scrambled to pick up the bits and pressed them back against the body of the thing.

It was a junkyard sculpture come to life. A

deformed giant of metal and meat. Slowly it turned, and great lantern eyes came into view, cutting through the gloom. He saw teeth like girders, great straining pistons, and wet flesh stretching at its neck. Wheezing and creaking, it hunkered down in the midst of the Infected's feverish activity and let them attend to it.

Like a queen ant and her workers. I know what that thing is. What did Radley call it? The Alpha Carrier. The mind of the network.

It reached out a limb like the arm of a crane and snatched up one of the Infected that scuttled nearby. Its victim went limp as the Alpha Carrier raised it to its mouth. It bit down, and the Infected was torn in half with a wrenching sound. Cables snapped and fluid spewed, though whether oil or blood or some other liquid, Paul couldn't see in the blue light.

He looked away then, but he couldn't shut his ears to the crunching.

It's absorbing them. Assimilating them, so it can grow. Just like that rat in the basement.

When it was done, he dared to look through the grate again. The Alpha Carrier shifted itself, moving its vast body restlessly. The movement stirred the steam-haze in the air, and for an instant Paul saw its face clearly.

Though it had changed almost beyond recognition, there was still something to it that was familiar. A fringe of tendrils above the mouth. A bull neck and smooth head with a horseshoe of ratty hair above where its ears should be. And though it was a grotesque distortion of the man he'd known, somehow Paul was certain that he knew that face.

The dominant male, Carson said. The dominant male becomes the Alpha Carrier.

Mr Harrison, the head teacher. Mr Harrison.

It was too much. The whole thing was too much. Paul backed away from the grate. How could they fight monsters like that? Even if they escaped, what hope did they have? The walls of the air duct felt like they were closing in on him. He reached the junction, turned and scrambled away, and didn't stop until the dark had swallowed him completely.

He knelt there, huddled up, calming himself. *Don't think about it. All you have to do is get Adam out of here and get to the helicopter. After that . . . who knows? But you'll cope. You'll cope.*

He felt a little better then. He picked up the torch, muffled it with his hand, and turned it on.

Crouching in front of him, its nightmare face centimetres from his, was one of the Infected.

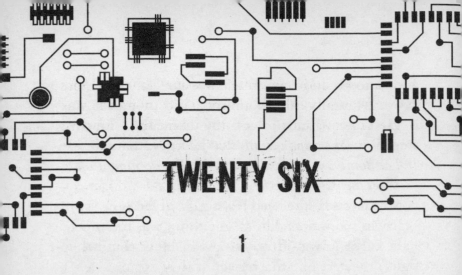

TWENTY SIX

1

Paul drew breath to yell, but the Infected moved first, slapping a hand over his mouth.

A *warm* hand.

Something in that touch killed the terror inside him. It was a human touch. Skin and blood and flesh. Realization slotted into place.

Caitlyn.

The thing that had been Caitlyn saw the recognition in his eyes. She shrank back from him, withdrawing her hand, averting her face as if ashamed. Her straggly hair hung over the machine half of her features, a curtain to cover them up. Paul couldn't help the horror and revulsion he felt at the sight of her, but he managed to keep from showing it.

This is Caitlyn. Don't look at the Infected part. This is Caitlyn, and she's as scared as you.

He swallowed. It was hard to overcome the fear of infection, knowing that the merest scratch could end his life. He didn't know how much of her was the girl he'd known and how much was the nanomachines now. She might lash out at him at any moment.

His skin tingled unpleasantly where she'd touched him. *Just your mind playing tricks*, he told himself. He hoped so.

They faced each other on their hands and knees, confined by the tunnel. Two rats in a maze, both searching for a way out.

"Caitlyn," he said quietly. "I'm sorry. I'm so, so sorry."

Her human eye welled up, and she pressed a finger to his lips. His instinct was to pull away from her touch. He made himself stay. After a moment, she pulled her hand back. She ducked her head and looked away, unable to hold his gaze. Even changed as she was, he knew she had something to say, something she could barely manage to force out.

When the words came, it was a synthesized wheeze so strange that he almost didn't understand her.

LOVE . . . YOU. . .

Of all the things he'd expected to hear, that had been the last. He just stared at her. He felt like he should say something, but nothing came.

I KNOW . . . YOU . . . DON'T. . . she said. She finally met his eye and held it. HAD . . . TO. . .

Out of the turmoil of emotions he felt in the wake of her words, one emerged, like an iceberg breaching the surface of a stormy sea. Pity. Pity so sharp and terrible that it could cut him or crush him.

You didn't deserve this. You didn't deserve any of it.

But she didn't want his pity. There was nothing he could say that would make anything any better. So he said the only thing he could think of.

"Adam's trapped. He needs our help."

She gave him the faintest of smiles, grateful that he'd changed the subject. It was the least he could do for her.

SHOW . . . ME . . .

2

"Adam," Paul's voice called quietly through the grate.

Adam hadn't moved from his warm spot by the radiator. He was quite relaxed, considering. There was something about that Paul kid, a manner that reassured him. He was a good sort, Adam had decided. Not the kind who'd run off and leave you.

It had crossed his mind that Paul had given him the hardest job on purpose, sending him down into the basement just out of spite, or some kind of revenge for their past fights. But that was stupid, of course. He might have believed that of other people, but not Paul. He didn't know why. He just didn't seem that way.

Besides, he'd come all the way down here to help Adam out, hadn't he? And since he'd managed that much, Adam had faith that he could pick up a wrench from somewhere.

"Do me a favour, Adam. Turn off your torch for a minute."

Adam frowned at him, narrowing his eyes. That old suspicion stirred. He didn't like to be made a fool of. "What for?"

"Just trust me, okay?"

Adam considered that for a moment. He *did* trust Paul. So he stifled the urge to ask any more questions, reached over and turned off the torch.

In the darkness, he heard shuffling. Movement in the air duct. Someone crawling.

Why would Paul ask him to turn the light off?

There was a *screech* of metal. Adam jumped. He scrambled for his torch, picked it up, found the press-stud and turned it on.

The grate covering the air duct had been ripped free from the wall, the metal slats mangled as if crushed by some incredible force. He stared at it. Faintly, from the shaft behind, he could hear a noise, a breathy mechanical sound like someone sighing through an out-of-tune harmonica. And he heard Paul say something in response.

"Paul?"

Warily, Adam crouched down and shone his light up the air duct. Paul was at the end, squashed up at the junction. He was looking off in another direction. There was the sound of someone moving quickly away down the shaft on their hands and knees, but it wasn't Paul.

"Someone in there with you?" he asked.

Paul looked over at him and beckoned. "Come on," he said.

Adam squeezed himself into the shaft and crawled towards him. He didn't like not knowing what was going on. It made him suspect a nasty surprise was in store.

"Follow me," said Paul. "The ducts come out fairly near the stairs. I think we can sneak it from there."

"How'd you do that with the grate?" Adam asked.

"I'll tell you once we're out of here," said Paul. "Right now, we've got to hurry. Really hurry."

"Why? What's gonna happen?"

There was a strange look on Paul's face. Worry. Fear. Sorrow? Adam wasn't good at reading people. Whatever it was, he was looking off up the air duct again, but when Adam looked there was nothing there.

"I don't know," Paul said. "All I know is, we'd better not be here when it does."

3

Erika stood on the edge of the sports hall roof, hugging herself against the blustery wind. Behind her she could hear Mark and Carson tinkering and clattering as they fixed up the engine of the helicopter. Carson was still woozy and had a darkening bruise on his forehead, but he hadn't stayed unconscious for long. Johnny was elsewhere, sitting on his own, obsessed with his own thoughts. Just as Erika was.

The campus was quiet. The Infected had stopped shrieking some time ago, their grief and anger spent, and gradually they'd dispersed and scattered. The occasional Infected still wandered about here and there. She'd seen some heading off towards the lake and the old ruined chapel. Others ambled aimlessly around the tennis courts at the far north end of the campus. The few that were left had been easy enough for Mark and Johnny to avoid on their way over from the school.

The Infected seemed to have lost their direction now. Perhaps their appetite for recruiting new victims had run out. Whatever the reason, they were apparently content to stay inside the campus walls and drift about. Erika occasionally caught sight of one of the creatures absorbing another, but mostly they did nothing.

She wondered why they didn't leave. If they broke out through the gates, they could spread over the countryside. Perhaps they didn't want to stray too far from each other. What was it Radley said? They're smarter when they're together? And something about an Alpha Carrier? Maybe it was that which kept them here.

Are they just waiting around while the network builds? While they get smarter and evolve? Maybe they've used up all the resources nearby.

It sickened her to think of people as resources,

but that was how the Infected must have seen them. Hosts. Carriers. Raw material to be processed.

Caitlyn.

No. She wouldn't think about Caitlyn. Not now. She needed to be strong.

She felt in her pocket for her cigarettes, found them, and then patted about for her lighter. It wasn't there. She remembered it had fallen out of her hand in the swim hall. Too much trouble, she decided; she put the cigarettes back.

"*Those things'll kill you*," Paul had told her once. The thought brought a tiny smile to her face. She remembered him grinning at her on the rooftop of another building, the science block, which was still burning nearby. The wind down the valley carried the smoke south and away from her.

Paul, she thought. *Where are you?*

Mark and Johnny had told her how Paul had gone down into the basement after Adam. It seemed like the kind of stupid heroics she'd often scoffed at in the movies that Tom liked to take her to. Pumped-up jocks running through a hail of bullets to save their buddies. When she saw it in the cinema, from the luxury of her nice safe world, it had always seemed laughably dumb.

But this was no movie. The world was no longer nice and safe, and she didn't laugh at things like that any more. She didn't think Paul stupid. She thought it was the bravest thing she'd ever heard.

I did my part, she thought. *Now you do yours. Get out of there alive.*

She turned away from the edge of the roof and walked towards the chopper. Mark and Carson were just closing up the engine compartment. Mark got up and grinned at her.

"Done," he said.

"It'll fly?"

"She'll fly," said Carson. "Not gonna know for sure if everything's alright till we get her up in the air, but I've checked everything. I'm as certain as I can be."

"Shouldn't you try out the engine or something first?"

"Last time I started those blades spinning, every Infected in the area went for us. Might be they haven't noticed us up here yet, but as soon as I fire up that chopper, they're gonna come running." He clapped his hands together. "So I want everyone in. Let's get to it."

Mark looked puzzled. "You just said—"

"Right," said Carson. "Once we turn on that engine, we're taking off. So let's get her going. Won't be a second chance."

Mark looked to Erika for support. "But. . ." Then his expression hardened. "Paul and Adam aren't back yet."

Carson gave him a sympathetic look. "They ain't coming back."

"They'll be here," Mark insisted.

"If them creatures come swarming at us, how long you think we'll have, huh? They can climb walls now. It's only a matter of time before they notice there's four juicy humans up here. I ain't going out like Radley did."

Mark's hands had bunched into fists at his side, and his normally weak chin had gone firm. "They'll *be* here!"

Someone banged on the roof hatch, making them all jump.

"There!" said Mark. "See?"

Mark ran over to the hatch. Muffled voices were calling from beneath. There was a heavy metal box full of flight equipment lying on top of it, which they'd taken from the chopper to stop anything coming up from below. Mark heaved at it, and Johnny joined him.

"Careful!" said Erika. "What if they're—"

But they'd already shoved the box aside, and pulled up the hatch.

Mark's face fell as he looked inside. Erika felt a cold dread touch her.

Infected? Please, no. Not when we're so close.

And then two kids scrambled up through the hatch and on to the roof. One skinny, one fat. They looked around excitedly, then both exclaimed, "Yeah!" and they fist-bumped.

Freckles and Pudge.

"How . . . er . . . how did you. . .?" Mark was saying. He was fighting to conceal his disappointment.

Freckles shrugged. "Hid in a cupboard till they were gone. Sneaked out under cover of the smoke while they were all going crazy afterwards."

"Just like *Metal Gear Solid*!" beamed Pudge, his chubby cheeks swallowing his eyes.

Carson was leaning against the side of the chopper. He gave Erika a look, as if to say, *Well?*

"They'll be here," she said.

Carson sighed and looked away.

4

The door. The door with the blue light.

Caitlyn was finding it hard to think any more. She loped along the pitch-black corridors of the basement, but they were not pitch black to her. Her Infected eye glowed blue, and that provided light enough for her amplified senses. Through the blue darkness she went, searching.

She passed other Infected. She didn't fear them. They didn't acknowledge her.

The whispers in her subconscious were louder now, but they really weren't like whispers at all. No words. Just . . . *knowing*. And with each passing minute this new way of thought was taking her over, replacing the clumsy join-the-dots intelligence of humankind.

She was not alone any more. No longer would she be left to pick her way through life, making her own path to revelations. She was suspended in a cloud of knowledge, and she was everywhere within it.

No, she thought. *Not yet.*

She struggled to keep her mind on track. She was human, human, human. And there was one thing she had to do before she could rest.

Love you.

She heard herself say it, the words mangled by her new vocal cords. What must he have thought, hearing those words from her, seeing her like this? But it didn't matter. She'd told him. That was enough.

The thought sharpened her mind. She found the door she was looking for. The door with the blue light. She opened it and stepped into the boiler room.

The nanos had removed the fear from her, in order to ease her change. That was good. Without it, she might not have managed to enter that place, that infernal, steaming stew of black pipes and lurching metal bodies.

She moved warily inwards. The presence of the Alpha Carrier was impossible to ignore. Though she could only see it as a shape in the fog, she was uncannily aware of it. It was more solid, more real, more *there* than any of the other Infected. It was important to her.

Important to the Infected, she told herself. *Not to me.*

Why was she here again? Oh, yes. . .

She moved among the heating tanks and pipes, reading the old stamped-iron signs there. PUMP CONTROL. STOKE HOLE. STEAM RELEASE. Lanterneyed metal creatures slunk and shifted around her. She saw the Alpha Carrier pick up a runty Infected and crunch it down. After that, she made sure to stay far away.

She drifted, lost focus. It felt like slipping back into sleep when you were trying to get out of bed. She only knew she'd done it when she found herself on the other side of the boiler room, not sure how she'd got there. It alarmed her. Soon there would be nothing left of her, and only the Infected would remain.

One thing to do before that. Just one.

She concentrated, searched, and found what she was looking for. The main gas valve that fed the boiler. A metal turn-wheel projected from a thick pipe that came from the ground. She rolled it; it turned easily, driven by the strength of her metal limb.

There was a series of *whuffing* sounds as the boilers went out. All across the vast hall, the growling sound of gas flames died. After half a minute, all that was left were the eerie ticks and groans and creaks as the tanks cooled.

The Infected paid no attention. They ignored what she was doing. It didn't matter to them whether the heating was on or off.

Now, she thought. *Now.*

It felt bad. It felt wrong. At first she couldn't even bring herself to do it. Something was stopping her, some instinct. The Alpha Carrier! What about the

Alpha Carrier?

She gritted her metal teeth, and forced out all the hatred she could manage. She thought of all the things she could have done in her life. All the joy she might have experienced. She might even have won over Paul, given time.

But the Infected had taken that away from her.

So she turned the wheel again, all the way open.

Sssssssssss...

The hollow, throaty hiss of gas.

She stepped away from the valve. It was not fear she was feeling now, but some other emotion, somewhere between guilt and disgust and self-loathing, something that begged her to undo what she'd done. But she wouldn't. She moved off between the tanks, into the blue mist.

Gas, hissing from a thousand holes. The gas burners beneath the vast tanks. Once they were turned on, the operator was supposed to press the ignition to light them, just like a burner on a stove. Perhaps there was even some automatic safety system hidden among all this ancient Victorian pipework which would trigger the ignition automatically.

But there was no electricity. So the ignition couldn't spark. And the gas kept coming.

Everyone who'd been at the academy long enough had heard the story of Billy McCarthy. The boy who'd died down in the boiler room, choked by gas. And everyone had heard about the caretaker who went down into the gas-filled basement the next morning, and came a hair's breadth from blowing up the entire school.

She reached into a pocket with her human hand and took out what was inside.

Erika's lighter.

A sense of unease stirred across her consciousness. A swirl in the cloud. She was not fully part of the network yet: it didn't know her mind, couldn't process her human thought. But in their vague way, the Infected sensed danger.

The creatures stirred as the room began to fill with gas. There was a sense of disquiet in their shuffling movements. Violent squabbles broke out here and there. The Alpha Carrier shifted its enormous body with a clattering of metal, as if discomfited.

The air became sharp and choking and it stank, but the Infected didn't notice. She wondered if they could smell it at all. Many of them didn't even have noses, and those that did were metal.

Caitlyn began to go light-headed. She felt herself slipping, her thoughts becoming fuzzy, and she bit her lip hard enough to bleed. The pain brought her back. If she let go, if she let her Infected side take over, she'd go back and turn off the gas. She had to keep control.

Think, she told herself. *Think of anything. Anything but what you're about to do.*

What came to her was netball.

She remembered the game they'd played that morning. She remembered Soraya's smiling face, Soraya, who'd thankfully gone home for the weekend and hadn't been caught up in this yet. *Oh, Soraya, I hope you'll be okay.* And she remembered Erika, Erika as goal shooter, receiving a pass from Caitlyn, coming to a halt, then her long limbs stretching as she popped another ball through the hoop.

Except in her memory there was no resentment, no hate, no sour jealousy in her heart. There was only the joy of the game, the pleasure she took in the way they worked together, how they'd pass and move their way up the court, cutting through opponents like a hot knife through butter. Caitlyn, making the plays from the centre of the court. Soraya, racing along the wing. Erika, on the spot to finish it off.

And so what if Erika took the glory? So what if she had the final shot? She'd never have even got there if not for Caitlyn and Soraya and the others.

We made a good team, she thought. *We really did.*

She clutched the lighter tight in her fist. Erika's lighter. She remembered Erika's tearful face, as she was pinned against the wall, a metal claw round her throat. *"What did I ever do to make you hate me so much?"* she'd asked.

Nothing. Nothing at all. It was always Caitlyn's problem, all along.

She heard a hiss nearby, a hiss louder and more sinister than the gas leaking into the room. She looked up, her vision blurring as her human and Infected eyes fought for dominance.

One of the Infected was looking at her. Looking right at her. A tall, scrawny nightmare of a thing with a face of warped metal. Ripped overalls clung to its body. A caretaker's clothes.

And as she stood there, another one nearby turned to her. Then the one next to that. She heard a shifting and a crashing of metal, and turned that way.

Across the length of the chamber, two huge eyes were staring at her through the mist. The eyes of the Alpha Carrier.

They know, she thought. *They've sensed it at last.*

She raised Erika's lighter, cupped it with her metal claw and held it up in front of her face. There was no fear. They'd taken it away. That was their mistake.

The Alpha Carrier screeched, and every Infected in the chamber howled at once, a noise like a hundred jet engines in a hurricane. They leaped towards her, gnashing, screaming, racing to tear her apart.

For us, she thought, and sparked a flame.

After that, there was only light.

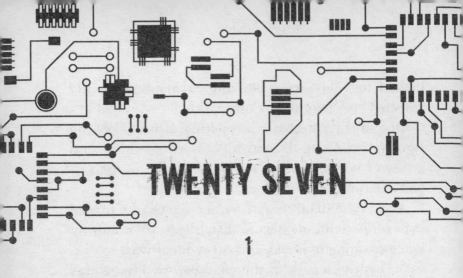

TWENTY SEVEN

1

Paul and Adam burst from the school and ran for their lives.

There was no time to do it any other way. Sneaking out of the basement had already delayed them too much. Paul had felt the urgency in Caitlyn's voice when she spoke her last words to him, and knew that something dreadful was going to happen any second.

Run, she'd said. *Run*.

There was a scattering of Infected wandering the drive in front of the school. Glowing blue eyes turned towards Paul and Adam as they came out of the main entrance. Paul lobbed a flash bomb towards them, its fuse already sparkling. The Infected had barely registered the attack before they were frozen into statues, and the boys raced past them at full pelt.

Run.

The flash bombs had become less effective every time they used them, and this time the Infected only paused for a few seconds. Paul and Adam had only just got by before they were mobile again. They turned and gave chase, screeching. Other Infected nearby, alerted by the noise, turned their heads and saw the humans in their midst.

Then the school exploded.

The blast of concussion and heat picked them up and flung them forward, sending them rolling along the gravel of the drive. Paul found himself on his back, looking up at the moon, stunned. He became aware of new bruises pulsing with pain, skinned hands singing, ears whistling. Everything was going in slow motion as he raised himself up on his elbows and looked about, dazed.

Flames licked from the windows of the lower floors of the school building. The walls bowed and the roof sagged. Stone cracked and split away as a section of the school collapsed inwards on itself. The Gothic facade bent and crumbled, toppling in a billow of flame.

Caitlyn, he thought, but in his confusion the name was just a name, and didn't mean anything.

Someone grabbed him and pulled him to his feet. It was Adam. He was yelling something, but the words didn't make any sense. Then he saw Adam was pointing towards the sports hall, towards the helicopter on the roof. That triggered something. Paul knew they were supposed to get there. He nodded, and began stumbling in that direction.

His senses returned as his head cleared from the blast. His face felt scorched and dry. Belatedly he remembered the Infected and looked to see if they were following. They weren't. They were screaming instead. And now he could hear them over the shrill whine in his ears: wild, feral howls, the cries of the newly mad.

They're in pain, he thought. *Look at them. They're in agony.*

There was no time to think about why. Together they ran across the darkened lawn towards the sports hall. The Infected nearby paid them no attention. They shrieked and thrashed. One of them attacked another, and they ripped at each other viciously. The dangerous intelligence they'd possessed was slipping away. They were like beasts now, mindless savages tortured by some unseen force.

From within the school there was a roar, a buzzsaw bellow that froze the blood. Paul looked back as he ran. Something shifted within the flames; an avalanche of flaming rubble fell as it moved.

Is that. . .? It can't be. . .

A massive black shadow, engulfed in fire, passed behind burned-out windows.

"Oh, no. . ." Paul murmured.

And then, with a roar that seemed to shake the earth, the Alpha Carrier burst through the wall of the school.

2

Erika screamed when she laid eyes on it.

Of all the awful things she'd seen tonight, this was the worst of them. It must have been four metres high, as big as a double-decker bus: monstrous, misshapen, cloaked in flame. It was melting and reforming as she watched, silver metal dripping and running down its face, solidifying into new forms and then melting all over again. It staggered out on to the driveway at the front of the school, and the great dark building caved in behind it, throwing up smoke and dust and fire into the night.

Tiny in comparison, Paul and Adam fled from it, sprinting towards the sports hall with all the speed they could manage.

"Run!" she shrieked at them. "*Ruuun!*"

Carson seized her by the arm and pulled her away from the edge of the roof.

"Come on," he said, his voice low and hard.

"What? Get *off* me!" she cried, angry at being manhandled.

Carson was relentless, doing his best to drag her towards the helicopter using only one good leg. "We're going. Now." He raised his voice. "Everyone! Get in!"

Freckles and Pudge scrambled into the helicopter and began strapping themselves in to the seats in the back. Johnny, who was standing nearby, said, "What about the others?"

"Get *off* me!" Erika shrieked again, and kicked

Carson in the shin. He let go of her with a curse, lost his balance and had to hop away a few steps to prevent himself falling over.

"Alright, you stupid cow. Stay here," he snarled. "I'm going." And he hopped towards the chopper.

"Hey! What about the others?" Johnny demanded again. But Carson was already settling himself into the cockpit, flicking switches, pressing buttons. The ascending whine of the helicopter's engines kicked in, and the rotors began to slowly turn.

Erika looked back at Paul and Adam. The bigger kid was dragging behind, tired. Paul was forced to slow down to the same speed.

Faster! You need to go faster!

At the sound of the rotors, the Alpha Carrier turned its huge malformed head, its blue eyes staring out from beneath dripping curtains of melted metal. Its gaze fixed on the chopper, on *Erika*. She quailed beneath that dread regard.

It began to lumber towards them. Staggering forward on all fours, cable-like sinews straining, silver skin running like wax, it set off across the lawn, following Paul and Adam.

Erika looked back at the chopper. Her arm still hurt from where Carson had grabbed it. Was he really going to take off? Was he really going to leave them there? And yet if they stayed to wait for the others, would *any* of them make it?

The beast was coming for them.

3

Adam felt on the verge of a heart attack by the time he climbed through the broken window and fell into the back office of the sports hall. He lay on the ground gasping as Paul climbed in after him. His whole body was burning. He'd already thrown up once as he ran, a thin stream of bile that splattered his thighs, and he felt like he was going to do it again. His head felt light; every part of his body ached. This was worse than any beating he'd ever taken.

"Get up!" Paul yelled, already dragging him up.

Leave me alone. Get your bloody hands off me.

He was too weak. He couldn't get up again. He'd never in his life sprinted that hard for that long. Once out of the basement, they'd run all the way through the school and all the way across the lawn at breakneck speed. Even when they got to the sports hall, they'd had to circle round the back to find the way in, because the doors were locked. There was no strength left in him. His body just couldn't push out any more.

"Get up! Get up!" Paul was trying to haul him up, but he was dead weight.

"Can't..." he gasped. "Let me catch my..." He threw up again before he could finish.

Paul was frantic. He didn't even let him finish being sick, but was tugging at him again. "Come on! Didn't you see that thing? We have to get to the chopper *now*!"

"I can't. . ." he gasped, and that was when Paul hit him.

It wasn't particularly hard. He'd taken harder punches and laughed them off. But the pain of it shocked him. Paul had hit him round the head. Paul! Paul, whom he thought he trusted. Paul, whom he'd begun to think of as a friend.

He just stared, surprised. Paul hit him again.

Dark anger curdled in his gut. He was just like the rest. Just like everyone else who pretended to be on his side, pretended to be his mate. They were just waiting for the moment to stick the knife in. Waiting for the right time to ridicule him, to beat him, to leave him behind.

Paul hit him a third time. Adam lunged at him, grabbing at his feet, but Paul stepped back and out of the way, and Adam fell on his face.

Rage and frustration flooded through him, driving him to his feet. His eyes narrowed, his face reddened, his fists clenched. His blood was hot, and there was new strength in him now. He'd batter that bastard for what he'd done.

"You mad yet?" Paul cried at him. "You wanna hit me, you stupid arse?" Paul gave him a desperate grin. "Try and catch me, then."

Paul ran, out of the office and into the corridors. Adam gave a cry of pure hatred and belted after him.

4

The Alpha Carrier had almost crossed the lawn to the sports hall. Behind it were furrows in the turf that flickered along their length with flaming gobbets of metal. The campus echoed with the screeches and howls of the Infected, writhing and gnashing, crazed with pain. They felt what the Alpha Carrier felt as the creature burned.

But it kept on coming.

"No!" Erika shouted at Carson. She was struggling with him in the cockpit, fighting to wrest the controls out of his hand. "No, we're not going yet!"

But Carson was twice her weight. He grabbed her shoulder and shoved her, sending her tumbling out of the chopper.

"You wanna stay, stay!" he yelled. "We're going up!"

Freckles and Pudge were already in the back, strapped in. After one look at the monstrosity heading their way, Johnny had joined them. "Get in!" he yelled at Erika and Mark. "We have to go *now*!"

Mark stood off to the side of the chopper, paralysed by indecision. Why was Carson acting this way? The pilot was really going to leave without them? And yet that creature was close enough to smell the flames coming off it now. Johnny and Freckles and Pudge were frantically beckoning to him through the chopper's sliding passenger door. If he didn't get in right now, Carson was going to take off, and he'd be left behind. Erika had fallen out of the cockpit and was picking herself up off the roof. The rotor blades whipped past overhead, blasting his hair about everywhere. And where was Paul, where was Adam?

Wouldn't Paul want them to save themselves, rather than wait for him?

Carson reached over and slammed the passenger door shut, locking Erika out of the cockpit. "Get in the bloody chopper!" he yelled at Mark through the window. Then he turned back to the controls and Mark heard the chopper begin labouring as it clawed at the air and began to lift.

Doing anything was better than doing nothing. Mark sprinted towards the chopper.

Johnny reached out a hand to help him in, but he ran past it, round the front, and threw himself up on to the helicopter's nose. His scrabbling fingers hooked on to the underside of the windscreen; his feet found a small projection that would give him leverage. He hauled himself across and lay spreadeagled across the fuselage, face to face with Carson, who was staring at him in amazement through the glass.

"What are you *doing*?" the pilot yelled at him.

"We're not going yet!" Mark shouted over the deafening noise of the blades. "He'd wait for us! We're waiting for Paul!"

"Get off the damn chopper!"

"*We're not going yet!*" he screamed.

Paul could hear Adam hot on his heels as he threw himself up on to the ladder and began clambering towards the roof. Adam was wheezing fit to die but he wouldn't give up, he wouldn't stop, not when there was still the possibility he could get his hands round Paul's throat.

That's right, you keep chasing, Paul thought. *Just a little further.*

He shoved up against the hatch and it burst open in a blast of wind. His clothes and hair lashed about his face and body as he clambered up and into the night.

He saw the chopper immediately. Then he saw Mark spread over its nose, hanging on for dear life, and Carson reaching out through the pilot's door, whacking at Mark to dislodge him. Erika was beating at the pilot's arm. Johnny was in the back, with two other kids, Freckles and Pudge. Where had *they* come from?

He stood there for a second, trying to work out what on earth was going on. Then he saw a huge movement out of the corner of his eye, something massive and bright, and an enormous hand reached up and slammed down nearby. Flaming, melting fingers slithered for a grip, and dug in with a crunch.

The Alpha Carrier was clambering on to the roof.

"There he is!" Mark squeaked, pointing at Paul. "There he is!" And they all started shouting and beckoning him, even Carson, who looked like he'd been about to take off moments before.

Paul ignored them all. He dropped to his knees and reached down the ladder. Adam was climbing up, eyes glittering with rage.

"You made it!" he cried. "Come on!"

Adam hesitated for just the barest of moments. And maybe it was something in his voice, or something in his expression, but in that moment Paul saw Adam realize what had been done to him. He understood that Paul had goaded him to get him moving, when it seemed he couldn't do it himself. Paul *had* tricked him . . . but he'd done it for his own good.

And he was smart enough and big enough to swallow his pride and reach up his hand.

Paul hauled him through the hatch, propelling him with a strength borne of desperation. Mark slid off the fuselage; Erika was climbing in the back; Carson had shut the pilot's side door and was back on the controls. Another blazing hand crashed down nearby.

"Going up, going up!" Carson yelled.

Paul and Adam pelted across the roof, sprinting for the open side door of the chopper, where the others were urging them on. The chopper lifted: an inch off the ground, two inches, three. And then they were there, their feet on the landing skids, launching themselves up, where grasping hands latched on to them and pulled them inwards. Paul clung on the nearest secure object he could find as the sports hall roof dropped away beneath them.

But they were not safe yet. They heard a bellow loud enough to rattle the helicopter, and the head and chest of the Alpha Carrier rose over the side of the sports hall, its eyes blind, its face a flaming, sagging ruin. Yet even though it couldn't see them, it seemed able to hear them. Paul watched in horror through the side door of the chopper as the creature raised one great arm and swung it back, ready to bring it down on them.

We're not rising fast enough! We're not going to make it!

They yelled as the Alpha Carrier hauled itself up on one arm and swept the other towards them, a deadly club to swat them out of the sky. Then Carson yanked the flight stick, and the chopperlurched and tilted, swinging sideways. The thundering tonnage of the creature's hand swept past them, close enough so they felt the wind of it on their faces.

But it missed.

The Alpha Carrier's desperate swing had taken the last of its balance. It toppled backwards, the edge of the roof crumbling under its weight. With one final, agonized shriek, it toppled backwards, and disappeared beneath an avalanche of brick and steel as the side of the sports hall slumped down on top of it with a crash that seemed like it would never end.

6

What came after was a strange peace, the shared disbelief of survivors. The chopper lifted into the sky to the steady beat of the rotor blades, and with every metre they rose, Mortingham Academy shrank beneath them. The Alpha Carrier lay where it had fallen, unmoving, smoke seeping through the rubble that had buried it. The Infected ran about the campus mindlessly, reduced once more to simple, bloodthirsty, brainless things, their purpose lost as their network collapsed.

Eventually, Johnny leaned over and slid the door shut. They laughed and congratulated each other, and excitedly told their stories, and some wept for joy that their ordeal was over, and others wept for the ones they'd left behind. Adam punched Paul in the arm and cursed him out for what he'd done back in the sports hall, but he ended up hugging him afterwards. The others told how Mark and Erika had kept Carson from taking off, and Adam hugged them too, and Paul did the same.

By the time that first flood of relief had subsided, they were skimming over the dark valleys of the Lake District. Paul looked out, and saw small towns nestled in the folds of the mountains. Some of them were ablaze.

Carson leaned back in his seat and called over his shoulder.

"Everyone alright back there?"

Paul looked around at the dirty faces of those who'd made it out. Some were red-eyed; some stared bleakly out of the windows. But all of them were alive. "We're alright," he said.

"Getting a lot of chatter on the radio. Ain't much of it that's good. Looks like they haven't been able to keep it under wraps as well as they'd like. Clips turning up all over the net."

Erika glanced at Paul. She knew. She'd always known, even before the rest of them had realized.

At least I saved you, he thought. *Doesn't matter that you didn't want to be saved. Doesn't matter that you didn't even need it, in the end. You're safe. That's enough.*

Then he dropped his eyes, embarrassed at himself, afraid that she might read his mind if he stared too long.

"Any ideas?" Carson prompted.

It was directed at Paul. He sensed that, just as the others sensed it. They looked to him. Even Carson, who clearly didn't want to take on the mantle of leader himself. Paul felt Mr Sutton's hand on his shoulder for an instant, but then it was gone, and he knew it was only his imagination.

He met their gazes one by one. Where now, indeed? Some of them had family they might want to go to. Some of them believed in the safety of institutions, the police or the military. But it was like Radley had said: nowhere was going to be safe for long.

The collapse would come fast as the virus spread. By tomorrow the whole country could be in a panic. Congestion, looting, riots. By the end of the week, no phones, no emergency services. By the end of the month . . . who knew? It would be a bloody summer, Paul had no doubt of that.

He had to keep them together. That was the important thing. Whatever this new world would bring, it belonged to them now. Not the adults, not the ones who'd unleashed this catastrophe. They'd had their chance, and now all their towers were toppling, and all they'd leave behind were ruins.

But the new world would be faced by the new generation. A generation that would grow up in it, live it, make it their own. If there was a war to be fought, they'd fight it. If there was a way to survive, they'd find it. The adults would squabble and fight and talk politics until it was way too late, but the kids . . . well, the kids might just do better.

As long as they stuck together. That was all they needed. They could do anything together.

"Hey, you hear me?" Carson said, interrupting his thoughts. "We got out of there. We got us a chopper. What do we do now?"

Erika gave Paul a small, encouraging smile. Paul smiled back.

"Keep flying south," he said. "I'll think of something."

ABOUT THE AUTHOR

Chris Wooding's first book was published when he was nineteen years old. By the time he had left university he was writing full time and has been ever since. Chris is now the author of twenty-one books that have been translated into twenty languages. His books have won many awards, including the Nestlé Smarties Silver Award and he has been shortlisted for the Arthur C. Clarke Award. Chris also writes for TV and film.

Everyone's heard the rumours. Call on Tall Jake
and he'll take you to Malice, a world that
exists inside a horrifying comic book.
A place most kids never leave.

Part story, part graphic novel. This gripping tale
will have you on the edge of your seat.

Look out for the thrilling sequel to *Malice*.

Part story, part graphic novel, find out if there really is a way to escape the terrifying world of Malice.

When a young woman is rescued from the demon-infested Old Quarter, her troubles are thought to be over.

But beautiful Alaizabel Cray hides a dark secret. One that could unleash the most terrible evil of all ... and bring destruction to the world.

A fantastical and award-winning gothic thriller.

IT WILL TAKE YOUR BREATH AWAY

STORM THIEF

CHRIS WOODING

Rail is lucky. The Storm Thief only took his breath. He wears a respirator now, but at least he didn't die.

There's little hope in a city where strange, dangerous storms rearrange the streets and turn children into glass. That is until Rail and his friend Moa unearth a mysterious object. One that might be their way out...

Get ready for a breathtaking adventure in this powerful blend of fantasy and science-fiction.

When Poison's sister is stolen by Phaeries, she begins an incredible journey to get her back.

But Poison soon discovers that her destiny – and her story – is out of her control. She will need all her wits about her to survive.

This is a fantasy where the power of story may be the only thing that will save you.